Lost
River

Lost River

four albums

*lives and images
lost and found*

Simone
Lazaroo

UWA PUBLISHING

First published in 2014 by
UWA Publishing
Crawley, Western Australia 6009
www.uwap.uwa.edu.au

UWAP is an imprint of UWA Publishing,
a division of The University of Western Australia.

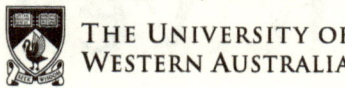

National Library of Australia Cataloguing-in-Publication entry:
Lazaroo, Simone, 1961– author.
Lost River: four albums / Simone Lazaroo.
ISBN: 9781742585390 (paperback)
A823.3

Cover image 'River near Manila, 1925', courtesy Scott Henderson
Cover design by Anna Maley-Fadgyas
Typeset in Bembo by Lasertype
Printed by Lightning Source

This project has been assisted by the Australian Government through the Australia Council, its arts funding and advisory body.

*For my friends who've faced death in ways
that have taught me much about life.*

When people we love disappear too soon, we long to see them more clearly. These stories and images are guesses in the dark at what might have been. Sometimes you have to imagine the colours.

– Dewi M, 2013.

Unexposed

How does a mother tell her child she might die soon? Ruth wonders as she hangs the closed sign on the door of the Lost River Opportunity Shop. The dusty glass door won't shut properly, jammed by a new cardboard boxful of donations: a reel of tangled fishing line; assorted floats and sinkers; an unopened set of false eyelashes; an incomplete set of china flying ducks, the smallest one beakless, the second broken-winged, the largest absent; a travel guide for Bali; and four slim empty photograph albums, their marbled vinyl covers grey, blue, green, white. An *Oriental Wisdom 1976 Pocket Diary* falls from an anodised aluminium flour canister. A few years out of date, and someone else's appointments are scribbled under most of the quotations, but it sits easily in the palm of her hand.

Sure need some wisdom right now. Anyway, spent time can't be sold at any price, Ruth concludes, pocketing the diary. The travel guide? No-one's looking. And the photo albums. *Somewhere to store all those memories for Dewi, just in case the worst happens.* They slide easily into her knapsack.

A couple in a sparkling-white four-wheel-drive stare at her as she steps out onto the footpath and closes the door behind her. She's used to this; no woman in this town looks more out of place than Ruth Joiner.

PART ONE

The Grey Album

Some kinds of waiting

February, 1982
(developing solution too diluted)

Dewi turns to the first page of the grey album. A black-and-white photograph of the rock-pool below the cliff, the only one Ruth's put into the albums so far.

'1982,' reads Dewi. 'So this photo's about eleven years old, like me. Is it one of his?'

'Yes. He shot it about ten months before you were born.'

'Why didn't you *do* something to stop him from going?' Her small fingerprints already mark its edges.

'I didn't know him well enough.' The waves arriving and departing from the shoreline. *He wasn't mine.*

'But he was my father. You should've done *something.*'

'He told me he was going just for a while. I thought he'd be coming back soon.' The pool in the photo mirrors fragments of windblown cirrus clouds in a bright sky. More hope than despair in those reflections.

∞

Ruth'd lain awake late at night in those first weeks after he left, searching for clues as to where he might've gone, listening in case he returned in the dark. She'd drift to sleep just before dawn, an hour or two before the alarm clock woke her for work.

As she repaired and cleaned garments in the op shop, she left the street door wide open so she'd see him if he went past. She hid in her knapsack the best garments in his favourite colours, for when he came back. An ultramarine wrap falling like water, a cobalt shift.

She checked the roadside mailbox a few times a day for a note, a letter, any sign from him. Only a few bills for him, spread thinly through the weeks. She approached the cottage with her pulse escalating, looked for him through the windows as she walked down the driveway under the wind-tossed eucalypts. But inside, his home looked more abandoned every afternoon. She listened for hours to his only record, as if it might provide clues about him. Bob Dylan's declarations of sadness seemed almost joyful compared to her unspeakable desolation.

In the living room, his paintings of their path through the dunes to the bay, the forest in shadow, the river valley hushed by retreating daylight. How dark they were, despite their colours. She marked each day since he'd gone with a scratch on the verandah post where she sat in the twilight, willing him to return. She would wait for him. Then she'd carry armfuls of light to him, somehow.

∞

Five weeks and he hadn't returned. His faded, navy-blue dressing gown hung on the bathroom door hook where he'd left it. She'd put it on for comfort. Way too big for her; his scent of broken saplings almost too faint to smell.

She pulled the gown tightly around her on the verandah. The opalescent sea beyond the river mouth. Where did it end and the sky begin? All her horizons unreadable. But the early autumn morning was so windless she thought she could hear the water trickling and dripping at the base of the cliffs, painstakingly developing its new geography.

∞

In their short time together, David had taught her nearly everything she knew about Lost River and the rock it wound through.

'Water seeps through the space between granite bedrock and limestone along this coast. Sometimes it forms underground springs and streams. When these find their way to open air and light, like that little spring-fed pool in front of that cave over there, they deposit their loads of calcium carbonate as a film that builds around mosses, tree roots and other vegetation,' he'd explained on one of their early evening walks. 'See that green-grey substance edging the pool?'

'That slimy stuff?'

'It's called tufa. If it's allowed to grow undamaged, it sometimes forms those ripple-shaped growths called rim-stone.' She'd reached out to feel it, but he'd stopped her hand.

'Its formation is slow and delicate, and it's easily damaged. If you took photos of that pool over ten years and compared the first photo to the last, you wouldn't be able to see much change in the formation.'

'What about the rock behind it?' she'd asked, hoping for something she could touch.

'It's called aeolian calcarenite because it's formed by the action of winds on ancient seabeds built from centuries of dissolved shell. Most of the caves around here are made of that rock. Easy to forget such hard stuff can collapse.'

'Why's this place called Lost River?'

'Apparently there was another river that met this one before the white settlers came and built all their dams and wells. They named this place after something they were destroying. Sorta like the property developers are doing now with the new subdivision names. Wilderness Gardens. Blue Waters. Paradise Estate. Jack Murphy next door reckons the local Aboriginals believed the sound the wind makes in the caves along this valley is the spirit of that vanished river calling out to this one. Reckoned this river changed course hoping to find its lost mate.'

Maybe there's still a chance that what was lost might be found again, she'd hoped, scratching another nick into the verandah post to mark the five weeks and one day since he'd left.

He'd been gone for long enough for her to expect him to reappear any minute. Who could she talk to about him? Ruth had lingered at the broken wire fence when she saw one of the neighbours hanging out her washing. They'd only waved to each other some mornings after David left for work. Now the woman threw another yellowed sheet over the line, turned and approached across the bleached summer grass. Skin freckled densely as granite, creased and careworn face contradicted by her nonchalant drawl, she offered her tobacco-scented hand.

'Name's Roberta.'

'Ruth.'

'Ruth, ay? Nearly as daggy as my name. Thought about changing mine to Rain Forest or something, like some of the other women around here. Couldn't be stuffed.'

'Don't really like my name,' Ruth concurred.

A little, blonde-haired boy pointed to the two wattlebirds squabbling in the tallest gum tree as he ran towards Roberta through the creamy filaments of blossom drifting down.

'*Pacman! Pacman!* The birds say Pacman! P-*leease* Mum, can I getta Pacman game in town?'

'I told you, we're not buying all that capitalist crap, Finn!'

'Aaww! I hate you!' he yelled; a smell like rotten fruit wafted towards them as he drew closer. 'I can't hear you anymore!'

Roberta sniffed, wrinkled her nose. The child had stared at Ruth with belligerent grey eyes, one finger in each ear as he stepped gracefully out of his soiled red shorts.

'Haven't seen David around for a few weeks, Ruth.'

'He went away. But he should be back by now.'

'How long's he overdue?'

'A week at least.'

'Did he say where he was going?'

'No.'

Roberta looked across towards the shed. 'He didn't take his ute. So he's probably walked or hitched a lift somewhere. Or maybe he took the Greyhound up to the city.' Roberta frowned. 'He usually drives up. His ute's pretty clapped out, but. Maybe he didn't want to risk driving it so far. He's probably just hanging out somewhere with his brother and friends in the city. Reckons he doesn't like their lifestyle, but I'll bet he's kicking up his heels with them.' She picked Finn's shorts up gingerly by the waistband. 'He'll get tired of it again, sooner or later. He'll be back.'

Ruth had decided Roberta was probably right, and went back to waiting.

∞

She'd seen him on the footpath outside the op shop only two days later. His dishevelled, sun-bleached halo, his elongated limbs. She ran to the door, her pulse accelerating. Called his name.

The man turned, glanced indifferently at her, slid into his Kombi van. Just a city surfer down early for the weekend. She hid the day's meagre takings under the pile of *Women's Weeklies* and *New Ideas*, turned the sign to closed, and left the shop an hour early. Walked home so low her feet dragged in the dirt.

Approaching the cottage across the paddocks, she'd thought she saw him hovering by the stove. But inside, his traces remained in exactly the same places he'd left them all those weeks ago.

∞

The next morning, as Ruth hung towels on the clothesline, Roberta had wandered up to the rusty wire fence with three brown glass phials no bigger than her thumb.

'Rescue remedies. Homeopathic. You seemed a bit off-colour yesterday.'

'Still not feeling the best,' Ruth agreed.

'Slip a drop of this under your tongue.' Roberta unscrewed one of the phials.

'Actually, Roberta, my period's overdue. Pretty sure I'm pregnant.'

'Ohh. How old are you honey?'

'Seventeen.'

'Thought you were young. You wanker, David,' she muttered under her breath. She patted Ruth on her forearm. 'Well. At least he makes Jack look good.'

'What d'you mean?'

'Pissing off and leaving you like this. Jack sort of lost the plot when he lost his job, but at least he hasn't left me. Not since I was pregnant with Finn, anyway. Not a totally unkind man, Jack. Just a bloody lazy one.'

'David didn't know I was pregnant.' Ruth glanced downriver towards the path they'd walked that night. 'What job did Jack have?'

'Park ranger. Only job that really ever suited him. Walking around the bush, finding lost people, checking the fire breaks. Giving people the benefit of his wisdom,' Roberta smirked.

'How'd he lose his job?'

'Boss found him watering coupla dope plants in a corner of the park.' Roberta glanced at her, sidelong but fierce. 'Don't jump to any conclusions.'

Ruth ran her finger along a slender dried reed on her side of the fence.

'Funny. Thought these only grow in water. D'you know if a stream ever flowed through your block to this one?'

'David's told you about the water dispute he had with us last year, right?' Roberta narrowed her eyes. 'Accused us of damming a stream some fool told him once flowed through this block.'

'Maybe we could check with the farmer who owns this place.'

'Merv Ferguson? Forget it. That old codger's probably senile by now. David was probably just jealous of our profits,' Roberta shrugged. 'As for you. You've got more serious things to worry about. I'm the last person you'll ever tell yer age to, Ruth honey. Watch out Child Welfare or the churches don't try to get their hands on yer baby, y'know? I know what I'm talkin' about, trust me.' Roberta's voice sounded forced, as if she was fighting to make herself heard. 'Had my first baby when I was only a bit younger than you. Jack was only nineteen then, didn't know what to do. Went to work on a prawning trawler up north before the baby was born. The hospital social worker persuaded me I couldn't give my baby as good a life as a married couple could. Doped me up with sedatives and some pills to dry up my breast milk. Persuaded me to sign some papers. I never saw my baby again.'

'Oh Roberta. That's…'

'I tried but couldn't get her back. Even when I got back with Jack and married him a coupla years later.' Ruth saw that the vertical lines running from either side of Roberta's mouth had been deepened by grief, not just too much sun. 'Another teenager I met had her baby in one of the church hospitals in the city a few years ago,' Roberta continued. 'Her family and the nuns persuaded her to sign on the dotted line. The churches are still pretty big on adoption. But it's Child Welfare you hafta watch most these days. I'm not only talkin' bout when I was a naive young thing. I'm talkin' here and now, honey. Don't let the pregnancy hormones send you to sleep.'

'What happened to the teenager?'

'Think it made her a bit crazy, y'know? Met her on the Greyhound bus comin' down here. She had a bit of a motor mouth. Reckon she talked to cover up all her pain. I said, "you can stay with us on the block if you like." Felt sorry for her, y'know? But wondered how I'd put up with her talking. I like to keep pretty loose. Everyone on our block does. But she didn't get off at Lost River. She stayed on the bus at the station in town until it turned around and headed back to the city. Maybe the adoption'd driven her mad. Lose your baby, lose yourself, I reckon. Knew how she felt. Seemed she didn't know where she was going, just catching buses back and forth, never knowing where to get off.'

Ruth had already known from her childhood on the mission up north that the churches and state had taken away the babies of unmarried Aboriginal women, but Roberta's stories had shown this could happen to other young women, too. What might the authorities do to the baby of someone like herself, not only unmarried but sort of foreign and sort of homeless?

∞

Roberta, Jack and their neighbour Pete had knocked on the cottage door the next day. Pete stroked his goatee thoughtfully, smiled circumspectly at her, his hazel eyes candid. The red bandana tied over Jack's lank, brown, shoulder-length hair accentuated his dark intense gaze. He carried an axe, and spoke like a man looking for a sense of purpose, a man wanting to be liked.

'Thought we'd do a bit of a search for Davo. Show us where he went on his walks?'

She led them along the trail she'd walked with David towards the beach. Approaching the round dune, the wind sighed in the high branches of the marri tree they'd lain under those two evenings just before he'd left.

How had she and David lost their way so soon after that?

Her pulse roared in her ears like a warning; a cloud of black cockatoos rose from the tree's branches, cawing in consternation.

'Feeling dizzy,' she murmured to Roberta.

'It's probably the anxiety and the hormones,' Roberta told her, 'pregnancy's nauseating. I'll walk you home.'

∞

The men returned home late in the afternoon as strong winds and rain blew in from the sea, pushing the trees and grasses almost horizontal, whipping the river surface into whitecaps.

'We scoured the valley for five kilometres. Not a trace of him. Do us a favour, babe?' Jack put his arm around Ruth's shoulders. 'Don't tell the cops he's gone unless you give us plenty of warning. I've got a dope crop downriver with some nice thick heads nearly ready to harvest. Don't want the pigs sniffing that out. We'll search for him again tomorrow once this cold front's passed.'

She hadn't told Jack she'd never approach the police because she had things to hide, too. The horizon and sea bled into each other; blue, purple, grey. All the colours a bruise turns.

∞

Early the next morning, after a few hours of restless sleep, she heard the men pacing the verandah boards early the next morning. A thick, white fog hung over the river valley. Jack, wearing his red bandana again, knocked on the door and explained that they planned to cross the river and fan out around the hills on the opposite side.

'Pete's brought his dog along. Best hunting dog around.' He lowered his voice. 'I need you to get an item of David's clothing. One with his smell still on it.'

'He didn't leave any dirty clothes behind. Maybe he knew...' Ruth couldn't bring herself to finish the sentence. She remembered his dressing gown, ran and grabbed it from her bedroom door. Pete called his dog over and held the gown under its nose. The dog sniffed and, almost immediately, turned and jumped up at her.

'You poor girl,' said Jack, pulling the dog back by its collar. 'Your smell must be on it, too. Well. Glad yer had some fun with him.' He averted his eyes as he handed the gown back to her.

She retreated inside, burning with embarrassment. She pressed the sleeve to her face. Jack was right. Her smell was stronger on the gown than David's now.

As the two men and the dog set off, questions had cut insistently through the fog and her fatigue. *Is Jack just pretending to search for him? Is David near or far? Does he love me or hate me?* Like the young woman on the Greyhound bus in Roberta's story, she didn't know where to go or get off, either.

∞

'Given it our best shot.' Jack had looked towards the ocean at the end of the second day of searching. 'Never find his body if he drowned out past the reef. If he left any traces on the land, last night's rain probably washed them away. Only way to tell if he's around here is look for the eagles and crows circling. That's how you'll find him if he's dead nearby.'

'Dead?'

'They go for the softest parts first. The eyes. The mouth.'

∞

When Ruth had looked out the window and seen a dense cloud of eagles and crows gathering further along the valley a few days after Jack and Pete stopped searching, she'd rushed towards it through the bush, heedless of the sword-sedge scratching her shins. As she drew nearer to the birds, she smelled something rotting; forced herself to keep going. Approaching the thick black cloud of flies concealing the body, she dry-retched. The biggest eagle rose with a round white morsel in its mouth.

Not his beautiful eyes. Please. She put her hand over her mouth and nose, sunk to her knees on the spiny sheoak needles.

The carcass was a kangaroo's. Most likely bowled over by a car on the nearby track. Too much of the face had been taken by the birds to make much sense of it.

Just visible beyond the bay as she headed back, fountains of spray from two whales migrating north to escape the coming winter.

∞

Ruth writes on the album page under David's photo of the rim-stone pool: *There is nothing resigned about some kinds of waiting.*

Last of the light, Lost River

February, 1982
(focus set to infinity)

∽

The newly handwritten note underneath his photo of the river valley reads like an echo of his voice from the evening they'd met.

∽

A laconic truck driver had first dropped her off in Lost River town that afternoon. He was returning to a timber mill further down the highway, and he'd played the same country and western tape repeatedly during the five-hour drive from the city freeway.

'*Don't take yer love to town,*' he'd droned one last time as they crossed the timber bridge. 'There y'ar Ruth. Lost River's main street. Can't get what ya want here, it's not worth having.'

'Thanks. Very much…' She'd tumbled from the high cab but landed on her feet on the kerb outside the red-brick Federation hotel, looked the other way as a few locals in the beer garden stared curiously at her. She barely recognised her reflection in the grocer's window, drained by the four-day journey from the mission up north. What on earth had she thought she was doing, going forth into the world with nothing but a pocketful of coins stolen from the chapel, a few scraps of donated clothing and untested hope? Still the child of missionaries, after all.

The grocery store was closing. Just in time, she bought her first bottle of Fanta from a gum-chewing teenage girl with a mascara-smudged stare. Ruth'd only had over-diluted lemon cordial, for special occasions, on the mission. The Fanta hissed agreeably against her tongue as she walked down the street to a narrow dirt path winding through more trees than she'd ever seen in her life: some with twisted dark branches weeping tear-shaped leaves; others more upright with trunks the colours of a struck matchbox side branching into blue-green foliage; taller creamy-trunked giants tossing their crowns of gilded khaki high in the breeze.

Ten minutes down the track, the undergrowth became so dense she couldn't see where she was going. It smelled of nectar and mouldy bread. The path ended abruptly. She clambered over a fallen tree into a thicket of shrubbery and sword-sedge, and couldn't find a way forward. Turning to retrace her steps, she couldn't see the track back. The shadows were damper and colder than any she'd felt before; it would be night soon. Panic and Fanta stung her sinuses.

Then, glinting like an answer between the leaves, the river. She pushed through the shrubbery to a loamy foot-trail, walked it a few miles along the bank, watching the rushing water cradle reflections of the sky towards pale limestone cliffs before widening and releasing them to the sea. In the rippling mirror she glimpsed her own reflection; already the river carried her.

A bird call, rising and falling like a child's swing through the cool air. Emerging suddenly into a clearing, she was startled by a man pointing a small black rectangular box in the palm of his hand towards the river mouth. He'd turned, nodded absentmindedly at her. Eyes the blue of distance, long, straight nose, lines on his forehead that didn't quite meet in the middle. Not as young as her, but not all that old. Sun-streaked hair stiffened by salt into a dishevelled halo. He ran his hand hastily through it, as if not quite resigned to its unruliness. Fingers so long they appeared double-jointed; torso narrow and elongated. His skin almost the same colour as the sunlit patches of tannin-stained river.

'Quite old-fashioned technology,' he'd murmured finally when he saw her scrutinising the little black box in his hand. He glanced curiously at her face and clothes before looking shyly at the ground and muttering something underneath his breath.

'Pardon?'

'Just reading the light.' He held the small black box up.

'Oh, yeah.' As if she knew all about it; but he must've sensed her ignorance.

'My camera has a built-in light meter. I just use this old meter when I want to get an accurate reading on some particular part of the picture.'

'I get it.' Though she didn't understand at all.

'The golden hour,' he said, looking downstream.

'I like this time of the day, too,' she said lamely, following his gaze to the late sun pouring like honey over grass-tussocked dunes and into the river valley; spilling into the sea. The radiance of the world. It'd been there all along but he'd helped her see it, despite her weariness.

'Taking photos helps you see the light. Even better than religion.' His smile, so fleeting you could miss it.

'Uhmm,' she nodded, but she didn't get the joke, quite. 'What are you actually taking photos of? The river? The dunes and trees? The ocean?'

'All of them.' He pointed to the little white settings on his lens. 'Sometimes you have to set the focus on infinity. Then everything will be reasonably clear, from the closest things to the most distant.' He squinted at her. 'You're new here. Where you staying?'

'Don't know. Just arrived an hour or two ago.'

'Where from?'

'A long way from here.'

'Can't say I know where that is.' His shy smile again.

'Up north.'

He'd looked at her face carefully, as if weighing her up against something.

'Bit late to look for a place to stay tonight. Spare room in my cottage. C'n stay there till you find yer feet. Won't cost you anything.'

The remaining stolen coins too light in her pocket.

'Uhm…'

'Up to you.'

The sun sank behind the ridge, darkening the valley suddenly.

'Actually, that'd be a big help. Thank you. Thank you so much.' Almost blubbering with gratitude. This man too kind to dismiss her, though she felt herself fading by the minute.

'Name's David, anyway.'

'Ruth.'

'Not far to go, Ruth.'

He'd led the way past a rounded dune and reeds; climbed the riverbank to half a dozen gnarled fruit trees and a small vegetable garden in front of an unpainted weatherboard cottage, simple as a young child's drawing of a house. Deep, rectangular sash windows either side of the front door, single-pitch tin roof, chimney. Alongside the orchard, two corrugated-tin outbuildings subsided under an ancient stone-pine's branches; a rusty Metters windmill clanked and flapped in the breeze.

The narrow planks on the cottage's front verandah rose and fell under their feet. He opened the four-panel wooden door onto a twilight smelling faintly of turpentine; led her past a threadbare couch and matching armchairs, their springs showing through patchy russet velveteen. Pushed open the door to the room on his right, so sparely furnished his voice echoed slightly in it.

'Make yourself at home.'

∞

White walls; dark, unpolished floorboards. A rusty iron bed-head over calico sheets so thin they showed the black-striped mattress ticking underneath. A chipped chest of drawers, cream paint peeling from its bevelled edges to reveal the duck-egg blue and eau-de-nil paint of earlier decades, one of its ornate U-shaped brass handles missing. A yellowed lace tablecloth hung over the window, its smells of starch and dust mingling with breeze-blown eucalyptus. Ruth had placed her empty Fanta bottle in her knapsack and hung it on the engraved iron hook on the back of the door, too inhibited to put her few clothes into the drawers. Sat on the firm mattress edge a few minutes to catch her breath.

When she'd entered the small kitchen, he'd looked at her too long without speaking.

'Nice house,' she'd remarked nervously.

'Rent it for a song from an old dairy farmer. You hungry?'

'A bit.'

'Feel free to take a shower while I cook. Like fish? Catch of the day.'

She nodded, though she hated canned sardines, the only fish she'd had on the mission. In the kitchen window reflections, she'd glimpsed him watching her as she'd left the room.

The bathroom door wouldn't close properly; she'd pushed her pindan-stained sandshoes and clothes against it to keep it shut. A sliver of starry sky in the gap between the window frame and tin roof; the waning moon haloed by vapour, unlike any moon she'd seen before. A shower curtain hung over the scratched enamel bathtub, its mildewed plastic printed with white swans, pillared white mansions, mauve willow trees. The water was cold and wind blew in through the cracks between the weatherboards, but she would've sung under that shower if she hadn't felt so shy. Velvet Soap, Home Brand

Shampoo, unstained water. More luxury than she'd ever had.

∞

A sleek tortoiseshell cat had slunk past her and yowled around David's ankles as they ate the mild fish and buttery potatoes.

'Don't mind her. Name's Yoko Ono. Because of her voice and opportunism.' Ruth smiled though she didn't recognise the name, didn't get the joke again. 'Hitched a ride with me when I was taking photos miles from anywhere and gave birth to her kittens that night in my motel room.'

'Really?' She scooped the last piece of potato from her plate.

'Starving, aren't you?' He pushed another potato towards her.

'Oh no, no, no.' She pushed it back towards him. 'It's yours.'

'You look kinda thin. Eat it,' he said, feigning sternness.

She finished it in three bites, feeling she might sink under the weight of so much pleasure and fatigue. The window reflected him watching her again when he thought she wasn't looking. She flinched at a sudden crack like a gunshot outside.

'Just the cliffs releasing the day's heat,' he said. 'They get direct light nearly all day in summer. You're really tired, aren't you?'

She smiled warily, cleared the table.

'Leave the dishwashing to me and the drying to the weather. Your bed's already made up.'

'Sure?'

'Sure. Sleep in. I leave early for grape picking.'

'Thank you. For everything.'

'That's cool.' His shy smile. 'Sleep well.'

The spare room echoed slightly as she walked across its floorboards to the narrow bed, but she wasn't fazed by the frugality of this house. She'd slept on harder beds; her missionary adoptive parents Fred and Grace Joiner teaching her that prayer was more comforting than money or other soft things. As she'd lain in David's spare room looking out at the sky that first night in Lost River, she'd felt certain that she no longer believed in their God, but in the light this new man had spoken of.

He'd beamed and pulled out a chair for her when she came into the kitchen early the next morning.

'Sleep okay?'

'Thank you. Only woke once. Something in the roof.'

'The possums. Forgot to warn you. And a piece of it bangs a bit when the wind's strong. Fixing that's next on my list.' He pushed a plate of toast and cup of tea towards her. 'Well. Help yourself to anything.' He glanced at his watch, stood abruptly. 'Late for grape picking. Sorry about the tools everywhere. I'm trying to fix this place up, bit by bit. They don't build them like this anymore. Make yourself at home. Just don't disturb the darkroom over there,' he'd warned, 'need to keep the dust out.'

'Sure.' She stood at the back door chewing toast as he drove his rusty ute along the gravel track towards the road, waving at her as he swung out onto the bitumen.

Her forearm still felt warm where he'd patted it on his way out.

Had she found her first real home? Silver diamonds of early light shimmering on the river between the trees. How long had she watched it for whatever might happen next?

∞

When the sea breeze is strong like this, pieces of corrugated tin creak on the cottage rafters as they did during her time with him. Those unsecured roofs past and present, threatening to unhinge her whenever she's off-guard.

Your father was a private man and shy, Ruth writes in the album underneath David's photo of the sun retreating over the river the evening they'd met. *He felt things deeply; kept them to himself.*

Her life with David, still beating inside her like another pulse.

Tea for two

February, 1982
(insufficient contrast?)

Lying in bed one Saturday evening, Dewi considers the photo he'd taken of Ruth pouring tea in the kitchen one afternoon. A table set for two people. Clean surfaces. She's smiling over the teapot. A life with some kind of unity and belonging, it appears. A home.

But just beyond the lens's sharp focus, the cracks already in the wall.

'Whatcha call this part of the picture that's clear?' Dewi points to Ruth's face, the teapot, the table edge.

'Depth of field or depth of focus, I think.'

'How'd you get that kind of focus with his old camera?'

'There's a setting on the lens. And if there's not enough light, you have to keep the camera and the other person very still when you take the photo.'

∞

'Back to painting once the grape-picking's over,' he'd said, after he'd taken that photo of her pouring tea. He was priming three canvases, running the roller methodically over the raw fabric from left to right, top to bottom.

'What're you going to paint?'

'The river here at different times of the day.'

'Could be a lifetime's work.'

The vertical creases between his eyebrows as he glanced sharply at her. 'The thing is, I don't feel there's much time left to get it right.'

'The property developers?'

'And other dangers.'

'What other dangers?'

His silence. The canvases, white emptiness waiting to be filled.

∞

Located between two capes projecting out into the Indian Ocean, Lost River is susceptible to sea-winds from three directions, rapid changes in the weather on any given day.

The unpredictability of his moods.

∞

She'd had no recipes to follow, only a few memories of Nelly cooking in the mission's corrugated-tin kitchen. She'd stood screened by the flywire door, watching David weed so the native plants could grow. Sun-burnished, hair the colour of the summer grass, he'd looked almost part of the landscape. Who would've thought that he was struggling to belong, too?

'Could've done with a bit more salt,' Ruth'd said to him as they ate her culinary disaster early that evening. The burnt potatoes like wrecked ship hulls; the oil slick in the gravy.

'Nah. Too much salt raises your blood pressure.' He rose and put his arm lightly around her shoulder. The gesture seemed more brotherly than romantic, yet she felt she might fly or sing.

'Warm milk and honey?' he asked.

'Thank you.' She tried not to purr.

He heated the milk in the old enamel saucepan and carried it to her in his blue ceramic cup, sipped his from a battered, green enamel mug.

'You have beautiful skin. Almost sepia coloured, like a historic photo. So'd you get your skin and eyes from your Balinese mother?'

'S'pose so.'

'My mother was from the Philippines,' he mumbled, taking a mouthful of milk. 'Mixed race, as they say. When I worked taking photos for the ad agency in the city, their market research showed most Australians prefer blue-eyed, blonde models, but I reckon that'll change. More Australians are beginning to connect with Asia. Faces like yours are the face of the future.'

'Heard a lady in the grocer's say she goes to Bali for cheap jewellery and massages.'

'Probably one of the councillor's wives.' He ruffled her hair. 'So. Gonna tell me where you lived before, and why you came here?'

She told him about Fred and Grace adopting her from the orphanage and a bit about her childhood on the mission. But she was silenced by a sudden memory of Grace's anger on the day before she left.

'Run out of steam, hey?'

'Tired. Need a wash.'

'No worries.' He went to the living room, lowered the needle on his Dylan record. Her shower water running down the drain had drowned out all those songs of love lost and found.

She'd re-entered the living room as the last lines of *I Want You* wound to their conclusion through the speakers' static. He'd looked swiftly away from her, pressing the heels of his hands into his eyes, as you do when you're trying to stop tears. Ruth tiptoed to her room, waited there until she heard him go outside. Because she'd sensed he was thinking about someone, and she'd known it wasn't her.

∽

The following afternoon, she'd smuggled home the items she'd slipped into her bag for him when no-one else was in the opportunity shop: an oak mantelpiece clock and barometer, a silver teapot.

She'd given them to him as he loaded a handline and bait into a bucket on the verandah.

'Thank you. The sort of things you can't really find a place for, but can't bring yourself to throw away,' he said, looking at her intently. 'Wanna come fishing?'

'Okay!' She scrambled down the bank after him as he headed towards the peeling, green wooden boat below. 'Whose boat?'

'Ferguson's. The old farmer who owns this place.' He climbed in, steadied the boat for her. 'You sit in the front.'

She gripped the seat, didn't tell him she'd never been in a boat before. Seams of water rose like quicksilver between the wooden planks under their feet as he rowed. By the time they rounded the bend to the end of the paper-bark island, her mission sandshoes were soaked.

'You sure this boat's safe?'

'Just a slow leak. Wanna bail?' He threw a rusty tin to her.

'You sure we won't sink?' She bailed fast.

'Dunno. Haven't been in it for a while. Don't worry.' He nosed the boat into a clump of reeds, lowered the oars. 'It's pretty shallow here.' He hooked up a piece of bait, threw in his line. They watched it lengthen and tauten on the current. A few fish jumped, gilded by the retreating sun. The concentric circles of their re-entries spread and overlapped, but nothing took the bait.

'What kind of fish?'

'Bream.' The air cooled suddenly as the sun dipped behind the cliff.

'You don't talk to the people next door at all now? Even though they seem friendly enough?'

'To you, maybe.' He looked downriver to where the sea breeze blew fragments of the sunset into the twilit water.

'You and me…don't know much about each other,' she faltered. 'Maybe we should talk more.' She watched him scrutinise her face bemusedly before looking downriver again. 'Maybe we both need to…*trust* people a bit more. M-maybe we could start with each other.'

He'd squinted as if he was trying to make out her face in the gathering dark, pulled in his line. The water had risen to the tops of her shoes again.

'Maybe you'd better just concentrate on bailing for a while,' he'd said, and began rowing back.

∞

She'd lain awake that night thinking about their conversation in the boat. Maybe he was trying to tell her he didn't really want her around.

The next morning, he'd barely spoken or looked at her. As he scrutinised his blank canvases, she quietly closed her bedroom door and packed her old mission knapsack. It was only slightly fuller than when she'd arrived. She slipped out of her bedroom window so he wouldn't see her leave, walked to the road and stuck her thumb out for a ride.

A few minutes after several sleek cars with city number plates sped past, a sunburned surfer in a battered van pulled up, leaned over and opened the door for her.

'Where to?' he smiled. She sat on the edge of the seat and thought too long about that. She had nowhere else to go.

'So sorry. I've changed my mind,' she said.

'Easy come, easy go,' he'd shrugged as she jumped out and shut the door with an embarrassed wave. She'd stood on the side of the road a long time after the van turned off at the intersection, watching people in cars heading towards destinations, the surfer's words resonating in her head.

Where to?

∞

When she'd returned to the cottage, David was so engrossed in his painting of the river that he'd seemed not to have noticed she'd been gone.

He glanced at her knapsack.

'More contraband?'

'Just stuff.' She pushed the knapsack quickly into her room, sidled tentatively up to the canvas. 'Is that how you start all your paintings?'

'Lots of ways to begin a painting. This is just one.' He dipped his chisel-edged brush into the saucers of warm blue and red.

'Why purple?' *Let me see what you see.*

'Shadows aren't really black. I use mostly a combination of ultramarine blue and alizarin crimson or burnt umber.' He dipped the brush quickly into his jars of turpentine and linseed oil, worked quickly from the top left to the bottom right corner. 'These make the paint runny enough to loosely brush in the dark masses and shadows of the landscape. And thin darks like this won't muddy your most vulnerable lighter colours. Not all colours are of equal tinting strength. Cobalt violet for instance. One of the warmer colours used to suggest faraway horizons, but it's not very strong.' She crouched to look at a smaller painting of the river in the corner.

'DRM.' The tiny tentative lettering in the corner.

'David Renaldo Mathews.'

'Renaldo from your mother?'

'Yeah,' he shrugged. 'That one will never sell,' he said. 'I did it a few months ago.'

'What's wrong with it?'

'Too dark. The subject was too dark to make a pretty picture from in the first place. Most buyers want pale paintings to match their interior decorating. Neutral colour schemes are big now,' he said, an edge of sarcasm in his voice. He put down his brush. 'The way to make a dark landscape painting paler overall is to lower your horizon and show a big bright sky. But I forget to lower my horizons, so lots of the paintings end up too dark. Ain't that just like life?' he remarked lightly, but his smile looked forced.

'Beautiful contrast against that pale yellow.' She pointed to the painting's sky.

'You like yellow.'

'One of my favourite colours.'

'Yellow is the most vulnerable colour in paint.' He smiled at her. 'It's the colour of royalty in some Asian countries.'

'Really? I like most colours actually. That blue.' She pointed to the painting's horizon.

'One of my favourites, too. The colour of distance.'

'As warm as blue can be.'

∞

In the photo, the woman pouring tea looks so young she could've been just playing house; not really ready to care for herself properly, let alone anyone else. It seems to Ruth there were three kinds of life present in the short time she'd spent with him. There was the life that a casual observer might assume they'd shared – these surface snapshots of domesticity. And then there'd been their less visible life: their struggles to mend deepening cracks and make ends meet over the gaps inside them. Even sharing those struggles with him would've been good enough for her.

But what about his third life, the one she'd sensed when he was unhappy, the life he'd wished he could live? The one she hadn't really put her finger on, until the flood revealed it and he'd already gone. Had that made sharing life with her impossible for him?

The flooded house

July, 1982
(reflected glare)

Dewi flicks quickly through the few black-and-white photos that are now in the grey album.

'What happened here?' She points to the photo of the cottage, submerged in bright water up to its threshold.

'The flood. One of the first photos I took after he'd gone. I set his camera on automatic exposure. Managed to keep afloat somehow.'

Months after he'd left and about midway through her pregnancy, Ruth had heard the surging wind and ocean waves increase to a roar late one afternoon. The roof banged relentlessly. She'd stood at the living-room window, looking downriver at the vegetation bent almost horizontally by the gale. Branches and leaves tumbled past. Just before nightfall, the breakers swept aside the sandbar separating the ocean from the river and rushed upstream, overturning dinghies, flooding the paper-bark island and reeds, breeching the banks, dumping seaweed and flotsam into the river. Ducks and cormorants struggling upstream to evade the torrent appeared almost stationary, suspended by the undertow. When it became too dark to see, Ruth went to bed and pulled the quilt over her head to muffle the din. The baby kicked and rolled in her waves of adrenaline.

∞

Ruth had been woken by her bedroom door creaking just before dawn. Dozing, she felt a tugging of the bedclothes around her ears. The cat, wanting breakfast early? Ruth turned away and pulled the quilt higher over her head.

She felt the cold wetness along her shoulders and neck almost immediately. Scrambling out of bed, her feet hit the floor with a splash. Ankle deep, wading towards the light switch near the door, it occurred to her just before she put her hand on the switch that she might electrocute herself. Wet clothing and magazines sucked at the soles of her feet like mud. Colliding against an unmoored chair and frying pan, she made her way into the kitchen, heard water fossicking through saucepans and crockery. She groped around for a candle and matches above the stove. The flame danced and sparkled on the rippling water like lights in a small harbour, illuminating a flotilla of cutlery and some of David's other possessions: his plates and blue cup, his straw hat, a whisk, a tripod, a broken-stringed guitar, a sieve, an Ilford chart showing development times.

An old enamelled-tin breadbox thumped against the kitchen table leg before taking on water through a crack in its base. As she lifted it onto the table, the candlelight revealed small, faded black-and-white snapshots too old to be David's: gowned women and tuxedoed men at a New

Year's dance in the town hall; a debutante sailing forth on a frothy tide of white taffeta; a man milking a black-and-white cow in a shed; a lip-sticked, permed woman and children clustered around a house-shaped birthday cake in the cottage's kitchen; a blonde crew-cut boy smiling on a shiny bicycle.

A shallower plastic box nudged her calf before foundering against the kitchen table leg and launching its cargo of photographs out across the water like a hand of large playing cards. The candlelight flickered fitfully over these newer black-and-white prints. Lifting them carefully onto the kitchen table, she separated them so they wouldn't stick to each other, but some of them tore. The river and beaches calm and stormy; paddocks and hills summer-bleached or winter-mantled; dense forests and sparsely covered dunes. All the places he'd taken her to.

As she'd retrieved David's landscapes, three perfect prints on glossier photographic paper emerged. A sleek, blonde woman sunbaking in a sharp black bikini; waving from a car; reclining in tight jeans and t-shirt on the cottage verandah. Ruth hung them from the kitchen curtain wire, her hand shaking.

Still standing upright in the corner of the plastic box was the only photo David had taken of Ruth and him together, rendered almost faceless by haste and insufficient light. She'd become accustomed since his disappearance to the past floating into the present, but suddenly it seemed that compared to the perfectly exposed blonde woman, Ruth was nothing but a dismissible blur in David's history. Still, it was the only photo she had of his face. She put the print on the high shelf facing the wall, away from the reach of the flood and the gaze of other people. As she waded to the door to shine the candle on what might be done to stop the water rising further into the house, the wind had swallowed her flickering flame.

∞

First light. Inside the cottage, it was as if all David's life and secrets had fallen open and spilled around her. She couldn't bear to look too closely.

Outside, the water subsided below the backdoor step. A bucket, a dead mouse, a piece of blue willow plate. A blowfish stranded in a knot of fencing wire and kelp. A slide transparency soaked to indecipherability. A handful of feathers. The wind had dropped to an almost balmy calm. An old white wicker pram floated like a small ark out of the rusty corrugated iron shed, a possum perched on its hood, a snake looped around its handle, tongue testing the air. She shut the door in case high tide washed them into the house.

∞

A few hours after she'd shut the door, there was a knock so quiet she didn't hear it at first. And when she'd opened it, there he was, face turned towards the river. He'd come back, after all. Pulse escalating wildly, she opened her arms to him.

But he'd stepped back and rattled the loose change in his pockets, embarrassed. Her pulse and arms fell.

This man who looked like David had a sharper gaze than him, and was taller. The lines on his forehead weren't broken in the middle like David's.

'Sorry. Wrong person. Can I help you?' she asked limply.

'I'm David's brother. Luke.' He stared at David's dressing gown stretched across her belly. 'And you?'

'I am...I am...' Who was she? 'I lived with him awhile.' Not: *He was the love of my life.* Because it would have been unbearable then to admit that.

Luke glanced to one side, as if he were recollecting something.

'You must be...your name isn't...Ruby? Ruth?' She nodded. What had David told him about her? 'He said you were staying with him.'

Was that all? Had she meant nothing to David, despite what had happened between them?

His car door slammed. A young blonde woman tiptoed carefully around the receding water, raising her finely plucked eyebrows at Ruth's globe-shaped belly. Ruth recognised her face instantly. The face that had floated on the flood. The perfectly exposed woman in David's photographs.

'This is a friend of mine and David's. Inga,' said Luke.

'Whose baby?' the woman blurted.

'David's.'

The visitors' eyebrows rose higher.

'Shit,' Inga muttered under her breath. 'Kinda wrecks the plans.'

Luke put his hand on Inga's forearm. 'Cool it. Thought you could do with some help, Ruth. The first flood in decades, the locals reckon.'

They walked past Ruth into the debris-cluttered passage. Luke began throwing some of David's smaller drowned belongings into a bucket: his straw hat, a sketchpad, a scarf. *You have no right to intrude like this,* she wanted to shout, but supposed being David's brother gave him that right.

'Please don't throw them away,' she begged. 'Not until I've had a go at washing and drying them out.'

'Save yourself the trouble. What use are they?'

'They'll help me remember him.'

'But they'll clutter the place and make it *ssmell*. Hardly de*ssira*ble,' said Inga, standing carefully on the step to avoid dirtying her white moccasins. She tiptoed over to the two photos of her hanging from the kitchen curtain wire and unpegged them. 'There are a few things the girl should probably be told about David,' she murmured. Luke put his hand on her arm firmly, as if to silence her. 'Think I'll go wait in the car,' Inga concluded, holding the photos carefully at arm's length.

'Won't be long,' Luke called to her over his shoulder. 'I've kept the lease going on this house, Ruth. Mind if I take a quick look around?'

She followed him as he picked his way over sodden paper and floor rugs. He paused at one of David's hung paintings of the river.

'He was way too shy, better at communing with the landscape than with people,' he murmured, blinking fast as he turned away from her. He touched the small damp brown patch between the dado line and the painting. 'That's always been there. Rising damp. David didn't manage to get rid of it. I told him it'd make more sense for Merv Ferguson to knock this place down.'

'But David loved this house.'

Luke swallowed.

'I live in the city,' he said finally. 'It's okay if you want to keep living here for a bit.'

'Thank you so much.' She couldn't keep the relief from her voice.

'I'll sublet it to you for fifty a week. I've been paying all the rent since he disappeared.'

'Ahhh,' Ruth replied. Fifty dollars was about a third of her weekly pay. Luke peered over her shoulder into David's bedroom. 'Feel free to go in. Find something to remember him by.'

'No, thanks. Can't handle that right now.' He bit his lip, pulled out his cheque book, scribbled a number down on the back stub and handed it to her. 'Here's my bank account details for the rent. If you don't want any help, we'll leave you to it, I guess.'

As Luke and Inga drove away, Ruth went back inside, looked at the confident flourish of Luke's signature on the stub. Nothing like David's small signature struggling for visibility in the corners of his paintings. She stood at the threshold of his bedroom. The hem of his quilt was still damp. In the living room, his handwriting on the Dylan record cover on the floor was blurred, but the Dylan record itself, his camera and his wristwatch remained dry on the high shelf.

She retrieved the bucket full of David's sodden possessions and pegged them to dry on the washing line outside. His damp clothes hung like effigies. They flapped against her in the breeze.

'Did you get flooded? Come and stay with us if you like,' called Roberta across the puddle paddock.

'Thanks, but I'll be okay. The water's already mostly drained away.'

Inside, David's paintings hung high above the flood-line, shining like offerings as the sun broke through the clouds and the living-room window. She found another photo of Inga washed up against the stove and hung it from the kitchen curtain wire.

She also found most of the prints she'd watched David develop, but when she shone a torch along the skirting boards of every room, taking special care in the darkroom, she couldn't find the negatives they'd come from. She guessed the flood had carried them away forever.

∽

Before Dewi returns from school, Ruth writes under her snapshot of the flooded cottage:

> **Three things are essential:**
> **Great doubt,**
> **Great faith, and**
> **Great perseverance.**
>
> **– Zen saying**
> – Oriental Wisdom 1976 Pocket Diary.

Dewi in her mother's belly

August, 1982
(problems with boundaries and ghost light)

'Did he take this photo of you?'

'No. He would've been gone for months by then.' In the photo she's dressed against the onslaught of that coldest winter. 'Roberta must've taken it.'

'Hah. That coat makes you look fat!'

'I was pregnant with you. The coat was the only one I could find that would cover us both.' In the snapshot, the daylight's behind her as she leans precariously on the fence-wire loosened by the flood weeks before; lozenges of lens-reflected glare are strung like a necklace from her neck to her growing belly. All the unweighable treasures.

The coat had come from the opportunity shop. Within a fortnight of meeting David, she'd found the job working there for Eloise Gilbert: serving customers, repairing and cleaning the most valuable items in the op shop so they could be sold at a higher price in Eloise's adjoining antique shop. The two shops had separate entrances, but were divided inside by a transparent nylon curtain hanging across a narrow archway in the weatherboard wall. Eloise was the wife of real estate agent Des Gilbert, one of the town councillors. Eloise's hair, suit, shoes and handbag were all shades of blonde. In the dimly lit op shop smelling of mothballs and dust, she eyed Ruth's baggy flannelette shirt and trousers disdainfully, stared at her pindan-stained sneakers.

'For God's sake. Choose yourself some clothes from the bargain racks.' Ruth shyly fingered a long flared skirt and woman's blouse with a ruffled collar. 'But they're from *years* ago,' Eloise shrilled, 'you have to look *fashionable*.'

Something saffron gold beckoned to Ruth from amongst the darks and neutrals on the closest rack. Partly obscured by the heavier fabrics, it looked to her the colour of something she'd lost years before but couldn't quite recall. She touched it tentatively. Eloise pulled the yellow silk dress off the rack, held it up against Ruth, pursed her lips.

'Yellow doesn't really suit you. A bit slutty. Exotic looks like yours are difficult to dress *tastefully*.' She grabbed another dress off the rack. 'This shift's about your size. You can't go wrong with grey. Doesn't show the dirt. Take this navy one, too.'

'Thank you.' They smelled of camphor and bicarbonate soda as Ruth folded them into a brown paper bag.

'And your *shoes* need replacing. If you can call them that.' Eloise gestured to the shelves of women's shoes. 'Try some on for size later. First, go through those boxes in the back room. Separate the antiques from the junk and the designer labels from the cheap stuff. Put the good stuff in the antique shop. Small change from this op shop goes to the Lost River Charitable Foundation to help the no-hopers. Profits from the antique shop are mine. Lots of city people wanting authentic country souvenirs now we're on the tourist map. It's your job to look after both shops. Too busy helping my other half with his real estate business these days. So many people from the city looking for holiday homes and lifestyle changes.' Eloise re-applied her pale lipstick in the change-room mirror. 'Property's really taking off around here.' Her pantyhose had hissed softly as she'd sauntered out the door.

In the dingy back room of the op shop, Ruth had found a wooden butter churn; tin stencils for marking farmers' initials on fence posts; a year of yellowed household bills rolled up in anodised aluminium flour and sugar caddies; calico mailbags from a couple of long-gone small-town post offices. In the back corner, she found rusty nails, screws and a war medal in jarrah-framed storage drawers made from empty Spam tins; a wooden fencing mallet, its head worn to a lopsided sphere. A broken cane laundry basket nearby contained a flour sack emblazoned with a blue lighthouse and the slogan *Empire brand – Leading Light in Flour;* a biscuit-tin lid bearing a print of a man embossed with the title *Down on His Luck*; and a serving tray made from an old tin shop sign:

WP James and Sons, Lost River
General Storekeepers and Produce Merchants.
District Agents for Westralian Farmers Cooperative
Limited, Yorkshire Insurance Co, McDonald Milker Parts,
Yates Seeds, Metters Windmills and Stoves.
Everything for Everybody.

∞

Early that afternoon, a stockily built woman, wearing a jacket with padded shoulders that made her neck look unusually short, had lugged a box from her new four-wheel-drive to the op shop counter. There, she poured out clothes and sundry household objects: psychedelically patterned polyester shirts, old Tupperware the colour of toenail trimmings, culottes, doilies, double-knit hot-pants, a rayon safari suit, a half-empty jar of Portia cold cream, pink plastic hair rollers, a green crimplene shift dress and two stained aprons.

'Mary Quant. Marimekko,' she'd recited proudly, staring at Ruth from head to foot before backing towards the door.

∞

Two dishevelled young women and four children had straggled into the op shop on their way back from the grocer's, their tie-dyed clothes creased and fading, their hair rat-tailed, mucous streaming from the toddler's nose.

'Newbie, arncha? What brought *you* here?' the plumper woman asked from the children's clothing shelves, adjusting the toddler on her hip.

'Chance, I s'pose,' Ruth smiled as the three biggest children bickered over the toys in the corner.

'Sure as hell wouldn't be family. You're the only Asian living in Lost River. Yer speak good English, but.'

'I've lived in Australia most of my life.'

'That's all right then.'

'Shut up youse kids if you want these. How much?' asked the other woman through her curtain of lank hair, pushing children's clothing, a plastic tea-set, a shaven Barbie doll, some nylon lingerie and a bluebird locket across the counter to Ruth.

'You can have them for twenty cents each.'

'Cool.' The woman dropped a few coins into Ruth's hands, taking a tarnished tin Buddha from the counter and stuffing it into her bag as Ruth turned to the cash box. Ruth bundled the purchases into one of the used grocer's bags on the counter, said nothing about the theft seen out the corner of her eye.

'Got anything nice to fit me?' the plump woman asked Ruth.

'Size sixteen, maybe? Rack of pretty dresses right there by the change-room. You can have any of them for twenty cents each.'

The woman tried on an armful of dresses behind the change-room curtain, emerged triumphantly in a full-skirted, pink cheesecloth dress and did a twirl before the dusty mirror.

'You look pretty, Mummy,' said the only boy, his eyes large in a face pale and innocent as a bowl of milk.

'I'll take them all,' she said to Ruth, dropping a few coins on the counter.

The op shop was so disorganised Eloise would never discover the thefts. By closing time at four o'clock, it had seemed to Ruth a place where she might make another world. *Maybe here,* Ruth'd thought, *I'll help lost things and people find one another. I'll give them all new purpose.*

∞

Eloise came into the shop to check on Ruth and the day's takings just as a tourist bus stopped alongside the pavement outside. Two Japanese tourists stood at the door and called:

'Roo?'

'They want toy Skippys,' called the bus driver, lighting up a cigarette on the footpath.

'Wrong shop. Grocer over the road's got kangaroo and emu souvenirs,' said Eloise. The driver ushered the tourists out. Eloise turned to Ruth. 'You'd think these jolly Asians would at least have the courtesy to speak good English if they insist on coming here.' Counting the small change, she looked sidelong at Ruth. 'Sorry. You're probably… What *are* you?'

'Whatever you want me to be,' Ruth had smiled.

∞

On the op shop's back step a few months before her baby was due, Ruth had found a box of unworn baby clothes. Soft white and yellow woollen booties, bonnets and jackets. Probably knitted by some farmer's wife for her grandchild, she'd guessed, bundling them swiftly into her shopping bag. At the bottom of the box, a soft coat in a flecked cream wool. Shaggy fake-fur cuffs and collar. Only a small tea stain on the fringed lapel.

She'd wrapped the coat around herself in the cold shop. Put five dollars in the till and keep the coat as well as the baby clothes? Or nothing, pay nothing; think of the baby, think of the expenses ahead, think of what it's cost her already.

Always this dilemma: was she asking for too much, or not enough?

'Looks like a cavewoman's coat,' said Eloise, rushing in to take the money to the bank. 'And stained. You can *have* it.' She pointed to a pile of rags and damaged household objects in the back room. 'Chuckem in the bin.'

A broken chair, cracked crockery, a bent television aerial. On the edge of the pile, a pointed piece of flint sat in the depression of a larger, flatter rock. The flint looked like one an Aboriginal woman from the camp near the mission up north had used for cutting.

'What're they doing here?'

'That's just rubbish some farmer found on his property.'

'I've seen rocks shaped like this into tools by Aboriginal people.'

'That'd be right. They're always leaving things behind,' Eloise had said impatiently.

The only Aboriginal woman Ruth ever saw in Lost River had first come into the shop weeks before Dewi was born. She'd looked dismissively at Eloise and Ruth, flicked nonchalantly through the clothes racks.

'Watch her,' whispered Eloise to Ruth. 'And keep your eye on the silver,' she warned as she sidled out the door.

The young woman completed her circuit of the clothes racks and came to the counter. Her broad smile reminded Ruth of Lizzy's on the mission, but she had more angular features than Ruth's childhood friend.

'Please sister. Give me your coat.'

'This is the only one that'll fit me.'

'You gotta whole rack full in here.'

'You can have one of those.'

'They old ladies' raincoats. Yours *s-o-o-ft*, nice colour. I'll give it back later. Please sister. I got no warm clothes for tonight.'

Ruth took the coat off and pushed it across the counter. The young woman startled when she saw the faded grey dress stretched over Ruth's big belly.

'I thought you was rich, sister. You look like a flash black.'

'It's just the coat.' They both grinned. The woman squinted at Ruth, her head slightly tilted to one side.

'You not one of us, but. Where you from?'

'Part Balinese. I was adopted by missionaries who worked up north.'

'What's your name, sister?'

'Ruth. What's yours?'

'Katy.'

'You come to Lost River much, Katy?'

'Every spring. Pick boronia to sell in the city. This my great-great-great grandmother Winnie's birthplace. One of the last children from the local tribe to live around here. Became a maid to the first white family in the district.'

'You might know what these are then.' Ruth pulled out the stones she'd retrieved from Eloise's rubbish pile. Katy whistled low between her teeth.

'Ay!' she growled, looking suspiciously at Ruth. 'These don't belong to you. Where you gettem?'

'Behind this shop.'

'They prob'ly from *my* old people.' Katy ran her forefinger around the impression in the largest stone. 'Grinding stone to make flour from seeds most likely.' She ran her finger along the sharp edge of the flint. 'This one for cutting.'

'You can have them.'

'Not that easy. I got no place to keepem here. I walk everywhere. One day I'll get a man with a car to pick these up for me,' she grinned.

'Okay. I'll look after them.'

'Till I get someone to fetchem. Why *you* living here, miss?'

'I met someone here.'

'Father of the baby in your belly?'

'Yeah.' Ruth turned towards the window, squeezed her eyes shut quickly to clear them.

Katy pushed the cream coat back across the counter.

'You gotta lotta coats. Gimme that one instead. Better camouflage and keep me dry,' she grinned, taking a green parka off the rack, pulling it over her as she slipped out the door. Within minutes, she'd disappeared amongst the trees along the riverbank.

∞

Ruth had dreamed of Eloise and Grace Joiner flattening out sobbing Aboriginal babies with a rolling pin to quieten them and make them take up less space. Once flattened, they handed them over to her.

'They're your responsibility now,' they said. 'Put them into this.' They pointed to a wooden filing cabinet like the one the mission records had been kept in up north, but its cardboard dividers took up all the space and Ruth couldn't see where to fit the babies. Picking the flattened babies up, she was unsure whether they could be revived. If only she could get them down to the river, they might give her a sign of life, she'd thought as she woke.

∞

That first winter in Lost River when she'd worn the coat, the granite boulders had worn mantles of green moss like velvet.

Adult lampreys waiting to spawn swam out of the sea and upriver, churning the water with their grey bodies. Ruth'd never seen them before, and thought they were snakes at first. She'd followed them a little way, her belly too big to bend and help them as they struggled up the concrete face of the weir near the town bridge, or when they attempted to bypass it along seasonal rivulets that would take them nowhere, strand them on dry land.

∞

Roberta had sidled up to the blonde woman's photo hanging from the kitchen curtain wire.

'One of David's photos. The flood washed it out of the darkroom,' Ruth explained. 'I hung it there to dry and forgot to take it down.'

'That's her-er!' Roberta whistled. 'That's the woman who broke his heart!'

'No it's not. She was his brother's friend. Inga. They came down the morning after the flood.'

'Whoa-ho! That's the wuh-hun! Inga the model and *life-ssstyle consssultant*,' Roberta hissed sarcastically.

'Ex-model, queen of the gym and cutting-edge interior design. David met her when he worked for the ad agency taking photos for the department stores in the city. She was his lover for a few months. He threw in his job with the agency and they came down here, but she left him soon after. After living with David in that crappy old rented shack, maybe she smelled money on his brother.'

After Roberta left, Ruth walked across the paddock. Had David made love to her with his mind filled with Inga's face?

Her belly no longer allowed her to slip under the fence wire using the shallow hollows the baby roos made to follow their mothers. There was no shortcut for her into the bush now, no quick escape. Some fur and feathers had snagged in the barbs of the wire. Ruth released a downy feather and tuft of fur, felt so ill and lightheaded she thought she might float away, too. David's photos of Inga, the visit from her and Luke, Roberta's revelations and the pregnancy hormones had saturated her, rendered her defenceless against sharp truths. Some people knew no boundaries, it seemed. She'd pulled the coat tighter across her belly, but it hadn't stopped the cold reaching into her like prying fingers.

∞

Ruth considers the photo Roberta took of her leaning against the fence when she was pregnant. The hand-me-down coat and dress, the bewildered expression of the orphan still in her face. She'd left the mission nearly a year before that photo, but had the mission ever left her?

Purpose, love, belonging; she'd never stopped searching for them. How can she give Dewi enough of them all? She flicks through the pocket diary.

Follow the river, have faith in its course. It will go its own way, meandering here, trickling there. It will find the grooves, the cracks, the crevices. Just follow it. Never let it out of your sight. It will take you.

- Sheng Yen
– Oriental Wisdom 1976 Pocket Diary.

She pastes the quote underneath the photo. **Everyone has a river inside them,** she adds in her own hand. But she knows the words won't be enough for Dewi.

Dewi, one day old: the bravest stars shine even in darkness

October, 1982
(subject luminance)

Dewi looks like some kind of small ghost in the negatives Ruth'd snapped in the hospital after her birth; swaddled in cloth, white-mouthed.

'Hey!' she laughs, looking at her open mouth in the negatives as Ruth holds them up to the sun coming through the kitchen window, 'it looks like I'm shouting light!'

∞

In the Lost River District Hospital labour ward, Ruth had refused all painkillers offered by the sturdy night nurse with the bobbed black wing of hair stark against her white cheek. The moon sank in the west, the contractions came faster. The clouded night sky through the window her only relief; starless and dense. She looked at it between contractions, until another wave of pain dumped her.

'Ruth. Listen.' Doctor Vincent, a smear of blood across her spectacle lenses. 'Your baby's in posterior position.

Sort of facing inwards instead of outwards. That's why it's taking so long. You need to keep pushing beyond the end of each contraction.' The doctor tapped the thin green zigzag on the heart monitor. 'We need to get your baby out before this heartbeat drops.'

Ruth pushed until she was out of breath. Just as she thought she would break, the words from Revelation came to her: *I am the offspring of David, and the bright and morning star.* A thin blood trail trickled down her thigh to her knee.

'Good news Ruth. Your baby's turned around,' announced the doctor. 'Keep pushing.'

'Breathe,' said the nurse. 'One in, out; two in, out; three…' How many more waves of white-hot pain? 'Good girl!' said the nurse. 'Head's crowning!'

A faint click, like a camera shutter closing, and it'd seemed David was nearby as their vernix-smeared star slid shining from between her legs on the long final wave. And it was as if they'd entered the heartbeat of their newborn together; and her first cry filled the room, the clear night air and the cloudy sky with dazzling light.

The prints of Dewi as a newborn, her vernix-furrowed face as contemplative as an old scholar's; her dimpled hand like a tiny starfish opening to the tides of her future.

Dear Dewi,

You entered the world on a red flood, your sky-blue eyes wide open. As you emerged, your hands were pressed together under your chin as if you were praying, forming a little shelter. Then you startled, sang one high surprised note and flung your arms out wide, and I saw you would not only seek love and shelter, but fly, too.

Merv Ferguson nursing Dewi

October, 1982
(poorly composed)

The baby, blue gaze candid like her father's, is nursed awkwardly by the old farmer on the torn vinyl sofa in a patch of gravel.

'Why was *that* man holding me?' Dewi asks when she sees the photo. 'And why's his forehead cut off?'

∞

Colic, meconium, reflux. They'd been the least of her problems.

Two mornings after she'd returned home with the baby, Ruth had dreamed of David sliding into the driver's seat next to them in his ute. *I'm coming with you,* he'd said. But her dream finished just as his words did, for someone knocked on her door.

'Yoo-hoo! Anyone home?' the child health nurse had called as Ruth rose from bed, the two wet patches on her nightie bodice spreading as the baby wailed next to her.

'Wait a minute!' She whisked the sodden nappy off the baby, shoved it under the bed and grabbed a clean one. 'Come in.'

'You okay?'

'Yes,' Ruth lied. *None of your bloody business.*

'No nappy rash. Good,' the nurse said as Ruth fastened the new nappy. But when the nurse ran her finger over the windowsill next to the cot, it came away grey. 'Watch the dust. She could get asthma. And you shouldn't really change her on your bed. Unhygienic.' She puckered her thin-lipped mouth and looked shrewdly at Ruth. 'You're more at risk when you're alone, love. Keep an eye out for post-natal depression. I can get you an appointment for the mobile counsellor for some mental spring-cleaning, too,' she smiled brightly.

'No, thanks. I'm fine.' *Keep your bloody diagnosis to yourself.* The nurse weighed and measured the baby, ticked her boxes and scribbled her notes.

'Thought of a name for her yet?'

'No.'

'You'll need to register one soon. I'll leave some pamphlets with you.'

∞

Ruth watched her daughter's pulse under her fontanelle. How was she going to be everything this baby needed? How was she going raise her, give her enough love, keep the house and herself from disintegrating around this soft, bald creature?

The baby started crying, too. Ruth walked her from room to room, rocking her. Though most of the walls had dried since the flood, the mushroom-shaped patch low on the living-room wall had spread since Luke's visit, Ruth was sure. She blew her nose and read David's *Complete Guide to Australian Home Maintenance and Renovation* while she breastfed.

Dampness in houses has many causes. Salt and rising damp are the most damaging and most expensive to cure. The more deceptive falling damp may appear low down on the wall, but finds its way down from a point higher up. For this, check the weeper holes to see if they have become blocked.

The section on condensation was particularly sobering: *Too much moisture inside the house causes soft things to rot, walls to stain, and, if allowed to remain, the health of occupants to be adversely affected.*

The nurse had left pamphlets about post-natal depression and breastfeeding. What if she *did* have post-natal depression? If she sought help, mightn't the nurse or counsellor notify the authorities Roberta had warned her about? Ruth screwed up the post-natal depression pamphlet. The diagram of the milk ducts in the breastfeeding pamphlet looked to Ruth like streams running into rivers. She had felt hers flooding as the baby's feeding slowed.

∞

The bass of one frog moaning under the higher percussive chorus of a more plentiful species as evening had approached. She'd put the baby to sleep, screwed up her used tissues and thrown them in the bin.

In the twilight outside, Ruth tunnelled her hands into the earth for the onions and root vegetables David had planted all those months back. Surely they'd be ready? Her fingers found three onions, but they were no bigger than marbles and felt shrivelled. *They probably died long ago. And maybe I'll never know for sure exactly what happened to him. What can I possibly learn from that?* Something to do with the importance of looking for another kind of wisdom, but she lost her grip on that too, and left it with the onions to lie underground.

Inside, she'd seized on a sentence from the *Guide to Home Improvements* and repeated it to herself: *There are times when the signs can be misleading and the problem might not be as bad as it seems.*

In the orchard, new green shoots had sprouted from the almond tree stumps where its limbs had been cut off. Ruth sat breastfeeding on the verandah, staring across the sun-bleached grass in the paddock to the river valley and the hills cushioned with foliage. They looked unscarred from that distance. But when she looked more closely, she saw the pale-grey sinews of the trees gripping the calcified spine of the closest hill. His body. Rising to empty sky, falling away to endless oceans.

The baby cried and fidgeted. Ruth walked her across the paddock. Roberta wandered over.

'She's *gorgeous* Ruth. What's her name?'

'Don't know. Not a biblical name like mine, that's for sure.'

'How about a Balinese name? Your heritage. And Asian names are *cool.*'

'I don't know any Balinese names. Haven't been there since I was born.'

'How about Dewi? Means goddess. Lots of upper-class women in Bali are named Dewi.'

'You know more about my birthplace than I do. But I don't think my mother was upper class.'

'No-one in Lost River would know or care about that.' Roberta had put her arm around her shoulder and brushed her fingers across the forehead of the sleeping baby. 'We're all goddesses, anyway.'

∞

On her first day back at work, she'd taken Dewi to the bus stop and op shop in the white wicker pram from the shed. The smells of breast milk and baby powder mingled with mothballs in the shop. Dewi waved at the garments hanging in the window and cooed herself to sleep as her small hands brushed against the scarves hanging above the pram.

Ruth rummaged through the boxes of household effects and racks of clothes. *What am I looking for? Some kind of revelation?*

Merv Ferguson, the owner of the cottage, peered around the doorway, his smile broad as a dinner plate in his red face; pterygia in the corners of his grey-blue eyes from years of sun.

'Got our old sofa out the back. Where'd'you wannit?'

'Shed might be best for now.'

His faded trousers hung low on his backside as he slid the sofa off his rusty old ute, a few stray pieces of hay stuck in the upholstery.

'Ow ya goin', luv?'

'Well, thanks.' Quicker and less painful to lie.

'Good on yer, luv. Ivy's bought a new velour suite for the living room. Strewth. Sore muscles. Me son took me out for a go at windsurfing the first time this mornin'. Didn't think an old bloke like me could, didja? Well. You might be right there. Bloody hard work trying to even stand up on the board thingo. Makes getting up every morning at four to milk the cows seem like a party. Took hours to get meself standing up, and when I finally did, me daks fell down in front of all the young blokes. No wonder all them windsurfers wear wetsuits. Hafta buy one, in case the wind carries me dakless to my death.' Ruth couldn't help but smile. 'Gotta laugh, luv. Ay?'

And she was laughing, in broken breaths sucked from her lungs as if by force. How long since she'd laughed? Merv chortled so fruitily that her laughter erupted uncontrollably. Until she remembered again, *David*, and her gasp broke into a sob.

'What's the matter, darlin'?' She couldn't find the words to answer Merv's alarm. 'It's everything, isn't it, luv? Everything. David. Yer little baby. The town gossips. Life. That's why yer beside yerself. Here, whyn't you sit on the sofa awhile. I'll push it under this tree. Jeez, good view of the river.' He pulled an oil-streaked rag from his ute tray. 'Here, blow yer nose on this. Strewth luv, you'll need a bath towel for all those tears. Ay? Gotta teabag or two in there? Getchou a nice cuppa.' Dewi wailed suddenly from inside. 'Stay there, luv. I'll get her.' Merv hurried in and came back holding Dewi awkwardly, handed her to Ruth. 'See you got the jacket and booties Ivy left for you on the back step,' he beamed, tweaking Dewi's toe through the soft wool. 'Now. Cuppa tea.'

He returned, slopping lukewarm tea from the mugs. 'Locked the front door and put the closed sign up. No-one'll know you're out here.' They sat on the couch in the patch of gravel, the teabag tags spiralling on their strings in the wind. And Ruth had seen that good occurs as unpredictably as bad and she shouldn't allow anything, not even grief, to obscure that for any longer than the clouds passing fast overhead.

∞

Watching the sun's journey over the river valley, we lost and found whole days. In our friends, we lost and found ourselves, Ruth writes under the photo of Merv Ferguson nursing Dewi.

Dewi four years old with Finn, Christmas Eve

December, 1986
(not enough of everything)

In the film negative of Dewi playing with Finn under the Christmas tree, Finn's smile appears devilish and satisfied. Dewi looks electrified, her smouldering eyes haloed by a cloud of hair, her wailing mouth white hot with hunger waiting to be satisfied.

'I don't remember that Christmas tree. Where was that taken?' Dewi asks her mother.

'You don't remember that Christmas Eve at the Murphy's? A couple of months before you began kindy. Do you remember when their bathroom had no real walls or door? We were scared to visit in case we found Jack or Roberta naked.'

∞

The only entrance to Jack and Roberta's timber and rammed-earth house in those years had been through their outdoor bathroom. Jack was just getting out of their rust-streaked tub when Ruth and Dewi went over that Christmas Eve. He'd waved airily at her when she called out.

'Go right in!'

Eyes averted, she'd rushed Dewi inside. The Murphy's living room was decorated with batik and Indian cushions embroidered with tiny round mirrors, posters of blue-faced Ganesha and Kali deities, two orange velour beanbags. Multi-hued saris covered an old sofa and armchair.

'Souvenirs from our youth in Asia,' said Roberta as Ruth admired the embroidered edge of the closest sari. 'Never wear them, so thought I might as well use them for decoration.'

On the cassette player, a deep-voiced American crooned earnestly about being given hell on an unmade bed. Ruth blushed and was grateful for the dim lighting. A silver cardboard lamp on top of the Christmas tree cast small star-shaped beams of light over Dewi and Finn's faces as they grabbed pretzels and dip from the kitchen counter. Wide-eyed, Dewi crammed three pretzels into her mouth before retreating to the garden with Finn.

'Coo-ee!' a man called from the front entrance.

'Yoo-hoo!'

'Howdy, Pete and Seagull. That's what I like. A girl who can do a good potato salad. Gotta nice slabba beer to go with it,' said Jack to his neighbours.

'Where'd ya get the Chrissie tree?' asked Seagull. Her vacuous pale eyes; a gull tattooed crookedly on her shoulder.

'Dug it up from the pine plantation,' said Jack proudly.

'Probably bad karma,' said Roberta.

'Nah, it's not a native tree and it looked like it was going to die anyway. What's new, Pete?'

'Everything. Did you know it takes seven years for every cell in our bodies to be renewed?'

'Can't you talk about something more interesting?' asked Seagull flatly.

'Like?'

'Music?' suggested Jack.

'Yeah.'

'Imagine music,' said Jack.

'I married John Lennon,' said Roberta.

'Seriously. I been thinking.'

'Always one of the great philosophers, that's Jack,' muttered Roberta.

'Here's an idea.' Jack tapped his temple. 'Wanna start up a band, Pete?'

'You can start up carrying the food to the table, Jack,' said Roberta, rolling her eyes and twisting foil into two curved stalks on either side of a dish of Jatz crackers spread with cream cheese.

'What's with the foil?' Jack asked.

'Decoration. It's a foil *gondola*.' Roberta placed it on the table with a greyish-pink gelatinous mound.

'Wow,' said Pete. 'Venice comes to Lost River.'

'And this is salmon in Liebfraumilch jelly,' said Roberta proudly. 'Spread it on the Jatz. Recipe's from *Len Deighton's Action Cook Book*. Op shop bookshelf. Time for something different. Jack found the Liebfraumilch and beer at the back of the pub. Probably bad karma too.'

'Tastes divine, but,' said Seagull.

As the women finished off the bottle of Liebfraumilch and the men drank beer, Pete told them he'd gone for a walk a few kilometres upriver the night before.

'Didn't stay long. The sea breeze blowing through the limestone overhang near the spring there sounded too spooky,' he said.

'There's some local Aboriginal story about that.' Already Jack slurred his words. 'It's supposed to be where two young lovers met when they were prohibited by their tribe from marrying one another. They reckoned that eerie sound the sea breeze makes there is the moaning of the young woman giving birth to their child after her lover died. Their spirits fly there at night. I know a lot about Aboriginal culture. Those two would've been prohibited from marrying because they were the wrong skin group for one another.'

'How would you know?' Roberta said crossly.

Jack tapped his forehead with his forefinger. 'Special knowledge.'

'Aboriginal skin groupings are quite complicated,' Ruth said politely. 'I know that much from living up north.'

'Yeah, but when you boil it all down, right and wrong skin is about whether or not two people are right for each other. Take you and David.' Ruth's face burned as Dewi burst through the door.

'Mu-u-*um*! Finn won't let me ride his bike.'

Ruth stood abruptly, took Dewi by the hand.

'Time to go to bed. So Father Christmas can come. Finn's probably going to bed soon too.'

'No he's no-o-ot. Finn *ne-e-ever* has to go to bed if he doesn't want to.'

'He does tonight,' said Roberta.

'I-i-i-i-i-i-' Dewi wailed as Ruth and Roberta exchanged goodbyes on the doorstep, 'I-i-i wanna stay with Fi-i-inn!'

Ruth took her by the hand and walked her across the moonlit paddock of yellowing wild oats, and opened the front door. The dead eucalypt branch she'd dragged up from the riverbank stood in a bucket, decorated with their paper cut-outs.

'I-i-i-i wanna Christmas tree like Finn's!'

'You can see your decorations better on this one, and this wood's a beautiful silvery colour.'

'That's not *silver*. That's *rusty*.'

After putting Dewi to bed, Ruth had arranged the brown-paper-wrapped op shop xylophone, blocks and doll underneath the dead branch, but she couldn't make it all look like enough, whichever way she put it.

Looking more closely at the glowing hole of Dewi's mouth in the negative, Ruth feels a pang of remorse, swift and sharp.

Building dreams on Dewi's fifth birthday

October, 1987
(underexposed)

Flicking through the album's photos of her fifth year – Easter, sandcastles, kindergarten – Dewi pauses at the dimmest one, directly underneath the photo of her blowing out the candles on her birthday cake. A gangly man huddled with Dewi over the block pile on the living-room floor, both of them intent on what they were building together.

'Oh, yeah, I forgot about that time he visited,' she says. 'A birthday surprise.'

∞

Ruth had invited only the people from the block next door for Dewi's fifth birthday, because she didn't want the mothers of Dewi's preschool friends to see their poverty. On the verandah, Seagull, Jack and Pete ate most of the fairy bread and fruit on toothpicks Ruth'd made for the two children.

'Wow!' exclaimed Jack when she brought out the round pale chocolate birthday cake. Dewi had topped it with a small plum from the orchard.

'*Gorgeous,*' agreed Roberta.

'Kind of looks like a breast,' said Jack.

'*Sshh!*' Roberta hissed at him, lighting the candles with her cigarette lighter.

'Bit of a crack in it,' blushed Ruth. '*Happy Birthday...*'

'Make a wish!' called Roberta when they'd finished singing. Dewi lifted the cake on its plate between her hands, closed her eyes, leaned in and blew out the candles. 'Don't fall into it!' laughed Roberta, but Dewi opened her eyes only briefly, to check she'd blown all the candles out. She didn't let go of the plate, closed her eyes again for nearly a minute, as if waiting in the darkness for her wish to come true.

'What'd you wish for?' asked Seagull.

'Something only I know,' said Dewi, putting the cake carefully back on the table.

'A secret,' nodded Ruth, cutting her a slice with the plum on it.

Cheeks smeared with chocolate icing, Finn and Dewi had played pass the parcel. Jack kept pressing the stop button on his old tape recorder whenever Finn held the newspaper-wrapped package.

'Jack, you dag,' hissed Roberta, 'Ruth's put a bubble-making set or a book in every layer of paper so they both get two prezzies each.' She stepped back and whispered in Ruth's ear. 'Jack always wants Finn to win every game cos he's a bit of a loser himself.'

The children took their bubble mix to the orchard. The adults sat on the verandah, watching them blowing and chasing the iridescent drifts on the early afternoon breeze.

'Me, Pete and some friends from the permaculture co-op other side of town've formed a band called The Night Mares,' Jack told Ruth. 'We've gotta laid back California-meets-west-coast-Australia sound. Can you sing? We need female backing vocals.'

'No, Jack,' said Roberta angrily. 'You want someone who'll do all the work and back you up while you take all the credit centre stage.'

'Cool it, Bobbie,' muttered Jack.

Finn yelled triumphantly and Dewi wailed as her bubbles drifted and impaled themselves one by one on the branches of trees.

'Don't worry, babe,' Roberta had called to Dewi. 'It's just the way the wind's blowing.'

∞

On the living-room floor after the guests left, Dewi had emptied the crate of op shop Lego Ruth'd bought her for a birthday present. She built a roofless house with two square windows on either side of a red front door.

'There are so many pieces you could build a little *neighbourhood* of houses,' Ruth suggested.

'Are Finn, Jack and Roberta our *naay*bours?'

'Yes.'

'I'm going to just build *one* house and *one* family. What can I make a family with? My Lego doesn't have any *people blocks* like the ones at preschool.'

Ruth gathered the old wooden clothes pegs from the laundry – the same kind of pegs with round wooden heads that she'd used to make dolls on the mission – and gave Dewi her sewing basket full of yarn and fabric scraps.

By the time Ruth finished washing the dishes, Dewi had made two dolls.

'A *girl* and her *mummy*,' Dewi said, holding them up proudly. She'd drawn them crooked red-texta lips and spidery black eyelashes, clothed them in the brightest strips of fabric from the sewing basket and given them long yellow woollen hair. She propped the dolls in the doorway of her house.

'They're waiting.'

'What for?'

'Their Daddy. He *left*. But they'll still always have their house, won't they?'

Someone knocked on the door. Dewi hid behind Ruth as she undid the latch.

His face was pinched and downcast. He thrust his hands into the pockets of his dusty, black jacket. He hadn't visited since the flood, though Roberta said she'd seen him in town some weekends.

'Hullo,' Luke smiled bleakly.

'Hi. Where's Inga?'

He ran his fingers through his fringe, looked at his unpolished shoes.

'She just came along for the ride last time. She was always just a friend.' The downturned corners of his mouth suggested he'd hoped otherwise. He looked even more like David. 'She's living with some stockbroker in the coastal suburbs now.' Behind him his old green Peugeot, the back fender dented.

'Oh. Come in. Come in. Cup of tea?'

'Thanks.'

'Who's that *ma-an*?' asked Dewi, clinging to the back of Ruth's dress.

'This is your Uncle Luke.'

'Why's he look so sad?' she whispered.

'I'm not sad anymore,' Luke smiled, ruffling Dewi's hair. As Dewi ran to her Lego house, he handed Ruth a cheque from his coat pocket. 'A refund. You don't need to keep paying me rent,' he said. 'Shouldn't ever have asked you to.'

His signature on the cheque wasn't the flourish she remembered from the morning of the flood. Cramped, barely recognisable, it looked as if it were struggling to find its way forward. Ruth had never held a cheque before. She put it hesitantly into a canister on the kitchen mantelpiece while Luke and Dewi added more rooms to the Lego house on the living-room floor.

A few discordant guitar riffs from Jack's new band drifted across the block as Ruth made a pot of tea. Jack's bass guitar and the drumming thumped loudly over the tinny riffs of the other guitars.

'Sounds like The Moody Blues on a bender,' Luke said.

'Yeah,' Ruth said, pretending she knew what he was talking about. 'What've you been up to?' She handed him the full cup. The tea slopped into the saucer as Jack's band played something she thought might be a love song, but the beat was too fast and the snare too loud to hear all the words until the last verse:

I wanna woman who won't do me no wrong

A woman who knows how to be soft yet strong.'

'He must've got that from the toilet paper ad,' said Luke.

A woman who knows how to heal scars

Hey baby come to me wherever you are. Yeahhh.'

'Well,' Luke concluded wryly over the top of his cup, 'rock on, I guess.' The guitars twanged into a new beat. 'Got some music to drown that out?'

'Sorry. Only Jack's tape recorder and the greatest hits from *Play School*.'

'Got some in the car.' He rose to his feet.

'Unca L-l-lukey,' stammered Dewi, running after him, 'd-don't go! We haven't finished our house!'

'Not going yet, Dewi!' He'd lifted her under her arms and swung her through the air and out the door, her single peal of joy purer than a bell.

∞

Dewi had dressed slowly in her new yellow duck-print flannelette pyjamas after Luke left. She bit her lip, brushed her hands over her eyes.

'Poor Dewi. It's late. You're tired.'

'Am not!'

Dewi stood looking at the Lego house with the two dolls in it. She took another peg, gave it two black-texta dots for eyes and a thin red line for a mouth. She put the peg into the house, unclothed and hairless.

'And the Mummy and the girl are happy, because the Daddy goes to work and makes enough money, and he comes home, every day he comes home.'

∞

Ruth avoids looking too long at the photo of Dewi making the Lego house with the man who wasn't quite her father; scrutinises the one of Dewi wishing, eyes closed, as she blows out the candles on her fifth-birthday cake. She's continued that habit of blowing them out with her eyes closed at nearly every birthday since, refusing to reveal her wish to anyone. As if it's too painful, or embarrassing, or more likely not to come true if she doesn't keep it to herself.

Dewi's fallen castle

December, 1987
(insufficient light)

Ruth and Dewi sit on the verandah in the morning sun, chewing on toast and flicking through the album. Middle-aged women's voices float up to them from the river.

'So I cooked up a leg of corned beef for meat for this weekend, always good for a weekend away, corned beef. I was just going to put it in the esky when two blokes knocked on the door and said, "got new dining room chairs to deliver," and I said, "you must be at the wrong address, I've never bought new dining chairs in me life," and Wayne pops his head outta the bathroom and says, "I did mate, you're at the right place," and the two blokes bring in these hideous orange vinyl chairs. They were that *cheap* looking. And I said to Wayne, "why didn't you let me choose?"'

'That's what men like ours do. Yer get sick of settling for the burnt chop, ay?'

'I'm fifty-five now and I've never bought new furniture in my life and I looked down and I was still holding the leg of corned beef in my hand.'

'Least he bought you *something*, I guess.'

The women's voices drop too low to hear. Dewi winks conspiratorially at Ruth, as if she knows all about such womanly matters now she's only a year or two away from high school. Looking at the photo of herself sitting alone amongst the scattered blocks of the demolished Lego castle when she was five, she asks Ruth, 'D'you still like Luke?'

∞

After Luke's visit on Dewi's fifth birthday, Ruth had cleaned the cottage obsessively each Friday after work and hoped he would visit from the city sometime on the weekend. But by Sunday evenings, all her polished surfaces looked cloudy. She gave up hoping after a couple of months, and the dust settled inside the cottage again.

Around that time, Dewi's preschool teacher had sent Ruth a note about getting Dewi's speech assessed by the travelling educational psychologist. When Ruth arrived at the preschool just before the assessment, Dewi sat next to the psychologist, sucking the end of one of her plaits, her hands and feet clenched.

'Can you tell me what these are?' asked the psychologist, holding up a laminated black-and-white illustration just below her hawk-like eyes.

'A *d-d-daithy*.'

'A daisy. And this?'

'A *c-cat*.'

'And this?'

Dewi hooked her forefinger from her lower lip as she stared at the picture of a wedding ring.

'D-d-don't know.'

The psychologist glanced at Ruth's bare hands.

'How about this?'

Dewi's forefinger tugged the corner of her mouth downwards as she stared at the illustration of the washing machine. The psychologist glanced at Ruth's dated dress, her sandalled feet. Her toenails badly needed trimming.

'Don't know? How about this one?'

'A d-dog.'

Dewi got all the rest of the flora and fauna right, but she remained bewildered and mute when shown the wedding ring and the washing machine again.

'Very good, Dewi. You can go out and play now,' the psychologist said. Dewi unclenched her hands and ran outside. The psychologist called the teacher in, turned to Ruth. 'Her stutter is only minor, but her language development isn't as good as it could be. Do you talk and read to her much at home?'

Ruth was too embarrassed to tell the psychologist that her daughter didn't know the words for washing machine and wedding ring because she'd never had either of them in their house.

'She's a single mother,' said the teacher before Ruth could reply.

Through the window, Ruth saw Dewi standing on the edge of the sandpit, looking at a small group of preschool girls spooning sand into plastic bowls. The psychologist made a note and closed her file. Outside, when the other girls ran from the pit, Dewi had just stood and watched them, her forefinger hooked from the corner of her mouth like a question mark.

∞

Early the next Monday afternoon, while Dewi was at preschool, Ruth had heard someone walking around outside, tapping on the cottage's side.

She opened the door, looked around the corner and there he was, scrutinising the weatherboards from top to bottom.

'Door's right here,' she called.

'Sorry!' he grinned as he came around the corner to the front door. 'Thought you were out. Just checking for damage. This place needs a lot of work.'

Don't take this personally, Ruth told herself.

'Cuppa tea?'

He sat on the verandah in David's wicker chair. They talked about Lost River real estate, conservation, the rising cost of living. He held the back of his forearm next to hers.

'Just a bit darker than mine and David's. David said you were part-Balinese.'

'Uh huh.' *Sepia skin,* David had called hers. *Historic looking.*

'Guess we're both specimens of the coffee-coloured people that politician Arthur Calwell said would result from mixed-race marriages. Remember Calwell? The guy who said, "Two Wongs don't make a white".'

Ruth nodded as if she knew all about that, but they'd rarely received newspapers on the mission and she'd never heard of Arthur Calwell.

'David said your Mum was from the Philippines.'

'Yeah. Our artistic inclinations probably came from her, too. She was quite passionate, married Dad in her late twenties, a mail-order bride, I suspect. Both of them desperate to escape one kind of poverty or another.'

'Your father was poor, too?'

'Poverty of the soul,' Luke said tersely.

'Did you and David get your blue eyes from him?'

'Guess so. He was a strict Englishman, stiff upper lip, ex–air force. Taught us a man should keep his problems to himself and sort them out for himself. Probably thought he was protecting us from Mum's ups and downs, helping us grow up self-reliant. Or maybe it was the only version of manhood he knew. S'pose that's why David found it hard to ask for help.' Luke spoke in a rush. *Like a confession,* Ruth thought. *Like someone with nowhere else to go.* 'Mum and Dad were incompatible really. We grew up in a mean little fibro-and-tin rental in one of those awful state-housing-commission suburbs east of the city. David was hopeless at footy, cricket – all those good Aussie sports. A useless, artistic, wog boy, Dad called him.' Luke looked at the hills across the river, creased his top lip between his forefinger and thumb. 'Poor old Mum. She worried about David. She hankered after a friendlier community than 1960s Australian suburbia could give her, felt things too keenly for her own good. Dad couldn't fly anymore because of problems with his vision. He worked in a factory making cardboard boxes.'

'Cardboard boxes?'

'For shoes, fruit and vegetables, removals, you name it. Boxes for everything.'

'Nothing as useful as a good strong cardboard box.' All those full cartons still waiting to be sorted in the op shop.

'And nothing as empty as making them. Dad kicked holes in the walls of our house, pushed us around a bit, drank himself to death by the time we reached our late teens. David didn't stand up to him like I did. Always a bit too sensitive and shy for his own good, David. He never really developed close friendships with other kids at school. I was pretty gutless when I look back on it, didn't want to hang around school with my daggy sensitive brother because my own standing with the other kids was sort of wobbly, though I was in the footy and cricket teams and had a few mates. But David and I were close in our own way. Talked about things to each other at home. Girls, music, that kind of thing.' Luke swatted at a wasp hovering over his cup of tea, lowered his head. 'I think I was the only person he really confided in, at school and when we grew up. Mum died when he was about fifteen or sixteen. When Inga and I became closer after she and David broke up, I s'pose he felt like he didn't have anyone in the world he could talk to about her. David was very close to Mum. She was a good person. But she felt the highs and lows of life too deeply for her own good. Got diagnosed with manic depression by Dad's Pommy doctor. Rightly or wrongly, who knows? Could've just been cultural differences. She was in and out of the psychiatric ward in her last years.'

'You don't think David inherited her...?'

'Who knows if it was mental illness or just her personality? They say both can run in families,' Luke murmured, looking across the river. 'I thought Mum was just...lonely.' He glanced at Ruth. 'Don't you reckon migrants from big families and close communities feel the great Australian loneliness more deeply than most?'

Ruth shrugged.

'What happened to her in the end?'

'David never told you all this?' He looked intently at her.

'No.'

'Then I won't either. He was so traumatised by it all he kept it pretty much to himself. It had long-term consequences for him. I promised him I wouldn't tell anyone about any of that.' Luke sighed, rubbed the lines on his forehead as if he might erase them. 'I hoped he'd get over it.' Luke looked at her almost beseechingly. 'I was the oldest by a few years, but there was nothing I could've done. I'd only just started uni. Trying to make my way to a better life.'

'Sure.'

Luke took a deep breath, as if the story now threatened to submerge him.

'David was smart enough to go to uni like me, but he couldn't stand school or living at home after I left. Dropped out of school when he was fifteen. He'd wanted to live in a house in the country near the sea since he was a kid. We both did. So we rented this cottage when I heard about it from Ferguson's grand-daughter Margo. She's a sort of…a *friend* of mine in the city. Looking back, I think David and I both wanted to get as far away as we could from the memory of our parents' unhappy lives.' Luke paused. 'One of David's biggest problems was his obsession with image.'

'Yeah? He *was* an artist.'

'I mean his obsession with his own public image. The image he thought others had of *him*. His low social status.' Luke paused. 'Probably why he fell in such a big way for Inga. Not only beautiful, but well-connected.'

Ruth glanced at the scratches she'd made on the verandah post to count off the days after David had left all those years ago. She waited for Luke to tell her more about David, his mother and Inga, but for several minutes, only the lengthening shadows of the trees filled the space between them. She didn't notice Dewi running from the school bus down the driveway until she'd almost reached the house.

'Unca *Lu-u-uke!*' she pealed, pulling his hand and dragging him inside towards the mound of Lego. 'I'm building a castle this time. See?'

'Wow!'

'For my family. They were too big for the house.' Luke sat on the floor, his long legs toppling a few blocks as she handed the clothes-peg family to him, one by one. 'The girl. The mummy. Betcha can't guess who *this* is?'

'Uhmm…' He turned the undressed, hairless peg over in his hands.

'Give you a clue. Someone to love the girl and the mummy.'

Luke rose awkwardly and ruffled her hair.

'I have to drive back to the city now. Before it gets too dark and the roos jump onto the road.'

'But you haven't guessed who the third person is. And the castle's not finished.'

'I'll be back. Promise.'

Dewi was silent and her eyes darkened, and she didn't follow Luke and Ruth out to his car.

'Her eyes are like…' he faltered as he opened the car door.

'David's.'

He got into the car, leaned on the steering wheel for a few seconds and looked out the window. He'd looked like he was avoiding her gaze.

'I'm going to be too busy in the city to come down for a few months. Take care of yourselves. I'll be in touch when I come back.' He had only turned to look at her briefly, near the end of the gravel track. The cloud of dust hovered between them long after he'd turned onto the road and out of sight.

> *The secret of contentment is knowing*
> *how to enjoy what you have,*
> *and to be able to lose desire*
> *for things beyond your reach.*
>
> *- Lin Yutang*
> - Oriental Wisdom 1976 Pocket Diary.

The quote seems apt for the photo of Dewi sitting in the ruins of the Lego castle she'd kicked to pieces after Luke had left, but Ruth can't make it stick with the last scrap of glue.

Ruth on the mission

1975?
(over-exposed)

Dewi opens the album at the creased, Kodachrome mission photo Ruth'd inserted over the page from the shot of the collapsed Lego castle. Ruth'd found this snapshot at the back of her dresser drawer only a few days before.

'Who's this?' Dewi asks.

'Me.'

'How old were you when this was taken?'

Ruth squints against the early sun slanting through the window. In the photo, she's wearing one of the awful mission dresses, her skinny knock-kneed legs just visible below the hem. Most of the red has leached out of the gingham checks and pindan earth in the background. The passing of time, or over-exposure during shooting?

'Roughly your age. About ten or eleven.'

'Where were you then?'

'On the mission up north where I grew up.' She points to the Nissen hut in the background. 'That was the girls' dormitory. And you can just see the old mission van on the edge of the photo.'

'Can I finish the Fruit Loops?'

'Okay. So long as you have some fruit and yoghurt.'

'There's only old bananas and they've gone black.'

'What about the apples in the fridge?'

'I hate apples for breakfast.' The Fruit Loops crunch as Dewi chews, reminding Ruth of unmade dental appointments.

'Don't forget to brush your teeth after.'

Dewi reads from the Oriental Wisdom diary quote below the photo.

'*May the fear-struck fearless be. May the grieving shed all grief. Zen chant.*' The tips of her dark plaits brush the cereal bowl. 'What's Zen?'

'Don't get your hair in the Fruit Loops.' Ruth tugs the plaits behind Dewi's shoulders. 'Some kind of Buddhism. Something to do with living in the moment, I think.'

'*Weird.*'

'Peanut butter sandwiches for lunch again?'

'Not much choice, is there Mum?'

'Sorry. I'll go to the shops today.'

Dewi crunches more Fruit Loops, looks out the window.

'Mum? What good's a photo album without the stories behind the photos?' Dewi picks up a stray Fruit Loop and peers through its hole. 'You have to write them down for me. Before you forget.'

Ruth can't get the scrapings from the peanut butter jar to spread far enough on the bread.

'Uh huh.' The purple lunchbox lid's always difficult to seal properly. 'Time for the bus.'

Dewi stuffs the box into her bag.

'Am I different to you, Mum?' she asks, hopefully but apologetically as they walk down the gravel driveway.

'In lots of ways.' *Happier, for a start. Let it be. Please*, Ruth prays as the orange school bus pulls up. She waves even after she can no longer see Dewi's face clearly through the rear window, carries her daughter's grinning after-image back inside to her own childhood snapshot. Her face has faded in the mission photo, but she can just make out the ghost of her smile, less certain than Dewi's.

∞

Her adoptive parents hadn't told her much about her beginnings. Fred and Grace Joiner. Gaunt, grey and hard as metal. Fred and Grace had themselves been the children of missionaries, unindulged except for the comfort of their faith, undoubting of the necessity to instil in the natives a strong sense of a Christian God and work ethic. When Fred and Grace were twenty-five, they'd met each other at a meeting of young missionaries organised by their church. They'd married within a month, *to permit our carnal desires to be consummated within the sanctifying union of matrimony*, Fred had told Ruth sternly during her mid-adolescence.

Fifteen years of marriage hadn't given Fred and Grace the child they'd hoped for. They'd found Ruth in an orphanage on the outskirts of Denpasar when they went on an evangelical tour through South-East Asia. Surveying the rows of cots in the orphanage, Fred and Grace chose her because she was paler than most of the other toddlers tethered by their ankles with string to their cots. They hoped her paler skin would get her through a loophole in the White Australia immigration policy. She was the illegitimate child of an Australian tourist and a teenager from some distant Balinese village who'd died a day after giving birth to her, the manager of the orphanage had told them.

Ruth had asked them once why her mother had been far away from her home so young. Fred and Grace had commented cryptically that there was something cheap and weak about her mother and something undependable about her father.

'You were born out of wedlock,' said Grace, as if that summed it all up. Fred added that her mother had given her more names than usual. The manager of the orphanage had told them that Ruth's mother had been found wandering the streets in her last days of pregnancy, and that she had gone quite crazy just before she died.

Had no-one led her mother in from the wilderness until it was too late? And what if she hadn't really been crazy, just sick or sad? Fred and Grace had dismissed all Ruth's questions and all her Balinese names.

'They were so unpronounceable.'

'Frivolous and unnecessary. We'd already forgotten them by the time we left the orphanage.'

'Left the photo of your mother behind so the immigration department wouldn't start asking questions about how much Asian blood you had in you.'

'And the dried umbilical cord behind, too.'

'A curious Balinese custom.'

'Unhygienic. Never would've made it past the Australian customs blokes anyway.'

'Not a chance.'

They'd renamed her Ruth after the gleaner maid in the Bible. Had they hoped that by making her a hard-working citizen of God, they'd erase any traces of her mother's weakness and cheapness? They read to her from a children's Bible illustrated with images of garishly haloed saints, white-robed angels and rag-clad sinners battling. In one picture, blackened sinners burned in flames erupting from their loins. *Serve something greater than yourself and your base desires*, Fred and Grace enjoined her over the thin stew Nelly the cook made, with an extra dispensation of biblical quotes to take the place of cake on her birthday.

∞

Ruth couldn't remember laughing much with Fred or Grace. There was always too much work to be done in the name of God. When Ruth wasn't in the mission classroom, Grace expected her to help with chores. Ruth's favourite task was unpacking the items donated by the city congregations of their church for their *less fortunate Aboriginal brothers and sisters*. You never knew what'd turn up. Worn flannelette pyjamas too hot for the mission climate; a box of used teabags some charitable parishioner sent every few months, their strings wound carefully around their middles to enable re-use, smelling of mildew. But the second-hand women's magazines seemed more like revelations to her than anything Fred preached. Inflamed by the frivolity of the flounced necklines and hemlines, Ruth'd put the magazines under her bed to read with a torch at night. In her first nine years, they were the closest she'd had to a vision of a different kind of good life.

∞

The van on the edge of that Kodachrome photo. Fred and Grace had painted the old white Dodge with biblical quotations and a crooked timeline that looked a bit like a barbed-wire fence. The timeline began with *Creation and Adam 4000 BC* at the rear tail-light, through *Seth, Enos, Cainan, Mehaleleel, Jared, Enoch, Methuselah, Lamech* and *Noah;* and on to *Stonehenge, the dinosaurs, the pyramids, the Roman Empire ('He is not here for He is risen');* with centuries of European saints and wars spanning most of the van's sides. *Still to come, the great hope of all Christians, the promised return of the Creator,* the black lettering at the end of the timeline read. *OUR JOURNEY CONTINUES TO ETERNITY,* proclaimed the driver's door.

'What's eternity?'

'The biblical Ruth was an outcast from society. But she gave unselfishly to others and was eventually rewarded for that,' Fred replied. He never let her questions get in the way of his sermons.

When he went into the chapel, she scratched a gap near the end of the van's timeline and dreamed of finding a place for herself beyond its barbs. Forever and ever. Amen.

That photo of her would've been taken only a few months before Lizzy had arrived. A welfare officer had brought Lizzy to the mission with a couple of younger boys, their hair and clothes reddened by pindan dust. Lizzy's parents had recently died from an illness in their camp on the edge of a cattle station further inland. Every morning Ruth sat with her on the wooden bench outside the classroom, holding her hand and talking to her until she stopped crying.

'You brown orphan girl like me,' Lizzy observed at the end of her first week, during the Friday afternoon art lesson. Using the worn stubs of second-hand oil pastels on the butcher's paper Grace gave them, Lizzy drew stick figures hunting near a river lined with pandanus palms.

'Where's that?' Ruth asked Lizzy.

'Back of my family camp. Near the cattle station,' Lizzy nodded towards the ranges, 'that way.'

'Thought there was only pindan and spinifex out there.'

'Big green river full of barramundi and cherabin in the wet.'

'Cherabin?'

'Like freshwater prawns.'

'Prawns?'

'You never had no good food, girl?'

Grace had already taught Lizzy to draw her people as black stick figures, but the rivers and ranges Lizzy drew around the stick figures were richly detailed with animals and strange haloed creatures whose names Lizzy kept concealed from the Joiners.

'What are they?' Ruth asked.

'Spirits. Ours stronger than the Joiners' God,' Lizzy had murmured to Ruth.

∞

The year they turned twelve, Ruth, Lizzy and the other mission girls had been expected to launder the dormitory sheets and their own dresses after school while Fred and the boys tended the vegetable garden. Each girl owned two red gingham dresses, which they'd hand-sewn themselves. Occasionally those dresses were supplemented by the second-hand garments sent by the city parishioners, but the donated garments were usually so stained or overworn that the girls refused to wear them.

'Rubbish clothes. They think we too dirty to care.' Lizzy masked her sharp observations with a slow smile and drawl. 'And this rubbish food make me *fa-a-at*,' she complained to Ruth over their lunch of bread and dripping. 'Or maybe my body already becoming a woman's.'

Grace too must've noticed Lizzy's body had become fuller. That afternoon as the two girls finished showering in the corrugated tin bathroom, she tossed Lizzy a few second-hand brassieres and a couple of *Women's Weekly* magazines from the latest boxes of donations.

'Can I have a bra, too?' asked Ruth shyly.

'Don't need one. Give thanks to God for your small Asian chest,' Grace declared, hurrying away.

'Don't worry, Ruth. One day yours'll grow too.' Lizzy kept only a clean cotton bra and threw the overworn nylon ones into the water heater fire after Grace left. 'More rubbish clothes. Make me itchy and sweaty. N*i-i-ce* dress,' Lizzy commented over Ruth's shoulder as she paused at a heavily made-up blonde modelling a tight silver ball-gown in a *Women's Weekly*. Lizzy had glanced at Ruth's towel-wrapped chest, pulled her own towel tighter around her own waist and chuckled. 'But we both too shamed to wear that.'

∞

Every few months, Lizzy's Aunty Elsie had visited from her camp and, through a gap in the cyclone wire fence, handed her food that Lizzy ate straightaway, her back turned to the mission buildings. During Lizzy's fifteenth year, Aunty Elsie came more frequently. She'd shifted to a new outstation camp only about ten miles away, at the foot of the low ranges rising from the plain.

After Aunty Elsie left one afternoon, Lizzy offered Ruth a small spherical red fruit as they sweated over the laundry copper. Even the laundry water contained pindan dust, tinting sheets and any other white fabric a pale orange.

'Quandong. Careful of the stone. Keep it for making necklace or playing marbles.'

Ruth bit into the firm flesh, winced at the astringent flavour of her first bite before her mouth filled with a sharp sweetness.

'*Skudda?*' asked Lizzy.

'*Skudda,*' agreed Ruth, throwing the wet sheets into a basket. '*Really* good.'

'Like all bush tucker. One day soon I'm leaving this stinkin' mission and its stinkin' food,' Lizzy muttered. 'Don't tell Mr and Mrs Joiner.'

'Where'll you go?'

'Aunty Elsie's camp.'

For a few seconds as she chewed the rest of the quandong, Ruth wished she could go with Lizzy, but she knew she didn't belong to that country around the red hills.

'When?'

'Maybe next time Aunty Elsie come.' Lizzy screwed up her face, scrubbed the yellowed collar of a visiting minister's robe with a nail-brush full of bicarbonate soda.

'Better than living in this mission my whole life. Maybe I get a husband out there. Long time ago I bin promised to a man to be his wife.'

'What do you mean, promised?'

'Old fashion way of marrying for my people.' Lizzy rinsed the wet powder off the collar.

'Which man?'

'He old. But he nice enough.'

Ruth stared at the quandong stone in her hand. It looked like a miniature globe of another world, round and pitted with unknown terrain she could only see from afar.

One morning a few weeks later, Ruth had woken to the sound of the Joiners' murmuring.

'That Lizzy's disappeared. Not in the dorm or anywhere else I can see.'

'The outstation natives have probably taken her. Those blokes can sense an adolescent girl a hundred miles away.'

'Shouldn't we go looking for her?'

'No point. She was too old when welfare brought her in. Once they've had a taste of the bush for that long, you can never really tame them. Her old aunty from the camp's been visiting her lots lately, sticking her beggar's hand through the fence.'

Pining for Lizzy's slow, sure smile, easy companionship and sharing of bush tucker and other secrets, Ruth wondered if somewhere much further along the road there might be another life to which she, too, could belong. She began waking before dawn and climbing the small outcrop of umber-hued rock behind the chapel to get a view beyond the mission fence. How unimportant its little buildings looked against the ranges and rocky outcrops sweeping east towards the red desert, the spinifex-silvered plains rolling west towards the sea. Better things surely happened elsewhere. On the road heading south, a few sparsely foliaged boab trees bottled up against the day's impending heat; a Peaceful Dove murmured its condolences from a stunted acacia tree nearby.

As she'd braced herself against being obliterated by insignificance, it'd seemed that the land beyond resonated with something more powerful. God, stronger spirits, eternity? Or maybe even her future.

Closing the grey album on the uncertain girl in the mission snapshot, Ruth still feels it, that sense of not having found where she belonged.

Too many goodbyes

1988
(problems with the negative)

The last scrapings of peanut butter on toast for Saturday breakfast.

'What do you want to do today?'

Dewi shrugs, opens the album.

'No-one to muck around with now Finn's hanging out with the boys.' She scrutinises the newly inserted snapshot Ruth had taken of her on their back doorstep years before. 'Who was I waving to? Why was I looking so sad?'

'I can't quite remember. Might've been me when I had to go to hospital. You would've been in grade one, I think. You called it the big school.'

'With Miss Carr, my big teacher.'

'Yes. Nearly six years ago. Time flies!'

'She was so huge she blotted out the sun.'

'Well. It was hard for you around that time.'

'What do you mean?'

'You had to say quite a few goodbyes.'

∞

For weeks after Luke's previous visit, Ruth had thought it was just the fear of being abandoned again that made her left breast ache. *Closeness to the heart,* she'd thought, *give it time.* But the pain had worsened over a month. She made an appointment with Doctor Vincent.

'Any family history of breast cancer?' Doctor Vincent's silver-streaked hair glinted in the glare of the examination light as she pressed her fingers against the underside of Ruth's left breast.

'Family history? I have no family history. It begins and ends with me and Dewi.'

'What do you mean?'

'I was orphaned just after I was born.'

'Ah.' Doctor Vincent checked the rest of Ruth's breasts with her cool fingertips, paused them on the underside of the left breast again, peered through her spectacles at it. 'This is probably just a fat cell in this bottom quarter, nothing to really worry about, but I'm giving you a referral to a specialist in the city. Just to be on the safe side.'

∞

In white medical rooms overlooking the freeway exchange where she'd been picked up by the truck driver going to Lost River about six years before, Ruth had braced herself for the cold touch of more examinations, mammograms, fine-needle aspirations. David's scratched old watch hung loosely on her wrist, its ticking louder than she'd ever noticed before.

Late in the afternoon, wearing a dark suit and a five-o'clock shadow, the oncologist pointed with his pale manicured hand to the claw-shaped white patch in the scan of her left breast. *Another negative,* she'd thought, looking at the illuminated scan, *lights and darks reversed.*

'You can see the calcification here. A tumour,' he'd said. 'Unfortunately. For a tumour like this, we usually recommend a full mastectomy and removal of the surrounding lymph nodes. Get it quickly. I have a space available on my surgery list Friday.'

∞

Stitches, catheters, analgesia. More lost days.

She'd mislaid David's wristwatch somewhere between the anaesthetic and the post-operation painkillers. Nausea, Maxilon, hormone receptor tests. Under the clear solution of the methadone drip, she'd dreamed the vanished river had returned to fill the empty valley where her breast had been.

∞

A cotton-covered lambs-wool insert from the hospital's women's auxiliary, *to take the place of your missing breast.*

'The wound's healing up nicely,' the oncologist had said a week after the operation. 'We usually prescribe women with your kind of breast cancer another drug to be taken at home.'

Tamoxifen, to be taken daily for the foreseeable future. Panadeine Forte for the pain.

'You'll need follow-up tests annually. The hormone receptor and other test results indicate your survival chances are fair.'

Fair. What might that mean? *Fair.* She'd turned the word over. It could mean good. It could mean not good enough.

∞

On the Greyhound bus back to Lost River, she'd written Luke a short note to let him know she'd had a mastectomy. But she couldn't work out what to tell Dewi. *How much should a mother tell her five-year-old daughter about this kind of thing?*

The bus driver dropped her off at the intersection just up the road from home. When she reached for her bag, the stitches pulled at her skin where her breast had been. As she walked up the driveway carrying her bag on her right side, the cottage door swung wide open in the breeze, as if no-one lived there anymore.

'Mummy!' Dewi rushed in from the orchard, her hair unruly and unwashed, pecked Ruth perfunctorily on the cheek, rushed out to play with Finn again. Unpacking and doing the hospital physiotherapist's exercises, Ruth watched the two children through the living-room window. They poked sticks into cocoons, made mud-cakes and attempted to feed them to Yoko the cat.

'Be careful,' Ruth had warned Dewi as they wandered further along the riverbank. 'Don't go near the cave. Look out for snakes. Don't get into deep water.'

∞

The lambs-wool prosthetic had shrunk when Ruth accidentally washed it in hot water. When people in town stared at her chest, she felt like a scarecrow with the stuffing knocked out.

'You know you can always get boob jobs done on private health cover,' confided Eloise. 'Thinking of doing it myself now I'm beginning to go saggy. Just cosmetic reconstruction for me, of course.' She patted her chest proudly. 'Piece of cake. You should get yerself a full image makeover in Myer at the same time.'

Private health cover, cosmetic reconstruction, image makeover. It had sounded to Ruth like a foreign language from an unreachable destination.

∞

As she'd sat at the kitchen table looking in her empty purse after shopping for groceries the next morning, someone had knocked on the back door. She opened it to Luke. He stood side on to her, as if ready to make a quick getaway. He held a bunch of slightly wilting yellow roses. His face looked weary yet determined. He glanced at her chest and winced almost imperceptibly before handing her the flowers at arm's-length, as if across a barrier.

'Thank you!' No man had ever given her flowers before. 'Come in!' Too eager, she realised as he took another step back.

'Nah. Can't stay.' Ruth held the roses to her face, covering her disappointment. 'Dewi?' Luke asked, glancing around the kitchen and living room.

'At school.'

He looked relieved, put his hands in his pockets, shifted uneasily on his feet. She could hear spare change shifting in his pocket as he told her that he was getting married.

'Congratulations.' She smiled as sincerely as she could.

'Margo. Merv Ferguson's granddaughter I mentioned to you a while back? Nice family.' His embarrassed glance.

Everything I can't give him.

'You don't have to feel too sorry for me,' she said. 'I'm not dying, you know.'

He pressed his fingertips against his temple. 'I hope you and I can stay friends.'

'Of course,' Ruth replied. A small grey wren flapped hard against the window pane, mistaking its own reflection for a mate.

'David did tell me something important about you the last time we spoke,' Luke said softly, sidling along the step.

'Don't tell me.'

'You don't want to know how he felt about you?'

'No. Please don't.' Because it would've been more painful than the stretched red scar on her chest, whether David had cared for her or not. She'd put her finger to her lips and slowly shut the door on Luke.

∞

The following Saturday afternoon, Finn and Dewi had disappeared from sight for more than an hour. Ruth walked onto the verandah and called them. No answer.

The water. The cave. The dangers. She ran through the orchard and along the track shouting their names, until finally Dewi replied from across the river. There they were, between two trees on the island of paperbarks, a makeshift roof of twiggy branches suspended between the forked trunks.

'How did you get there? The river's flowing too fast!' Ruth yelled.

'It's only up to my chest. We're building a house,' Dewi replied.

The paperbark trees grew together so densely you couldn't see more than a few feet into them. David had told Ruth a visiting botanist had once calculated the biggest of those paperbarks were at least five-hundred years old. Her feet sank into silt as she waded across the river and into the reeds. On the island, water pooled around her feet with every step into the black mud. Both children were wearing only their underclothes, wet from swimming. Finn kept glancing at Dewi's nipples, just visible through her singlet. The wind murmured like a jury through the trees' creamy branches.

'Come back, right now,' Ruth snapped, grabbing Dewi by the wrist and putting her dress back on.

'See ya later, alligator,' said Finn.

As they waded back to the cottage, Ruth steadied her trembling and Dewi whimpered. She ran Dewi a bath, added bubbles for a treat. She realised she'd let anxiety get the better of her, because she'd been unsure exactly how far back in her own past the darkness had really begun, when it would finish, and what lay on the other side.

∞

'Don't do anything like what Lizzy did,' Fred had warned her sternly when he and Grace saw her return from one of her early morning walks to the rise on the edge of the mission. 'Lots of the girls from the outstation camps get involved with men years before they should.'

'No good Christian man will marry you if you behave like that,' muttered Grace.

*'And he said, Blessed be thou of the **Lord**, my daughter: for thou followedst, not young men, whether poor or rich.* From *The Book of Ruth,'* Fred concluded, wiping his feet on the chapel doormat.

As a child, Ruth had believed everything Fred preached to the Aboriginal people about the importance of walking the Right Path with God, sticking her arm out rigidly in front of her like all the other young children in the pews of the tin chapel, demonstrating how straight that path was. How she had wanted to embrace the white plaster Christ, His attenuated limbs bleeding pindan dust when the chapel roof leaked in the wet season. But in the year after Lizzy left, the path to God looked less straightforward to her. She couldn't shake a feeling that she'd not only lost her best friend, but that something even more important had been missing throughout her childhood. This feeling intensified when Grace criticised her.

'Weakness of character can be inherited as much as weakness of the body,' Grace had warned, staring at Ruth's chest. 'Only God can help you overcome that.'

Theirs was one of the last missions in the state to shut down. The day after the mission children had been sent to boarding schools in the closest town hundreds of miles away on the coast, Ruth gazed through the cyclone wire fence towards the intersection of the gravel track and the bitumen road shimmering in the heat, while Fred and Grace packed and cleaned. A road train roared northward along the bitumen towards the town hundreds of miles away. In a few days, they, too, would travel to that town, to be house-parents in one of their church's boarding schools.

'Ruth! Don't just stand around at the fence showing yourself off to the world!' snapped Grace. 'We didn't bring you up all these years to sell yourself cheap!' Crows cawed over the Peaceful Doves' murmured condolences. When Grace slapped her cheek and strode towards the dormitories and every other thing needing cleaning before the mission closed, Ruth only glanced mutely at her. The road south was far more compelling, wavering and beckoning beyond the mission fence.

∞

Joining her at the fence a few minutes later, as the horizon creased under the sun's press, Nelly the cook had said: 'Grace only slap and yell at you because she busy and worried about bringing you up right way. Maybe she never had enough love from her parents. Them old missionaries real hard. Maybe she hiding something about herself, too. When someone too strict Ruth, they prob'ly shamed bout something they done themself.'

'How do *you* know?'

'Had too much shame, too.' Nelly put her hands over her face, spoke through the gaps between her fingers. 'A white man made me pregnant when I was just a bit older than you. I had my little baby boy *lo-ong* time ago, before Joiners came here.' She lowered her hands slowly, wiping her broad cheeks. 'The old missionaries sent my baby to a home in the city for half-caste children, they callem. Sent me to work here. Treat me like rubbish. I never saw my baby again. Anyone try to make you feel like rubbish, don't be shame like I was. Too long I felt shame.' Nelly had rubbed Ruth's cheek with her tough-skinned thumb. 'I'm leavin' to cook at the station where my brother works tomorrow. Might be we never see each other again,

Ruthie. But remember I tol' you this. Don't let anyone make you feel shame.'

∞

Ruth had left the mission before dawn, carrying in a donated knapsack a change of clothes and the snapshot. As she'd walked along the red dirt road, she'd felt much older than her seventeen years. She'd left her two gingham mission dresses behind and worn a baggy pair of trousers and man's shirt from the boxes of donations sent by the city churches. The weight of forty-three dollars and twenty cents stolen from the chapel's collection box in her pockets; the promise of the world beyond the mission in her sights.

As she'd turned at the end of the gravel track to look back at the dim mission buildings one last time, only a few things seemed clear to her: that Fred and Grace had faith in God; that she'd inherited nothing she wanted from them, least of all their kind of faith; that she never wanted to see them again; and that she had to put more than just distance between herself and the life she'd lived with them.

∞

The low cooing of a bronze-wing pigeon in the river gums beyond the orchard. Ruth had stood in the living room facing the river, doing her daily exercises to help the scar and muscles heal properly.

'Finn's playing with some boys his own age,' said Dewi. 'I'm bored. When's that funny man Luke coming to build Lego houses with me again?'

'Luke's getting married, Dewi.'

'To you?' Dewi's voice, small but brimming with hope.

'To someone else.'

'W-why?'

'Because he loves her, I guess.'

'B-but doesn't he love *us*?'

'Sort of, I think. But...'

'But not enough to *m-marry* you? Because you had one of your bosoms cut off?'

'Maybe. I'll build houses with you, Dewi.'

'Luke's are better.'

'Why?'

'He knows how to do things big.' Dewi paused. 'B-but *I* don't love *him* anymore.'

∞

Dewi, flushed and tearful when she emerged from the classroom at the end of the next day. She'd run to Ruth and hidden behind her as Miss Carr came out holding a firmly knotted plastic bag gingerly by the handles; handed it over to Ruth.

'Dewi wet her pants in class today. If you can launder and return the spare pair she's wearing.'

'Thank you, Miss Carr.'

The big teacher; the big school. The tiny wet garment in the plastic bag weighing so little, yet so much. A couple of mothers stared curiously at the plastic bag. Ruth shoved it hastily into her knapsack. Miss Carr dropped her voice.

'She's really a bit old to be doing this kind of thing now.'

Ruth felt Dewi's grip tighten on the back of her skirt.

'We're never too old to make mistakes and never too old to learn, I hope, Miss Carr,' Ruth replied, steadying her voice even as she wavered under the teacher's parting glare.

Dewi pressed her fists into her eyes and sniffed as they walked down the street.

'Sorry, I don't have a tissue, Dewi.' She squeezed her daughter's wet hand. When they reached the first paddock on the outskirts of town, Dewi began sobbing loudly.

'Don't worry. Don't be ashamed,' Ruth said, mopping her daughter's tears with the hem of her skirt. 'I know,' she murmured as her daughter's tears kept coming, 'I know.'

∞

Do not despair, saying "My life is gone,
and the Friend has not come."
He comes...and out of season.
He comes not only at dawn.

– Jalal ad-Din Rumi
– Oriental Wisdom 1976 Pocket Diary.

Ruth puts the quote under the photo of Dewi waving on the step, hoping it'll ring true for her daughter soon.

Luke and Margo

1989

(contrast appears stronger than it does in real-life)

'That dress I wore in that grade one photo nearly fits me now. See?' Dewi hitches up the bodice of the torn sequinned silver gown Ruth'd brought home from the op shop for a dress-up five or six years before. 'Remind me, who's that lady next to Luke in this photo again?'

'Margo. She married Luke, so she's part of your family too. If ever I'm...not here anymore, they can help you remember where you came from.' The lines on Luke's forehead, smoothed by his smile at Margo. 'Maybe even help you find where you're going.'

'When was that photo taken?'

'You were at school. I think you were in grade two.'

'Yay! Katrina and the Waves! My favourite song!' Dewi sashays across the living-room floor to turn up the radio volume on *Walking on Sunshine*, lifts her arms and twirls. 'I already know where I'm going! Dancing!'

Ruth lifts her arms and spins with her.

'Yay, Mum!'

'Don't know all the moves!'

'Pretty good for a Mum, though!'

'Where'd you learn those ones?'

'School.'

Dancing, one of those things she'd hoped to do with David. The late afternoon sun pours through the open door and it's almost as if she and Dewi are walking on sunshine like the song says, and embracing it with their outstretched arms, and for those few radiant minutes Ruth doesn't feel older than her years.

'Yay, Mum!' Dewi cheers again, 'you should always be like this!'

'After I've had a rest!'

Ruth drops to the couch. The sequinned gown's bodice is still a bit too loose when Dewi lowers her arms and she trips over the skirt once, but she picks herself up again and keeps dancing past the pile of grey photographs, through the open door and into the golden hour.

∞

Ruth's mastectomy scar had healed completely over the months before Luke and Margo's first visit together. Every few weeks, Jack dropped over leftover vegetables in a cardboard box. A few small carrots and potatoes, a cabbage or wilting plumes of spinach.

'Didn't sell at the markets.'

'Thank you!'

'Gotta juicer?'

'One in the op shop I think.'

'Lots of non-acidic vegetable juice's good to prevent cancer. Cucumber, carrots.'

'I'll try anything.'

'Naturopath friend recommends wheatgrass enemas.'

'Enemas?'

'S'when you shove it up yer arse.'

'Sounds tricky.'

'Yoga classes at the town hall Saturday arvo wouldn't hurt. Get the breathing going. Get some prana into you.'

'Prana?'

'The life-giving force in the air.'

'So long as the classes don't cost too much.'

'Not much money in the bank, ay?'

'Or much energy.'

'Your choice,' he shrugged. 'Your money or your life, I guess.'

No choice at all.

'Thanks for the vegies, Jack. So kind of you.'

'Nothing like good neighbours.' His gap-toothed smile full of pride, he looked a few inches taller as he walked back towards his block. 'Shit!' he'd yelled, tripping over the fallen wire fence. 'Never did work out who should fix that.'

∞

'Want some vegies from the Murphy's garden?'

'No, thank you,' Dewi had replied primly over the top of her latest Lego house.

'Why?'

'Don't like their *fertiliser.*'

'What fertiliser?'

'Their wee. Finn *said.*'

'Dewi. They pour it on the ground, not on the vegetables themselves.'

'Can we plant our own vegetable garden?'

'We can try. Trouble is, most vegetables need a lot of water. We don't have a dam like Roberta and Jack. There's not much in the rainwater tank for drinking water.'

'What about the river?'

'It's hard work carrying the water up the banks. But it *is* nearly winter. We could give it a try. Tomatoes grow easily from seeds. We could use the seeds from this old one of Jack's.'

'Yeah! Our own garden! With things that grow quickly. Just in case.' Dewi's shoulders, raised and tense.

'Just in case of what?'

Dewi twisted the hem of her dress.

'Just in case you die.'

'I'm not dying anytime soon, Dewi. You can live for years after a mastectomy. Lots of women grow old and don't die from breast cancer after they've had it once.'

Dewi's shoulders dropped.

'*Promise?*'

'Promise.'

∞

In the rain-damp earth they'd planted rows of tomato, corn and lettuce seeds dried from Jack's donations; a few of David's old seed potatoes she'd found on the orchard's edge. Probably long dead, but you never could tell. Their vegetable patch measured no more than four feet square, but Dewi marked the place of each seed obsessively with twigs.

'So they don't get lost,' she'd explained.

∞

The house had deteriorated so much that Ruth didn't know where to begin. She still couldn't control the rising damp, despite trying nearly everything Jack and Pete suggested. She dreamed of a permanent spring under the house and woke in the morning wondering if she'd solved their water shortage. Crawling under the house, she found nothing except small deposits of feathers, rodent and frog skeletons, deposited there by the cat, she guessed.

'I don't want to go to school anymore,' Dewi said when she got out of bed one cold morning, her skinny knock-kneed legs trembling.

'Why not?'

'My legs and feet feel too c-*cold*.'

'I'll buy you some stockings.'

'That won't help.'

'Why?'

'I really feel cold because Miss Carr doesn't like me.'

'Shall we pick her a bunch of flowers?'

'No flowers in our garden.'

'Well. Shall we just be brave?'

'Okay. But only cos I want you to be happy, Mum.'

While Dewi was at school, Ruth had consulted *The Complete Guide to Australian Home Maintenance and Renovation* again. How immaculate and tightly sealed all the houses in it looked, compared to anything she'd ever lived in. Built-in cupboards, smooth shiny surfaces, mood lighting. Money. Would she ever have enough?

She went into Dewi's room. Rising damp, falling damp or lateral damp? She'd tried drilling more weeper holes next to David's, added lime mortar on the ground between the walls and weatherboards and to the ground under the house. But the dampness remained over the following weeks, patches of mildew growing on the walls like cumulus clouds.

At the back of the bookshelf, Ruth found a magazine cutting showing how to make floor rugs from rags. All those unwearable clothes in the boxes at the back of the op shop. She followed the magazine instructions, hammering rusty old nails from the shed along the top and bottom of one of David's large picture frames. The scar on her chest still tight but no longer painful as she'd strung the frame up into a makeshift loom.

∞

Every day after work the next week, she'd carried some of the unwearable clothes home from the op shop. Faded floral housedresses and aprons, threadbare striped and checked shirts. She washed them and tore them into long narrow strips in the evenings. The next weekend, she wove them, running veins of vivid colour amongst the more faded. The slowly accumulating striations of cast-offs. The sedimentation of millennia in the cliff she'd walked to with David.

∞

'It's nice and soft and warm, even though the room's cold.' Dewi, barefoot on the finished rug on her bedroom floor. She'd lain full-stretch on the rug, blue crayon in hand, butcher's paper on the floorboards, and copied David's painting of the river valley on the opposite wall. Making do; they'd practised it all their lives.

∞

'*Gorgeous*,' crooned Roberta when she saw the floor rug, 'must be able to make money out of that. Weave some more and I'll sellem at our Saturday morning market stall. So long as you snaffle us some goodies from the op shop.'

Ruth toed the gaps between the edge of Dewi's floor and the wall, stuffed a few pieces of rag into them. Maybe re-using other people's cast-off cocoons might help carry Dewi and her across these crooked foundations and floors to a more secure future.

∞

The young Aboriginal woman had come into the op shop again while Ruth sorted the latest box of donations. She'd looked thinner than the time before, and she'd lost a tooth. Her green op shop jacket was stained and torn.

'Hi. Katy, isn't it?' The woman nodded and thumbed half-heartedly through the racks of clothes without talking to Ruth. 'How've you been?'

Katy didn't reply, took a half-smoked cigarette from her pocket, sat and lit it on Merv's old vinyl couch near the change room.

'Bit early for boronia picking?'

'Whatcha think?' Katy scowled.

'Things a bit tough for you right now, Katy? Life's hard sometimes, isn't it?'

'Whatcha know about life being really hard?' Katy's top lip tightened and deepened in the corners. 'You gotta job and a house.'

She couldn't bring herself to tell Katy about her mastectomy. Looking at her, she saw things could be worse.

'Family get sick or die too young. Those sorts of things are hard.'

Katy glanced at her, a flicker of recognition in her eyes.

'Yeah. No-one to look after the kids. 'Cept those white guvment pricks. Puttem in foster homes. Break 'em up from their brothers and sisters worse than the old missions. Happen to me. Seen 'em drive my sister and cousin mad. Then the loony bin drove 'em even madder.'

'Sorry to hear that Katy. When did that happen?'

'Still happening. Betta stay outbush.'

'Give me the bush any day,' Ruth nodded from behind the unsorted pile of handbags and high heels.

'True,' said Katy, helping herself to another jacket and a bright pink jumper on the way out. 'See ya.'

Ruth had watched her cross the gravel car park to the track upriver and out of sight. Maybe one day Katy might show her places you could get away from the glare of hard authorities.

༄

Only a few of Ruth's rugs sold, and frost killed their lettuce seedlings. Still not enough money to buy Dewi all the warm soft things she deserved. But in spring the seeds from Jack's overripe tomatoes sent out bursts of yellow, star-shaped flowers, and the almond tree blossomed more than it had for years.

༄

Ruth had gone into the darkroom with a torch that spring. *What am I looking for? Memories. A way to make extra money, maybe. Anything to carry us through.*

A thick web had hung across the few inches between the enlarger's lens and its base-board. The touch of her hand launched a flotilla of tiny newborn spiders across the dark space where David had printed enlargements from the negatives of his last weeks, his watchful face lit just a few seconds per print by the enlarger's timed light. She thought she heard something rustle briefly behind her. She shone the torch onto the shelves next to the enlarger, found only a few dusty rolls of black-and-white film. She pulled up the old wooden chair to check the highest shelf. Almost missed the slim narrow folder the size of a bookmark.

Outside in the morning sun, a small cloud of dust rose from the folder as she opened it to reveal the strip of black-and-white negatives. She held the film carefully by its edges up to the light. Even with the darks and lights reversed, she recognised them: his perfect exposures of the river valley, before the subdivisions and the holiday houses of the wealthy had marred the view upriver.

The morning sun's low angle showed her something else. There, on the unexposed black frames at each end of the negative strip, elongated fingerprints. Despite their fineness, the fingerprints were larger and more widely spaced than hers.

In the kitchen, she'd cut those last traces of his touch carefully off the film and put them in an envelope to keep them safe.

∽

'How much for five postcard-sized prints of each of these black-and-white shots, please?' Ruth had asked the new pharmacist's assistant sorting prints of real estate and happy families from the latest printing machine. *Mel!* her plastic name-tag read.

Ruth carefully handed over the envelope containing his negative strips.

'Single lens reflex photos. Don't get many of them these days,' said Mel, peering at them from beneath her frosted fringe. She'd lowered her chrome reading glasses on the end of her powdered nose, smiled beneficently at Ruth. 'Only five cents each this time. Use-by date on our black-and-white print paper's nearly up. Want to make it ten of each at that price?'

∞

The new prints of David's landscape photos had fit neatly into the empty bookstand at the front of the antique shop. Ruth fixed a sign to the top of the stand: **Postcards of Old Lost River $2.00 each.** She painstakingly wrote David's name and hers in small clear print above her postal address, in the bottom corner on the back of each postcard. A partnership more public than any they'd had before he left.

Most of the postcards sold that week to city holiday-makers. She'd order more prints from Mel straightaway. *Diversifying the income stream,* Des and Eloise Gilbert would call it. On the way to the bank to put the money into her account, she'd seen a tourist outside the post office sending David's last images into the future.

∞

The first day the weather had warmed enough to get the cicadas singing that summer, Dewi burst into the cottage with her hands full of red and yellow jewels; her cheeks smeared with tomato juice, corn kernels caught in the gaps between her teeth. Sharing the sweet flesh with Dewi, it had been easy enough for Ruth to believe that youth and rude good health would be theirs for years to come.

∞

By midsummer the weatherboards had become so dry that a few pieces had begun to break off on the western side of the house, which bore the brunt of the winter winds and storms.

'Used sump oil's the cheapest,' Jack'd advised. 'I'll get my mate Jim at the service station to deliver some to you tonight on his way home.' Jack said 'my mate' proudly, as if friends were his wealth.

∞

She'd dragged an old wooden ladder out of the shed, a rung or two missing, leaned it against the weatherboards above the verandah. Took the battered tin of black sump oil up with a stiff old paintbrush, gritting her teeth. Barely a clue, and no head for heights.

Halfway up, a remnant wasp's nest crackled under her hand like thin paper and blew away on the wind like ash. Cocoons nestled between the weatherboards, empty old yellowed ones, new white ones incubating life. She threw the old ones to the wind and painted carefully around the others, the dry brown jarrah soaking up the oil thirstily, darkening to almost black.

Underneath the verandah gutter, a swallow's nest with broken, blue eggshells inside. She put it in her pocket for

Dewi. Holding tightly to the gutter, she turned slowly, eyes closed, legs trembling against the top rungs, to face the view. The gutter creaked under her weight. She felt the sting of fear in her sinuses, but the gutter didn't give way. She'd opened her eyes to the river rushing through the rocks further upstream before lazing into loops; its serpentine green path cool amongst the dry yellow paddocks before it reached the cliffs and wound through the dunes to the bay. A revelation: this little world between the river and the sea, and her precarious place in it.

∞

When Luke had finally visited again that month, he'd stood at the front door with someone who looked nothing like Inga. Wearing a checked flannelette smock over her sturdy legs, she had a cheerful smile and skin as lightly freckled as toast.

'Ruth. Margo,' Luke murmured, his voice quavering slightly. The wind blew against her smock, revealing her pregnant belly.

'Ah. Hullo.' Ruth was surprised by a pang of regret. She felt thin and insubstantial next to his wife. *Seven-, maybe eight-months pregnant*, Ruth guessed, a hollowness in her own belly as Margo reached out to Luke's arm to balance herself on the step. What would it be like, to have someone to lean on like that?

'Good to meet you, Ruth.' Her face wreathed by fine lines running from her outer eyelids and corners of her mouth, her hazel eyes large and frank, Margo shook Ruth's hand firmly. Her fingers felt dry and chapped, the hands of a labourer.

'Cuppa?'

'Just had one.'

'Have another.'

'Only if it's not too much trouble. Just a teabag'll do. We're full of Gran's scones.'

'Good old Ivy.' Luke glanced at Ruth.

A few voices rose from the river.

'*Coo-ee.*'

'Forgot how much sound travels up here.' Margo eased herself into David's wicker chair.

Ruth heard the couple's low confidential murmuring on the verandah as she made the tea inside, but she couldn't catch their words. They hushed when she brought out the tray.

'Well,' she said, slopping tea out of the cups. 'Sugar?'

'One, please,' said Margo.

'No, thanks,' Luke said sternly, looking at the three ants in the sugar bowl.

'Sorry about the wildlife,' Ruth apologised.

'They don't eat much,' Margo said cheerfully.

'Margo does the garden design and planting for some of my projects up in the city,' explained Luke as Ruth whisked the sugar from under his gaze.

'Landscape design at tech's how we met,' Margo smiled.

'Margo grew up down here.' Taking it in turns to tell their story.

'We'd rather be living down here, but. One of these days.'

'What keeps you in the city?' asked Ruth, hiding the sugar bowl under her chair.

'Harder for me to make a living down here,' said Luke.

'Never mind. S'all good,' Margo beamed beatifically. The trees behind her filtering the sun's glare.

'How's Dewi?' asked Luke.

'Okay.'

'Your daughter. How old's she?' asked Margo.

'Six.'

'Luke says she's lovely.'

'Great fun,' said Luke, looking at Margo's belly.

'When are you due?' asked Ruth.

'Mid-March. We'll be snowed under by nappies and milk. Mum and Dad'll come up and stay. Help out. Do you have any family around?' Margo asked, looking at her levelly.

'*Coo-ee,*' the voices echoed again in the valley below.

'Just Dewi.'

'Ohhh,' breathed Margo. 'Must be hard. Especially after your illness and all.' She pressed her hands together.

'I'm better now, thanks,' said Ruth firmly.

Margo opened her mouth and closed it again.

'How'dya like living in the cottage?' she asked finally.

'Best home I've had.'

'I grew up in the house my Mum and Dad built up the road. Dad spent his childhood here, but. Said it was always bursting with family and visitors. Used to be a sleep-out right here on the verandah for the overflow.'

'Aah,' said Ruth. 'Just a sec.' She hurried through the cottage to the darkroom, opened the door onto an odour of mice and mildew. There it was, just visible on the table by the wall: the tin breadbox full of old photos she'd put there after the flood. She heard a quick, light scuffling behind the breadbox as she lifted it and carried it to Luke and Margo on the verandah.

'Bread?' queried Luke, tracing the green cursive script on the beige enamelled tin as Ruth put it on the small table.

'We-ell. Food for thought. Are these Margo's grand-parents' photos?' Ruth asked, lifting the lid with a flourish. Luke and Margo craned their heads expectantly.

Margo shrieked, clapped her hand over her mouth. The photos had been shredded into ragged strips of variegated grey, black, white.

'I'm so sorry!' Ruth took a moment to notice the two hairless, pink bodies, small as her fingernail, squirming in the corner of the box.

'Ugh,' said Luke.

'Baby mice,' said Margo, matter of factly.

'Mother must've got in through that crack in the base,' said Ruth. The translucent membranes over the babies' slightly bulbous, unseeing eyes. The baby mice waved their tiny forelegs, as if in supplication. 'Put them back so their mother can find them?' said Ruth.

'Sorry,' said Margo, her eyes red. 'Did you get emotional like this when you were pregnant?'

'The house'll be overrun by mice if you just put them back,' said Luke.

'You're right,' sighed Margo. 'Maybe we could put them back just long enough to capture the mother, drive them all into the bush further out and let them go?'

'Nah. Mice can travel miles. They'll probably come back or pester someone else,' said Luke.

'I know. I'm being silly.'

'Best to drown the babies straightaway,' said Luke.

'Not in the dunny like Dad used to but,' said Margo. 'Please.'

'The river?' said Ruth. 'We could let the river carry them away.'

'That way we wouldn't have to get rid of their bodies,' agreed Luke. 'No mess or smell.'

'So long as you don't put the breadbox in the river,' said Margo. 'Could hurt the swimmers or the canoes.'

'Easiest just to carry it down and tip them out,' said Luke.

'But then we'll have to watch them drown,' said Ruth. She thought she recognised a frill from a debutante's dress on a flood-mildewed scrap of photograph; a big hand on the udder of a torn black-and-white Friesian cow. Only two photos remained reasonably intact, apart from light mildew and a few nibbles around the edges. She fished them out by their corners. 'The mice mustn't like this glossier paper.'

'That's Dad with his bike. Musta been about ten. And that's Dad, Aunty Joan and Gran with one of her fancy birthday cakes.'

'A fairytale cottage?' suggested Ruth.

'Licorice allsort windows and Smartie flowers. Gran made a different shaped cake each birthday for Dad and his sister. A tractor cake for him one year. Gran was quite a looker in her day. Check out that perm!' observed Margo.

'Does anyone in your family have prints or negatives of these?' asked Ruth.

'I doubt it. Never seen these ones before.'

'Let me clean these two for you then,' said Ruth.

'They're probably too full of germs,' said Luke.

'A few germs never hurt anyone,' Margo replied.

'Vermin germs might.'

'He's right. Best to be careful when you're pregnant,' said Ruth. 'I'll put them in an envelope for later.'

'Got a light cardboard box? We'll send the babies down the river.'

'A box'll only prolong their misery. Best to just throw them straight in and drown them instantly. Best to get things like this over and done with quickly,' said Luke, lifting the breadbox and walking across the verandah.

'Thanks Lukey. Pregnancy hormones making me gutless.' Margo put her hand on Ruth's arm. 'I can't watch.'

Luke carried the breadbox through the orchard towards the riverbank.

'I'm so sorry,' Ruth repeated. 'You must think I... d–don't do any cleaning around here.'

'Don't worry,' Margo said, patting her on the forearm. 'Housework's boring. What happened to those photos is kinda what happens to a lot of old things down here. They either rot or get used to feather new nests.'

'By people or animals?'

'Same thing, aren't they?' Margo laughed. 'S'all good.'

Luke paused at the top of the bank.

'It's just the darkroom I can't face cleaning properly. David...stored a lot of his memories in there.'

'Lovely guy, David. You must miss him.'

'I didn't get enough time to know him very well.' They watched Luke clamber down to the river. 'Did you?'

'Only just enough to see some of the differences between him and Luke. Even though they looked similar, personality wise you wouldn't know they were from the same nest.'

At the water's edge, Luke took the lid off the box and tipped the old fragments and new lives into the water quickly. He stood watching until the river carried them around the bend and away.

'Is it hard, raising a child on your own?' Margo asked Ruth.

'It has its ups and downs.'

As Luke crossed the orchard with the empty breadbox under his arm, Ruth saw that his eyes were red and watery before he averted his face. He put the box down on the verandah, folded his arms and looked at the river again.

'I never did say goodbye to him properly,' he'd murmured, so quietly Ruth almost didn't hear him, 'I never did.'

∞

Life I coold live
by Dewi M.neerly 6 years old

When I was young I was a baby now I am neerly groan up. When I'm groan up I will be a happy wife with a big new house who wears beootyful cloathes. Or a bizness woman. Or a famus film star. I will not be sick. I will have lots of frends and munny. Hope that time hurrys up.

∞

Sitting in her bed, Dewi considers her crooked handwritten note Ruth's just inserted with the photo of her dressing up in the sequinned evening gown when she was six years old; the photo of Margo and Luke smiling on the verandah.

'Can we take some colour photos, Mum? Something *funner* to look at.'

'More fun. What a good idea. Maybe we could sell some colour postcards with your Dad's black-and-white ones.' A blessed relief, her daughter's inclination to happiness.

'Good idea, Mum. Make some more money. Well. Gotta get my beauty sleep,' Dewi winks, pushing hairclips into her damp fringe so it'll dry straight. 'Good night.'

'Sweet dreams.'

'Yeah, yeah, you too,' Dewi yawns, lying carefully on her back so the hairclips stay in place.

Out in the kitchen, it occurs to Ruth she'd never really felt entitled to happiness. Fred and Grace Joiner had emphasised the importance of being good, but never the importance of being happy. She flicks through all the photos in the grey album. *Where have I been? What have I learned? Something to do with living life as well as possible, despite everything. Something to do with finding the river inside us. Something to do with Dewi.*

PART TWO

The Blue Album

Dewi, 11 years old, in her new dress

October, 1993
('strength' in a photo lies in the juxtaposition of the brightest highlights and the deepest shadows)

Dewi enters the dark kitchen, looks at the late-afternoon photo of herself Ruth had put in the album the night before. The pearlescent sheen of her skin against the new dress.

'I chose the purple dress so nobody could see how small my boobs are,' Dewi says, scrutinising the photo critically. 'I'm one of the only girls in my class who's too small for a bra.'

'And the only one who looks beautiful in your special way,' Ruth smiles, concealing her apprehension.

A warmer-than-usual spring week. The crickets and cicadas practised their shrill song for summer; a bottle of Jack's home-brew beer exploded in the Murphy's shed; the cliffs released the day's heat with a cracking noise.

Finn had begun staying in town after school and on weekends. Dewi waited for him to return late in the afternoon and talk with her near the broken wire fence, but he stayed in town later each day. He'd grown into a lanky adolescent, often sullen, his voice on the edge of breaking, his feet restless. When it grew dark, Dewi turned sadly from the fence and retreated into her room.

By the end of the month, when Finn didn't return until after her bedtime, she stopped waiting by the road. Ruth had glimpsed her through the half-closed door, sitting up in bed, silhouetted against the twilight outside her window, looking at the road that led out.

∞

As she'd washed dishes the next morning after Dewi had left for school, Ruth's hand brushed against her right breast. That was when she'd felt the two pea-sized lumps. Through the window, a flock of white cockatoos erupted from the withered orchard plums into the cloud-strewn sky. She'd pressed the lumps. Moments, clouds, cockatoos reeled around her before lurching back into focus. The disease had returned.

Reflected in the clear water in the sink, her face wavered in a sudden gust of wind coming through the kitchen window. Another disrupted portrait.

∞

The day after her appointment with the city oncologist, Ruth had been surprised to hear Dewi's subdued voice on the verandah early in the afternoon, accompanied by a brisk clicking of heels. A professional woman's heels, she guessed, unlike the teetering of Eloise Gilbert's stilettos. She opened the door to Dewi and the upper-school teacher Mrs Robbins. Her ashen, tear-streaked daughter fell into her arms.

'We found this *alcohol* in Dewi's schoolbag,' Mrs Robbins announced crisply through her thin crimped mouth and small pointed teeth, drawing a dusty sealed beer bottle from a plastic shopping bag. 'She told me it's from home.'

Ruth recognised the bottle immediately. Jack's home-brewed beer. Mrs Robbins dropped the bottle back into the bag and dusted her hands fastidiously on a tissue from her blazer pocket.

'Please don't tell her where it's from,' Dewi mumbled wetly into Ruth's ear.

'Ah. Well, that's strange, Mrs Robbins. She certainly hasn't ever touched alcohol before. What was it doing in your bag, Dewi?'

'It must've got there accidentally.'

Mrs Robbins looked shrewdly at Ruth.

'Can I have a word with you, separately?' she asked.

'Go inside for a minute please, Dewi.' Ruth shut the door after her.

'I'll get straight to the point. Eleven's a bit young to be involved in this sort of thing. I'm suspending her for the rest of the day. I'll have to inform Child Welfare if there's another *episode*.'

'Well. I'm sure it was an accident. Like she said.' Ruth could see Dewi inside, peering at them through a gap in the living-room curtains. 'I'm sure Dewi's had enough humiliation for now.'

'You're referring to what's just happened?'

'That's the least of it.' She wouldn't tell Mrs Robbins about the oncologist's diagnosis, just in case it made the teacher contact Child Welfare.

Dewi ducked below the window sill as Mrs Robbins' eyes darted around the house. The rusty drainpipes, the gaps between the weatherboards, the loose verandah planks. The pilled bodice of Ruth's op shop shirt, the frayed cuff of her jeans.

'You know Dewi doesn't fit in with her classmates very well.'

'I gather.'

'May I suggest you and Dewi see the regional school psychologist next time she visits.'

'Sure.'

Pursing her lips, Mrs Robbins lifted the plastic bag handles primly between forefinger and thumb, being careful not to make contact with Ruth as she handed it to her. She walked to her car without speaking.

'You can come out now, Dewi. Who gave you the bottle of beer?' Ruth asked as Mrs Robbins drove away.

'Finn.'

'Did you ask him for it?'

'No. He saw me buying lunch at the canteen while you were in the city. He wanted money. He tried to sell me that pot Roberta and Jack smoke but I said I didn't like the smell. He said I had to buy the beer off him. Please don't tell the school.' She began crying.

'Poor Dewi. It's all a bit of a drag, isn't it? Especially Mrs Robbins, right? Cheer up, Brave Star. You never know what's around the corner.'

'Finn's the only one who sticks up for me and makes kids be nice to me. He'll call me a dobber if you tell the school.'

'I get it. Don't worry.'

'And it's free dress day tomorrow, and I haven't got anything nice to wear,' she sobbed.

'How about we go into town and buy you a dress from Pearson's?'

'A *new* dress? Not just one from the op shop?'

'I wanted to buy you another birthday present anyway. Sorry it's a bit late.'

'Have we got enough money?'

'You didn't want a party. And I've been saving the postcard money. They're still selling well.'

'But we shouldn't use it all up, Mum.'

'We won't need to.'

''Cos you never know what's around the corner.'

Dewi had chosen the deep-violet dress with the gathered bodice and flared skirt after trying on nearly all the dresses her size, and Ruth bought her the fluffy slippers, too. As if soft things could compensate for the hard news she had to tell her, sooner or later.

'How beautiful you look in that colour.'

'My favourite.'

'Purple's the colour of bravery, they say.'

'I'm tired of being brave. I don't want to go to school.'

'Why not?'

'Everyone'll call me a loser or a hippy for having that beer in my bag.'

'Mrs Robbins won't tell the kids about the beer.'

'What if Finn tells them?'

'I'll have a word to Roberta.'

'Promise?'

'Right after dinner.'

Arms outstretched, Dewi turned quickly back and forth in front of her bedroom mirror, making the skirt swirl and catch the electric light.

∞

'Little bastard,' Roberta said when Ruth told her about the beer that evening. 'But what hope's he got with a father like Jack? Please don't tell the school, Ruth. I'll talk to him.'

'Thanks. I haven't been feeling all that good since the latest prognosis.'

'What'd the docs say?'

'Cancer's usually terminal when it returns like this. Nothing they can do except get me on a trial drug program. Buy me some time if I'm lucky.'

'*Heav-vy*. How much longer will that give you?'

'No-one really knows. A year if I'm lucky. They're only on trial. So they mightn't work and they'll probably make me feel really sick.'

'Shit. Naturopath in the city recommends shark cartilage enemas for cancer. I'm really sorry to hear it's come back, Ruth.'

'Please don't tell anyone. I don't want Dewi to hear about it before I tell her myself.'

'Better not tell the school about it, that's for sure. Nothing'd spur them into contacting Child Welfare as much as a dying single mother with a misbehaving child.'

∞

Waking the next morning to the sounds of the day beginning: parrots shrilling, another bottle of Jack's home-brew exploding against the walls of his shed, a crow cawing doom. Dewi pouring cereal into her bowl in the kitchen.

Thank goodness for that.

'Good morning, Brave Star. Your new dress looks lovely on you. Let me do your hair in a nice plait.'

'You haven't done my hair for years. I'm not a baby.'

'I just thought a plait would look nice with your dress.'

'None of the girls in my class wear their hair in a plait. Who're you trying to impress, Mum?'

They both knew, and they both didn't say. Waving Dewi off to wait for the bus, Ruth wondered if Mrs Robbins had already told welfare about Dewi and her.

– *At risk.*

– *Single mother.*

– *And a foreigner.*

The voices of the authorities murmuring in her head.

The next morning, Ruth's headache is sharper and more persistent, and so are the voices.

– *Time's running out.*

– *Pull yourself together, you silly girl.*

– *You've got to put out into the world if you want anything back.*

As she pulls the sheets over her head to shut out the early-morning light, she's surprised by a lone woman speaking softly, unlike the others:

– *Ruth. Finding happiness isn't easy sometimes. But you can find something just as satisfying, even when your life's running out.*

Whose is that gentle voice? It sounds slightly playful yet knowing, like Nelly's or Lizzy's, but older. Ruth wonders if her true mother might've talked like that.

She tiptoes to the kitchen, puts on the kettle. Turns to the first pages of the blue album.

'What am I looking for?' she murmurs, stopping at the photo of Dewi in the purple dress. 'To love, despite everything. I choose to love today, and all the days of my life that remain, and always for Dewi.'

Her daughter shuffles in, wearing her new fluffy slippers; turns the radio on. The regional news. New roads, real estate, timber, milk and grape prices.

'*Boring.* Wish we had a *real* sound system and some music. Did Dad?'

'I think his Bob Dylan record's still around somewhere.'

'Bob *Dylan*? Isn't he one of those really *old* rock stars?'

Dewi looks over Ruth's shoulder at the photo of herself in the purple dress.

'I'm really...*something.*'

'You really are.'

'A good dress for dancing. Where's that record?'

Ruth goes to the living-room shelves, reaches up to the top one. The flood-wrinkled cover. *The Best of Bob.* The singer's surname and face have peeled away, apart from his nose and one shrewd eye.

'Mum! Why didn't you show me this before?'

'The flood wrecked the record-player. Before you were born.'

'Is that Dad's handwriting on the cover?'

'Yes.'

'*Cool!*' Dewi grabs it. Her face falls. 'You can't read his writing. It's gone all *runny.*'

'It got wet in the flood.'

'Where can we get a record-player?'

'There's an old portable one in the op shop. I'll go in later this morning. See if it works.'

'We can listen. See if we can hear what he heard.'

'Okay.'

Be careful. Choose the moment, for Dewi's sake. Who knows what sunken dreams might resurface with those songs from the past?

Dewi, 11 years old, listening to Bob Dylan

October, 1993
(stray light?)

Ruth's voice has become husky overnight, as if she's been shouting in her sleep.

'Why are you talking funny, Mum?'

'Probably just laryngitis or something.'

'You sound like you're trying to reach a high note but can't,' says Dewi.

'You have to hold records by their edges, like this, so you don't damage them,' she rasps, handing the Dylan album over to Dewi. 'That's right.'

'Which one was Dad's favourite song?'

'Not sure.' Not wanting Dewi to be haunted like her parents by songs of love lost.

'Does the record-player work?'

'It's fine. I tried it in the op shop.' There, Herb Alpert's Tijuana Brass Band's 1965 recording had sounded a bit hollow.

'The record's dusty.'

'Blow on it.'

Dewi raises the Dylan record reverently between her hands, closes her eyes and blows. The way she's blown candles out on her birthday cakes since she was a pre-schooler. As if she's still hoping in the darkness for her wish to come true.

∞

'Any pain anywhere else?' Doctor Vincent had asked, feeling around Ruth's neck.

'Just the lumps and a headache,' Ruth croaked. 'Nausea. Nightmares too.'

'All side effects of the drugs the oncologist gave you.'

Doctor Vincent washed her hands and went to the next room. She returned looking even more sombre.

'Ruth, I've just phoned the oncologist. He said one of the small lumps on your last scan could be pressing against your vocal chords, and that your voice will probably keep deteriorating. He said it's probably indicative that the cancer's progressing faster than he predicted.'

'How long have I got?'

'Hard to say exactly. Somewhere between two and six months, maybe. I'm so sorry. When it gets to this stage…' Doctor Vincent had pushed a few sample packs of Panadeine Forte across her desk. 'You'll probably need even stronger painkillers soon.'

∞

If I don't find the words to tell Dewi soon that my death's close, maybe I won't get to tell her myself, Ruth had reflected as she fixed price tags to garments in the op shop. *Any day now, my voice might disappear forever.*

Seagull came into the shop and tried on a pair of red patent stilettos and tight jeans.

'Pay you when I've got money,' she said as she staggered towards the door in them, 'which is never.'

Fifteen minutes later, Roberta came through the door.

'I'm going to a concert in the city.' She pulled a diaphanous gold dress off the rack and held it against herself. 'Do you think I look like the kind of woman a famous middle-aged singer would like?'

'Why not?'

'Your voice sounds weird, Ruth.' She stared at the small lumps at the base of Ruth's neck.

Ruth told her the oncologist's latest prediction.

'Hea-vy,' Roberta said, 'hea-vy.'

'Don't tell anyone. I haven't told Dewi yet.'

Roberta had hugged Ruth, but headed quickly towards the door when she saw Eloise parking her car outside the shop. 'Come over for a cuppa and talk this afternoon? And smuggle this dress home for me?'

∞

Finn had been playing Space Invaders when Ruth took the dress over.

'Hi Finn. Where's Mum?'

'She's already gone.' He blew up a neon green invader on the screen. 'What's wrong with your voice?'

'Just a sore throat. Where's she gone?'

'City. Says she's gonna run away with Leonard Cohen. Someone gave her a ticket to his concert in the city and she reckons she's going backstage to meet him after the show.'

One of my best friends, Ruth thought, *and I barely know her.*

'Oh really? Are you okay, Finn?'

'Whaddya mean?'

'How're you feeling about her running away like that?'

'Well, it's better than listening to the olds fighting.'

'Okay. Who's feeding you?'

'Seagull. Seagull's sorta been with Dad for a while.' Finn's impassive face gave nothing else away.

'Really? Still living in their own houses though, aren't they?'

'You know what I mean.'

'Yeah. I get it. Where are they now?'

'Dunno. Seagull's house I guess.'

'Okay. Come and stay with us if you like.'

'Nah.' He stared intently at his screen.

'Let me know if there's anything I can do for you? Even if you just want to talk.'

'Sure,' Finn said, before he'd obliterated a new onslaught of Space Invaders.

∞

Static or a scratch on the vinyl cutting into the opening chords of *Blowin' in the Wind,* the portable record-player's cheap built-in speaker hollowing out the instruments and voice.

'Do you like the Dylan record?'

'It's o*kay,*' Dewi says tactfully, leaning on the kitchen table, looking at the photo Ruth had taken of her listening to it. 'We learned *Mr Tambourine Man* in school. In grade *two.* All the songs on the record sound strange, like they're coming from far away.'

'Bob Dylan's accent and music always make me think of the rest of the world. How big it is. How far away it seems from Lost River. The other kinds of lives people live. Is that what you mean by sounding as if they come from far away?'

Dewi shrugs.

'I just meant it made me think of my Dad. What he might've said to me.'

Her father's eyes; her mother's knees; her own splendid hair

October, 1993
(Dewi)

Walking through the door after work, Ruth sees the album open at her latest snapshots of Dewi, just before she smells the bleach. Dewi puts the bottle of White King down hastily on the bathroom sink. Her hair's dripping with it.

'Dewi! Why are you putting bleach in your hair?'

'I want blonde hair. And straight. All the cool girls at school have straight, blonde hair.'

Ruth towels the bleach quickly out of Dewi's hair.

'Your father had wavy hair like yours.'

'You mean frizzy. What colour?'

'Sort of pale brown underneath, but the sun bleached it blonde on top.'

'I got the wrong mix from you both.'

'You're beautiful! Quick! Put your head under the shower before the bleach gets in your eyes. Press this flannel against your forehead.' Ruth turns on the shower. 'Tilt your head back. That's it.'

'Now my hair won't go blonde.'

'This stuff's poisonous.'

'*Der*, Mum. I know. I was being careful.'

'I'll make some rosemary rinse for you. It makes brown hair shiny.'

'I wish I knew my father.' Dewi twists a strand of her wet hair so tightly around her forefinger it turns red.

'I wish you did, too.'

'What did you and him *do* together?'

'We knew each other only a short time. But we did good things together.'

'What kind of things?'

'Gardened. Developed photos. We walked a lot and swam. And we made you!'

Ruth washes a few strands of Dewi's hair down the drain, their darkness and waviness persisting.

∞

Ruth had been surprised to see Roberta leaning on the fence post only two days after she'd gone up to the city for the concert.

'Back already, Roberta! How was the concert?' Roberta shook her head, closed her eyes. 'Sorry. You okay? Finn said something about Seagull and Jack.'

'Old news. Can't blame Jack really. He was pissing me off so much I wasn't giving him any.'

'Oh, Roberta. I didn't know things were so bad between you. Why didn't you tell me?'

'I figured you had enough to deal with.'

'Such as death? I'm still living. I still want you to talk to me like you usually do.'

'Sorry, Ruth. Well. Things've been bad between Jack and me ever since we came down here, really. Lost River's full of people who'd rather be somewhere else. Guess swapping beds is as far as some of us can afford to go.'

'But it's so beautiful here.'

'Too small and far away from the rest of the world. We're all getting long in the nose leading each other around the Lost River show arena, sniffing each other's bums. By the time you get to my age, Ruth…' Roberta struck a match, lit her hand-rolled cigarette. 'Sorry…' Exhaling, she suppressed a cough. 'They say positive thinking and wheatgrass can help with cancer. And Vitamin C.'

'You don't really believe all that?'

'Anything's worth a try. Go see that naturopath.'

'Well. The doctor reckons I'll be lucky if I get to the end of the year. The trial drug made me so sick I had to give it up. I'm sorry you're having such a tough time, Roberta. I know what it's like to want to run away.'

'Guess it's no wonder, really, that so many of us here want to do that.'

'What d'you mean?'

'Most of us who settled here over the past decade were running away from something in the first place. Maybe Lost River isn't far enough.'

'You mean…far enough from the city?'

'I mean far enough away from ourselves. I mean, maybe all you do is bring your old ways to a new address. Like the thing we're running from is inside us, y'know?' She dragged hard on her rollie. 'I was damaged goods when I came to Lost River, Ruth. Thought this beautiful countryside might heal me. Shame one or two other damaged people got in the way.' She blew a ring of smoke into the air. 'You know all about damage Ruth. How it doesn't always show. How damaged people and things can get used again and again until they break.'

'Yeah. Maybe most of us are wounded in some way. But something important about us keeps going, don't you think?' She had to believe that, despite her prognosis.

'What do you mean?'

'Whatever you want to call it. Our spirits?'

'Our spirits can break too. Mine did after my first baby was adopted out.'

'But you kept going. Look at everything you've made since. Finn. Your house. Your garden. A life!' Roberta shrugged indifferently, looked past Ruth. 'How *was* the Leonard Cohen concert, anyway?'

'It was kinda sad watching him up there on stage shuffling along to slower versions of the songs he wrote years ago. He looked...well...old. We're all getting old.'

'Is that a blessing or a curse?'

'Sorry, Ruth. I keep forgetting you're...'

'S'okay. The hardest thing is figuring out how to tell Dewi.'

'Maybe you should go to Bali for a holiday with her. Find your people. The Balinese see life and death differently to us. They balance grief with happiness, somehow. Maybe cos in Hindu religion there's an emphasis on light and helping each other. These days in Lost River, people think you need an architect-designed house to live in the light.'

'I'll think about it. But what happened after the concert, Roberta? Finn told me you were running away with Leonard Cohen.'

'Poor Finn. Heard me fighting with Jack. I was a bit off my face then. Just went to the concert, that's all. Called out to the famous man from my seat between songs. Not sure he even noticed me. Even in the sparkly gold dress.' Roberta kicked dirt over her cigarette butt. 'Bloody security blokes wouldn't even let me go backstage after the concert.'

'Sorry to hear it. And I'm really sorry to hear that things are so bad with you and Jack.'

'I'm sick of wasting my life with a lazy two-timer in this backwater the rest of the world's never heard of. Still, he reckons he's over Seagull now.' Her face crumpled. 'A few days ago I really felt like I was meant to leave and make myself a better life, you know? Maybe even find my soul mate. Or at least someone more romantic than Jack.'

'Like Leonard Cohen?'

Roberta's embarrassed half-smile. 'Yeah. But here I am, putting up with Jack the old bastard again. Is that karma or stupidity?'

'Maybe it's just commonsense. For now at least.'

'For now at least,' Roberta echoed, hugging her.

Though Roberta's situation had seemed different to any she'd experienced herself, Ruth had felt familiar enough with it as she walked back across the paddock. *If we don't make the most of the life we have, we start taking our longings and fantasies for real,* she'd reflected as she looked back upriver to all those years of yearning for David.

On her way to work the morning after Roberta's return, Ruth had called into the pharmacy with the colour negatives she'd shot in the weeks before. She held the film up to the window while she waited to be served. Talk about ghostly realities. A double exposure at the beginning of the strip showed the school bus arriving at the breakfast table. David's gaze in Dewi's eyes. Ruth's knock-kneed stance in Dewi's legs.

'What can I do for you today, Ruth?' Mel the pharmacy assistant had dyed her hair a paler shade of strawberry blonde to camouflage the grey.

'Can you print one each of numbers nineteen to twenty-four, please?'

'Sure. Your colour landscape prints are already done.' Mel pushed the prints across the counter. The morning fog in them softened the contrast between the stark blonde brick of the recently built holiday houses and the dark green valley.

'Ar*tistic*,' smiled Mel, 'like a painting.'

∞

Ruth had placed her new colour postcards of the river valley on the stand outside the antique shop, right next to David's black-and-white ones. They'd looked good side-by-side, but the wind had changed direction suddenly and mixed up the old and new, so she'd had to sort them out again.

∞

In the kitchen, Ruth considers her latest photos of Dewi. She's already halfway through the blue album, but two albums are still empty. *I can't just stop here. I have to last the distance as well as I can, for Dewi's sake. I have to save her as many good memories and as much time as I can.*

Memories and time, even harder to save than money. She listens to the ceaseless journeying of the river towards the ocean as the daylight and birdsong dwindle.

Dewi and Yoko Ono

October, 1993
(focus quite sharp, from the nearest to the most distant)

In the following week, the gentle woman's voice comes to Ruth in the quietest moments, especially late in the evening or early in the morning. Sometimes it seems to speak to her from the tree outside her bedroom window, sometimes from the stars hovering just above the tree, sometimes from nowhere in particular.

After waking several times to the woman's voice through the night and into dawn one Sunday, Ruth rises, lights the flame under the kettle. She adds to the album the latest print of Dewi holding Yoko, her black ears flattened by the baby's bonnet Dewi had tied under her chin. Someone knocks on the door as she presses the photo onto the page.

'Just me, Ruth,' a gruff woman's voice calls. She opens the door to Katy, pulling twigs out of her hair.

'Katy! Come in! Cuppa and toast?'

'Out here.' Katy stares through the doorway into the living room and backs away. She's sitting in Dewi's wicker chair when Ruth emerges with the tray. Katy dumps four teaspoonfuls of sugar into her mug, spreads the jam thick on her toast and crams it fast into her mouth.

'Couldn't sleep much,' Ruth yawns. 'Keep hearing a woman's voice talking to me.'

'Good voice?'

'Yeah.'

'Prob'ly one of your family's spirits. Don't tell the doctor about hearing voices, but. Put you in the loony bin,' warns Katy. 'Me and summa my family hear them voices. Fair enough. Course our old peoples' spirits talk to us. But the loony bin psychologist tol' my cousin we only hear voices cos we sick in the head from alcohol an' losing our parents too young.' She slurps her tea. 'Why you speakin' so rough?'

'I have...tumours in my throat.'

'*N-yoh*. That hippy Jack tol' me you had cancer bad. Never know whether to believe anything *he* says. Y'know spirits talk to you more when you're...really sick like you.' Katy rises suddenly as plates clatter in the kitchen. 'Anyway, Ruth. Goin' back to the city today. Came to say goodbye. Just in case.'

'Look after yourself, Katy.'

'You're the one needs to look after herself.' Katy scrounges in her pocket, retrieves a dozen small purple berries and places them in Ruth's hand. 'Lots of these nitre fruit in the rocks round the bay. Good for you. Don't work too hard, Ruth. Walk lots. And thanks for...everything.' Katy hugs her, squeezes her other hand, jumps off the edge of the verandah. 'And don't let anyone send you anywhere you don't wanna be, okay?' She saunters along the trail, turns once to smile and wave before disappearing in the undergrowth.

Not all the sugar's dissolved in Katy's cup. Ruth puts the berries on a plate, carries the tray to the kitchen.

'Morning, Dewi.'

'Who was that?' Dewi looks up from the album.

'Katy.'

'That Aboriginal lady? Wish I could meet her.'

'She never hangs around long.'

'Why?'

'Not sure. Bit scared or worried about something, maybe.'

'Maybe she's just shy.'

'She gave us these.' Ruth hands a berry to Dewi, bites into the salty tang of one.

'A bit sour,' Dewi winces.

'Ascorbic acid probably. Vitamin C. Good for you.'

'Yeah, yeah.' Dewi grins. 'Yoko's lying in my arms like a baby in this photo, but she looks a bit cross under that bonnet.' Scrutinising the recently built houses and apartments in the background of the photo, she says hopefully, 'Maybe there'll be some *real* babies and kids in the new neighbourhood. Someone to play with.'

'That'd be fun. Babies need a lot of looking after, though. You know you don't have to have babies of your own when you grow up. Not if you don't want to.'

'Don't *worry*, Mum. I *know*. We had those sexing lessons at school.'

∞

Another cold snap. Ruth had begun to swallow the new painkillers each morning before going to work. A few unemployed locals asked for blankets, complained to her about their aching bones and chapped skin as the southerlies increased unseasonally, of their clothes smelling like fungus, of the scarcity of firewood nearby since the property developers had cleared the trees for the new subdivisions. Eloise had gone to the city for the department stores' mid-season sales, so Ruth gave these customers the op shop's old woollen blankets, faded quilts, jumpers, pyjamas and jackets from the boxes in the back room. She closed the shop early after they'd left.

∞

Walking past the school on the way home early one afternoon, she heard the children singing the national anthem in bored voices. She wondered if Dewi's voice was amongst them.

She took her usual shortcut home, clambering over old wooden posts and rusty wire. Most of the bushland on the edge of town had been cleared and divided into neat parcels by more-solid fences and walls during the past few years. The newest developments had the grandest ones; limestone blocks, wrought iron or pastel-rendered brick bearing huge pretentious signs in heritage colours: **Green Glades. Crystal Brook Gardens. Riverview Estate.** On the edge of a paddock midway between Riverview Estate and the cottage, Lost River Council had erected a small sign invisible from the road: **Rezoning Application.**

How far would it go?

∞

She'd nodded off to sleep after returning home. The sound of footsteps outside woke her. They paused every now and then before resuming their slow circumnavigation of the house, breaking twigs and small branches. Someone treading heavily; a man, she guessed. Her throat tightened.

The gap down the side of the curtain revealed a freckled, square hand holding a clipboard against a khaki-shirted paunch. The breast pocket bore the embroidered blue and yellow logo of the Lost River Town Council. The double chin, the ruddy nose and bland grey eyes of Ron Hawkins the council ranger. Ruth lay still in her bed for a minute, wondering if she should pretend absence. The front verandah boards groaned under his boots before he knocked three times on the door. Pulling a pair of tracksuit pants under David's old t-shirt, she opened the front door just widely enough to reveal her face; heard the conspiratorial clicking of the cicadas.

'Just a routine council check.'

'I didn't know the council did those.' She couldn't make her voice louder.

He shrugged diffidently and kept his eyes on his clipboard.

'If we have reason to suspect...' his eyes alit on her chest. She pulled David's old dressing gown off the sofa and wrapped it around her.

'Suspect what?'

'Residents are contravening council health and safety regulations.'

'What? Who says?'

'You are contravening health and safety regulations. On several counts.'

'Tell me.'

He nodded towards the full garbage bags and empty bottles waiting on the verandah for someone to carry them out. Exhausted, she'd forgotten to take the rubbish out to the roadside for the garbage truck that week.

'An oversight.'

'And insufficient clearing of undergrowth,' the ranger added.

'For goodness sake. Isn't that just a *lifestyle* difference?' Resorting in her desperation to Eloise's and Inga's terms. 'We're living in the bush here.'

'More than a lifestyle difference, I'm afraid. A fire risk. Regulations stipulate a twenty-metre firebreak around house and garden and clearing of undergrowth further out.'

'Who are you to say what's bush and what's garden? What if they're the same thing?'

'No point in getting philosophical. It's regulations, proper boundaries around property. Simple as that. And you have waste improperly stored or disposed of.' He nodded towards the empty cat-food cans Dewi had arranged in a neat pyramid at the far end of the verandah.

'Attracts vermin. Mind if I take a look inside?'

He looked over her shoulder, waiting for her to step aside. The cicadas trilled louder.

'Yes, I do mind.' Her voice was even higher than it had been when she waved Dewi goodbye that morning.

Clear all safety hazards and health risks, he wrote on his card before handing it to her and mumbling something apologetic into his double chin.

'I'll come back at a time that suits you. If you could ring this number.' He stepped daintily through the overgrown weeds for such a big man, all the way to the council ute. Clutching the back door jamb for support, Ruth felt as scattered and insubstantial as the cirrus clouds above. She put the ranger's card on the pile of garbage.

Had Ron Hawkins been tipped off by the new neighbours? She pulled on her best dress, brushed her hair and teeth. What would she say to them?

Breathing deeply to calm herself, she picked an early branch of almond blossom from the orchard and dawdled upriver along the trail, composing greetings, an offer of friendship. Sun-gilded damsel flies drifted starlike above the river; magpies pealed and swooped. She saw a man standing behind the open back door of a silver four-wheel-drive parked in a gravel patch overlooking the river. Drawing closer, she recognised Des Gilbert. Though she saw his face clearly, he seemed oblivious to her.

Des had only spoken briefly to her in all her years working for Eloise. *Too busy diversifying his income stream,* Eloise had explained after he'd hurried through the antique shop one morning a few weeks ago. *Worries about money all the time. His father gambled away Des's inheritance. Have to give Des credit for being a self-made man.*

As Ruth glimpsed his stocky leg struggling to make its way into his permanent-press business trousers, a woman's shoe fell on the ground next to him. Not one of Eloise's neutrally hued shoes. A red, patent stiletto.

Ruth swerved away and hurried into a thicket of trees, wishing she could erase that image from her memory.

'Agonis flexuosa,' she murmured, plucking one of the long, dark peppermint tree leaves. 'Hovea, weeping wanderer, melaleuca.' How this leafier wilderness had grown over her dry mission prayers.

She reached the firebreak around the new neighbours' house just as a neatly moustached man in tennis shorts and polo shirt locked his wrought-iron gate from the other side. She cleared her throat.

'Excuse me,' she murmured. But he'd already turned away and hurried towards his house. She left the almond branch at his gate and sank back into the shadows of the track. The cicadas trilled; the voices in her head clamoured.

How much gossip about her had the new neighbours heard? For a few seconds she wished for higher fences, risk minimisation, stronger analgesia. Re-entering the cover of the bush, she recalled Roberta's warning years before. *Watch out for Des Gilbert. Gotta few dogs chained up around town.*

Eloise Gilbert's airs and graces seemed more like signs of vulnerability now Ruth'd seen the red stiletto falling from the councillor's car. Clambering down the bank, Ruth splashed her face in the river shallows, wished the water would wash these dirty new secrets from her.

After she heard Gilbert's car spin its wheels in the gravel and drive away, Ruth clambered up the bank to the shed. She rummaged around, found one of David's old brushes and a scrap of black paint in a tin. Empty grass-seed husks and a few stray damsel flies floated past her in the breeze as she painted on the big fencepost at the driveway entrance:

Private property
Keep out

But the wood had been so dry and rough it soaked up the paint, so her words had been all but lost there, too.

∞

She returns to the photo of Dewi holding Yoko. Despite her fierce gaze in the photo, Dewi looks too thin and vulnerable.

'Who will care for her?' Only the last stand of karri trees on the ridge across the river are listening, nodding their heads in the wind.

– *We are with you,* they murmur.

Ruth closes her eyes tight to try and clear the analgesic fog. Is Katy right about hearing spirits talk? Or is it only drugged or orphaned people who hear voices like this? Will stars, trees, wilderness speak to Dewi too, more alive to her than her vanished parents' stories and photos?

Dewi running for the bus

October, 1993
(increase shutter speed and aperture)

Dewi jumps, bare arms and legs outspread in a star shape, while Ruth hastily sews the top button back on her school uniform dress, trying to ignore the pain in the lumps near her armpit.

'Why are you sad so much, Mum? You should be happy like me!'

'You're right! Sorry, Dewi.'

'What makes you happy, Mum?'

'You!'

Dewi rolls her eyes, but grins. 'Besides me.'

'Friends.'

'But you don't have many friends, do you Mum? Just Roberta.'

'What about the people who come to the opportunity shop? And Katy.'

'I mean *really close* friends.'

Ruth cuts the thread.

'Quick. Put this on. Would you like to bring your friends home more?'

'Be easier if we had a Dad.' Dewi shrugs the uniform on. 'What d'you mean?'

'Everyone wouldn't think we're so *weird,* I guess.' Dewi glances at her, pats her consolingly on the wrist. 'At least I'll always have you, Mum.'

The floorboards creak as Dewi does another star jump and grabs her schoolbag. Would there ever be a good time to tell her that it wouldn't be so?

The dull, throbbing pain sharpens as Ruth raises her arms to take a photo of Dewi. As her daughter turns and waves at the top of the driveway, the wind-blown clouds casting flickering shadows across her give the impression of time moving even faster than usual.

Doctor Vincent's eyes narrowed as she ran her fingers over Ruth's armpits, chest and up her neck. She pulled off her rubber gloves.

'It's time to start doing what's really important to you, Ruth. Finish any unfinished business. Get your affairs in order. Maybe take a holiday with Dewi.'

'How long do I have?'

'Anywhere between a few weeks and a few months.' The doctor squeezed her hand, gave her some small white boxes in a brown paper bag. 'Keep your eye on these pills. Big demand for them on the black market. They may cause hallucinations but they should be safe enough if you take them as directed. They'll help with the pain. Ring me if anything urgent happens.'

Urgent? How much more urgent could it get? On her way past the travel agent's, Ruth picked up a brochure titled *Balinese Bargain Holidays*. Maybe a holiday there would give her and Dewi breathing space. Maybe she and Dewi would even find some happiness there. Maybe it would somehow give her the spiritual strength she surely needed, boost her immune system. Maybe she'd even find a miracle cure there. She'd flicked through the prices. Maybe they could just afford three days.

∞

'How would you like to come to Bali with me on a nice holiday?'

'Won't it cost too much?' Dewi had asked dubiously.

'This one's affordable.' Ruth showed Dewi the Nirvana Hotel page in the brochure. ***Find yourself. Be enlightened at the Nirvana,*** its slogan read. 'I've saved some of the rent refund Luke gave me ages ago, and the money from the postcards.'

'Will Luke visit again?' Dewi asked wistfully.

'He said he would. But it could be a long time now they have a little child.'

'What about the *dangers*?'

'What dangers?'

'The volcanoes and earthquakes in Bali, Mum. We learned about them in social studies.'

'The Nirvana Hotel's far away from the volcanoes. The Balinese are supposed to be very friendly.'

'Maybe we can find your *real* family there.'

'That would be too hard. I was left in an orphanage, and I don't know my Balinese name.'

'Can we go there, then?' Dewi asked, pointing to a photograph of an elegant family lounging in white swimsuits by the pool. The little blonde girl wore silver-beaded Balinese slippers and sipped a bright blue drink. 'Yes, a holiday like that. Minus the father.'

Ruth pointed to the pool's far end, where it appeared to merge with the horizon. 'It says here it's called an infinity pool. Because it looks as if it goes on forever.'

∞

Insects fly through the gaps under the windows. Mice and small frogs creep under the doors and between the cracks in the floor. Gaps between the bathroom and laundry weatherboards reveal shards of light she hadn't noticed a month ago.

The house David tried to mend is disintegrating, and she's too sick and unskilled to do anything about it. It seems she and Dewi don't have any dependable structure to live in; that they're inhabiting not much more than shrinking time and unsecured space.

Over in a flash, Ruth writes under the photo of Dewi waving. How will she find the time to do everything she wants to do with Dewi before she dies?

Don't forget to bargain hard for the best deal, the Balinese travel brochure advises.

Bali from the air

November, 1993
(dimmed by distance and window tinting)

A photo taken through their jet-plane window of the island, emerald-green in the tropical noon's gilded light, as the fine drizzle cleared.

∞

The Nirvana Hotel's courtesy bus had delivered them to the steps of the ornately carved main-entrance doors. In the gleaming, white-tiled foyer, a petite Balinese receptionist wearing a synthetic powder-blue sarong and white kebaya placed frangipani leis around their necks.

'Isn't this *Hawaiian*?' Dewi whispered to Ruth, fingering her lei.

'Selamat datang,' the receptionist murmured, pressing her hands vertically together under her chin. 'Mrs Ruth and Miss Dewi? I am Murni.' She smiled warmly, deepening the fine lines around her dark eyes and the bridge of her nose. Ruth guessed she would've been no more than twenty, but Roberta had told her Asians looked young for longer. Murni gestured towards a stocky young man wearing a shirt and sarong the same fabric as hers. 'Gusti will take your bags and show you to your villa.'

Gusti placed his hands together, bowed, and grinned broadly at them, sunlight glancing off his small round spectacles as he wheeled their suitcases through the side door and past the lotus pond.

'What were they doing with their hands?' Dewi whispered as Gusti led them to a cluster of grass-thatched villas. 'It looked like they were praying. Maybe your crooked chest frightened them.'

'They were just welcoming us,' Ruth replied, surreptitiously adjusting her bra. 'That's how the Balinese greet guests.'

Gusti ushered them through a pair of carved blue gates into a walled courtyard.

'Your villa, Mrs Ruth and Miss Dewi.' Balinese on the outside, but inside, a Western deluxe cocoon like the new apartment interiors she'd glimpsed back in Lost River. White walls and linen, mood lighting and air conditioning.

'Ohhh!' Dewi breathed. 'Like a rich person's house!' The large glass windows overlooked a narrow river running through a steep rock gorge. On the other side of the river, villagers toiled in muddy padi terraces beneath lush hills.

'Dewi is a Balinese name. You Balinese?' Gusti asked Ruth.

'My mother was,' said Ruth. 'But she died after giving birth to me.'

'So sorry. You come to see her family?'

'No. I don't know where they are. An Australian couple adopted me.'

'You know any of your Balinese family names? Maybe you can find them.'

'No. I don't even know my mother's name.'

'So sorry.'

'Can you tell me? Is there still an orphanage on the northern edge of Denpasar?'

'Orphanage?'

'A home for children with no family?'

'Ah. Only one in north Denpasar,' Gusti had said. 'I take you there tomorrow morning. Wait for me in reception at ten o'clock?'

∞

While Dewi bought herself a fizzy red drink at the bar that evening, Murni had glanced at Ruth's chest, smiled at her gently.

'You been ill, Mrs Ruth?' she murmured.

'I have cancer,' she whispered.

'Ohhh,' Murni exhaled softly. 'I'm so sorry.' She paused, lowered her eyes. 'I pray for you tonight at temple.'

Lying in bed back in their villa, Ruth and Dewi heard the night insects, birds and frogs trilling divergent rhythms over the river's rushing. What kind of timing was that? Ruth had given up trying to follow each song and drifted with Dewi into sleep.

∞

As Gusti had driven them towards the edge of the town the next morning, Dewi furtively ate the small banana pancake she'd smuggled from the dining room after their enormous breakfast, licking her fingers when she'd finished.

'What're they doing?' She pointed to a line of brightly dressed women carrying baskets to a cantilevered red-brick temple with an ornate curlicued gateway.

'Carrying offerings. We villagers always giving offerings and money to temple and ceremonies.'

'My friends in Australia say the Balinese are poor but happy. Do you think that's true?' asked Ruth.

'Rich Western tourists sometimes tell me that,' Gusti smiled wryly. 'Being poor doesn't make us happy,' he said, 'especially when we can't afford food or medicine. But giving to the village and the temple ceremonies makes us *good* poor.'

'Good poor?'

'At peace with ourselves for helping others.'

The dirt road passed through iridescent-green rice padi terraces and small villages of thatched concrete houses. Ducks quacked and dabbled next to farmers weeding in the flooded fields; children flew kites, or fished with pieces of string for eels in the muddy water. The road narrowed between small shops selling stone gods and goddesses, painted eggs and wood carvings before opening onto a wider bitumen road on the outskirts of Denpasar.

'Here,' said Gusti, pulling up at a squat concrete building covered in mildewed chartreuse paint. Three scrawny dogs, black, tan and brindle, circled them as they got out of the car. Bites, parasites, rabies. She clung for a moment to Dewi and Gusti's arm, suddenly afraid the dogs might kill her quicker than the cancer. 'It's okay,' said Gusti. 'I look after you.'

Someone in the closest compound whistled and the dogs ran off. A plump, middle-aged Balinese woman opened the thin wooden door of the orphanage when Ruth knocked.

'Tidak boleh,' she said irritably when Ruth told her she'd come looking for her birth certificate. 'Cannot. You see how busy.' Behind her, large-eyed children sat at three long tables, waiting patiently for their bowls to be filled by two women in aprons. Five infants were tied around their ankles by pieces of string to their highchairs. Two of them sitting nearby were pale-eyed and fairer than the others.

Tourism, indeed, Ruth thought.

Gusti leaned over and whispered into the woman's ear so Dewi wouldn't hear.

'I try,' said the woman, her eyes softening as she turned to Ruth and glanced at her chest. 'Leave your name and address and the year you were born. The names of the people who adopted you.' The woman pulled a blunt pencil and grubby piece of paper from her apron pocket. 'Can ask someone to look for you.'

'Can it be done soon?' Ruth asked.

'Tidak. I try soon.'

Please, Ruth prayed silently on the taxi ride back to the hotel in the foothills, *help Dewi and me find someone we belong to.* But even though she was closer to her birthplace than she'd ever been, she'd found no-one to pray to except herself.

∞

'What are those white things in the trees along the river there?' Dewi had asked when they returned to their Nirvana villa.

'Heron, maybe.'

'Way too fat, Mum.'

They walked out onto the balcony to get a closer look.

'Some kind of bird,' Ruth said.

'No they're not, Mum. They're disposable nappies. And plastic bags.'

Ruth felt almost hopeless. She'd so much wanted to believe that her origins were in some kind of paradise, and that Dewi had a place there too. Across the path from their villa, Gusti cleared plates from the steps of one of the River View villas.

'Which village do you live in, Gusti?'

He pointed to the cluster of small thatched houses and flowering trees across the river. Nearby, two women bent over clearing thick undergrowth with scythes.

'Do many of the village women have other jobs?'

'They help weed. They do all the cooking and house-work. The lucky ones get jobs as cleaners in the hotels around here.'

The still water mirrored the toiling women and tiny houses.

'How beautiful,' Ruth had said, like any tourist admiring the view. But she could see no place for Dewi there.

A bird had perched on the balcony of the adjacent villa. Ruth recognised its tail streamers.

'A red-tailed tropic bird! Haven't seen one of those since your father showed me some before you were born. Maybe it's flown here all the way from southern Australia to escape the cold.' How bent the bird's tail streamers were, and how downy and vulnerable its small white body and wings. 'Looks like an orphan,' Ruth croaked. 'Most likely blown off-course by strong winds.' It lifted off from the balcony and the wind buffeted it across the river valley. As it had disappeared from sight, Ruth heard David again: *Their parents abandon them. They have to learn to fly quickly.*

∽

Ruth and Dewi had eaten lunch at the thatched pavilion overlooking the two pools.

Infinity pool closed for repairs, a sign read. Ruth wondered if the wide crack in its tiled, blue interior could be properly fixed. *Please use plunge pool.*

'What's *she* doing?' Dewi asked, pointing to an old woman in a faded sarong kebaya at the spring near the pool enclosure gate.

'Most Balinese are Hindu. She's making offerings. Flowers and food.'

'For the guests to eat?'

'For the gods, I think. Or the spirits of the dead.' Some bamboo wind chimes rattled in the breeze, a sound somewhere between hollowness and promise.

'Mum, you went purple around your nose and mouth a moment ago,' Dewi muttered midway through her shoe-string fries.

'Purple?' Ruth could barely swallow her satay. 'I'm a bit cold. Maybe that's why.'

'In this hot weather?'

Though the air was humid and still, she began trembling.

– *Maybe your death's sooner than you think.*

– *A stitch in time.*

– You have to tell her.

– Tell her soon.

Ruth leaned her elbows on the table to steady herself. Dewi skipped blithely over to the small circular plunge pool, her flushed face and hair incandescent in the tropical light. Ruth pulled the camera from her bag and took three, four, five shots. Just in case she never had the chance to photograph Dewi happy again. She put the camera down as Dewi began speaking.

'Feel like a swim, Mum?'

'I'll watch you swim. I didn't bring my bathers,' she lied. She didn't feel brave enough to further reveal her chest to the sleek black-swimsuited couple lounging on the opposite side of the pools.

Jumping into the water, Dewi's body in her red-striped op shop bathers looked trusting and vulnerable to Ruth; lithe-limbed, flat-chested.

Dewi floated on her back before standing neck-deep on the step of the plunge pool.

'Come on, Mum. Be happy. Our first holiday ever, and in an *overseas luxury resort.*'

'What d'you like best about it?'

'Our beautiful room and sparkly bathroom. And the Balinese people. They're really nice.'

The couple stood up from the li-los. Staring as they retreated through the gate, the man ran his forefinger over his moustache and the woman snapped her black bikini over her tanned buttocks.

'Why do the Balinese people smile at us more than those guests?' Dewi asked.

'I don't know.'

'Doesn't matter,' Dewi said quickly. 'Why are you sad, Mum?'

Ruth took a deep breath. 'Dewi, remember I told you I had to see the cancer doctor again a few weeks ago?'

'Uh huh.'

'Well. He told me the cancer's come back. And he told me that when cancer comes back a second time, it usually...' Ruth's voice skittered higher. She took another deep breath, 'can't be cured.'

'But it can go away for years,' Dewi smiled. 'Until you're old. You told me years ago. And I read it in an encyclopedia in the school library. Permission? No. *Re*-mission, the encyclopedia called it.' Dewi watched her mouth carefully. Was it turning purple again?

'Maybe not this kind of cancer, Dewi. Not when it comes back again like it has. The specialist said Mummy probably has only a few months to live.'

Dewi's face fading against the hard aqua of the plunge pool as she tried to reach the bottom with her toe. She stared at Ruth and her outstretched hand, yet seemed not to register her. So this is what it's like to begin dying, Ruth thought. For my daughter, I'm already no longer here, in a way.

'But we still have time together,' Ruth said desperately. 'A few months at least. Longer if the new drugs work. I'm doing everything I can to get more time.'

Dewi's hands suddenly looked too small to keep her afloat. The pinkness had left her cheeks entirely, and she breathed deeply. As a long-distance swimmer begins her race. As women enter labour. Or the dying enter their last minutes, Ruth imagined. *She's in shock,* Ruth realised, reaching out to grasp both Dewi's hands. As if this might keep the bad news from overwhelming her, as if this might make her future look less lonely and precarious.

∞

Her daughter had curled up on the teak four-poster bed, facing the wall.

'What're you thinking, Dewi?'

'This isn't *quite* the kind of holiday I thought it'd be, after all.'

'I'm so sorry. Would you like to go shopping? We could get you a sarong.'

'Maybe I could get silver slippers, like the girl in the brochure had,' Dewi had whispered, as if she hardly dared hope.

∞

They'd taken the hotel's courtesy bus along a dusty road into town. Little offering-baskets of cracker biscuits, flowers and rice sat on the dashboards of cars and the steps of shops. They paused outside a grandly carved temple gate and watched a priest sprinkling holy water over a small congregation kneeling on the ground, their palms pressed together in prayer. I'm surrounded by faith, and yet so far away from finding my own, Ruth reflected.

At the crossroads, a raggedly dressed young woman holding a wailing infant thrust her empty palm towards Ruth. She was gaunt, more obviously poverty-stricken than the local villagers, with sharper facial features and several missing teeth. But there was something besides supplication in the beggar's outstretched hand and eyes. It was almost as if she'd recognised Ruth's urgency, too.

Would her own mother've looked like that if she'd survived? Ruth placed a few coins on her palm and hurried on with Dewi to a glass-fronted shop with designer watches in the window. She never had replaced David's wristwatch, lost in the analgesic fog of her mastectomy years before.

'Was she begging?' Dewi asked.

'Yes. She's poor.'

'You should've given her more.'

'We might need more money ourselves,' Ruth murmured, guiltily scrutinising a ladies' Timex. Cheaper than back home. But was its authenticity guaranteed? And would measuring time make her life go faster or slower?

– *Time to do what's important to you, now,* Doctor Vincent's voice echoed, but Ruth felt more unsure by the minute how to apply the doctor's advice.

Dodging scooters precariously loaded with passengers, caged roosters and sacks of rice, she steered Dewi across the road to some makeshift market stalls. A middle-aged vendor, her gap-toothed smile emphasised by fluorescent pink lipstick, grasped Dewi by the wrist.

'Hallo, hallo! Beautiful girl! Blue eyes! Come. I give you good price on sarong.'

Frightened, Dewi withdrew her hand. Ruth took it firmly.

'No, thank you,' she said.

'Why'd she grab me like that?' Dewi murmured as Ruth steered her away.

'Just being friendly. And maybe because she's desperate for money.'

Ruth bargained with a nonchalant youth around the corner for a purple sarong, a yellow paper festival umbrella and a silver pair of beaded slippers for Dewi.

'You want more?' he asked. 'This blue sarong nice. This pink one. I give you three for the price of two.'

'The blue and pink ones. Pleeease Mum!'

'Okay.' Ruth handed over the money. The youth held their thousand-rupiah notes in one hand and flicked them like a feather duster across his piles of sarongs and slippers.

'Why's he doing that?' murmured Dewi.

'Brings more good luck,' he grinned, handing them their purchases. 'More money.'

Ruth bought herself a small Buddha statue from a middle-aged man at the next store, but she didn't bargain for it. Anything for a glimpse of wisdom. They just made it back to the Nirvana's courtesy bus on time.

'Selamat datang,' Murni sang from the reception desk when they arrived back.

'Selamat datang,' Ruth had replied. But she couldn't copy Murni's prayer-like gesture, for her hands were full of shopping.

∞

Sitting on their villa balcony that afternoon, they heard gamelan music and shouting from the road leading to the closest village. A column of people followed an open-sided tower of bamboo-and-wood strewn with silver tinsel, its five pagoda-like roofs ascending from biggest to smallest. A long bundle wrapped in white lay on the highest platform of the tower. The men bearing the tower cheered as they ran.

'What are they doing?'

'I don't know. Maybe some kind of celebration.'

'A cremation procession,' a voice called out from the path below their balcony. Gusti, gathering half-empty plates from someone's room-service meal.

'Oh. I'm sorry,' Ruth replied to him. 'They seem so happy.'

'They are. Because soon the soul of their dead relative will be released to the next life. No need to be sad.' He scraped the remains from the plates into a small bin on his trolley.

'What's the next life?' Dewi whispered to Ruth.

'The Balinese believe that after you die, you're reborn into a new life here.'

'Is that *really* true? Do you believe that?'

'I…It would be nice if it's true.'

Dewi turned from her mother and called hesitantly down to Gusti. 'Excuse me.'

'Miss Dewi. How beautiful you look in your sarong and silver slippers.' He put down the plate and smiled up at her.

'Thank you,' she smiled, shy but satisfied. 'Excuse me. Where's the dead person?'

'See that bundle high on the tower?'

'That thing that looks like a big white present?' Dewi asked.

The waiter laughed. 'That's right. That's the body wrapped in white cloth.'

'And who're all those people?'

'The villagers, Miss Dewi. They help the dead person's family.'

So much shelter.

Suddenly, the men bearing the tower shook it vigorously and ran it around in circles a few times, cheering loudly before reversing direction.

'They do that to make sure the dead person can't find his way back to the family house to disturb them.' Gusti leaned his forearms on the handle of the trolley and smiled up at her.

'But what if they *want* him to come back?'

'When people die, we hang a lantern at their gate for some days to show their souls the way home before we bury them. A lantern and a white paper damar kurung bird. But when we dig their bodies up for cremation a few months later, it's time for their souls to go to the next life. Usually the dead return as one of their grandchildren.' *I'll have to wait a long time to return,* Ruth thought. Gusti glanced at her. 'You want me to take you both closer to watch the cremation?'

'No, thanks,' Ruth said, shivering despite the humidity.

The procession moved into a valley behind a screen of trees, until only the smallest, top-most roof of the tower remained visible. They watched for a minute or two, but the procession didn't reappear.

'Well,' said Gusti. 'Work to do! Selamat malam.' Gusti bowed and pushed the trolley past the lotus pond towards the dining room. Dewi went inside and lay on the bed, staring up at the mosquito net.

'Mum. You know how your voice sounds funny? What if it's…because your soul's trying to escape through your mouth already?'

'It's just…my voice getting tired. I'm still all here,' Ruth murmured. 'Promise.'

Dewi looked doubtfully at her chest.

'You won't come back to me after you die, will you Mum? Even if I *really* want you to. Even if I leave the lights on every night to show you the way. Even if the funeral people don't run your body around in circles.' Dewi pressed her hands together vertically in front of her face, as the praying congregation in the temple had, but her fingers curled helplessly against her abrupt tears.

'Probably not. But you'll still be able to talk to me if you want.'

'But you w-won't talk back to me,' she sobbed. 'Your voice is already going.'

'You'll have to sort of feel what I might say. You might have to practise a bit.'

Dewi closed her eyes tightly, but her tears kept coming. 'I can't,' she whispered after a minute.

'Don't worry. You don't have to. Because, you know, you'll probably have better answers than me, anyway.'

Lying on the bed listening to unfamiliar birds and insects calling outside, they saw the cremation tower ignite against the dark indigo frieze of distant mountains.

∞

No-one was at the reception desk when Ruth and Dewi went down to check on the shuttle-bus times early the next morning, but someone had left the computer on. A photo of a Balinese woman illuminated the screen. From that distance, she looked like a villager making an offering. Dewi and Ruth went closer, as if they might find some answer there.

'The Nirvana Hotel website,' Ruth said. *The Nirvana, proudly owned by your Australian hosts Mick and Rhonda Evans,* the first line of text read.

'Murni!' Dewi murmured, pointing to the woman's face. Underneath the hotel's gold-lettered name and address, the receptionist carried a tray of cocktails towards the elegant family they'd seen in the travel brochure back in Lost River. Her face appeared paler and heavily made up. Cosmetics, computerised image enhancement, instant makeovers. Only the sky on the screen looked anywhere near authentic to Ruth, almost the colour of Dewi's eyes when she'd told her she was dying soon. Ruth's vision blurred for a moment, but she held fast to that blue. But her daughter was more than one step ahead of her.

'Don't worry, Mum. I'll be all right.' She squeezed Ruth's hand. 'Will we get this?' She pointed to the last lines of the gold text on the screen:

Find Yourself
Limited Time Only: Child Stays Free

'We'll find a way to get it,' Ruth had replied. 'We'll get it, somehow.'

Closer inspection of that first Bali snapshot taken through the plane window shows a distant volcano smouldering in the centre of the velvet-green island, veiled by a glittering sun-shower. So much fire and rain in one moment. In Lost River's colder dawn, it looks like a trick of the light, or fantasy.

Bali snapshots and souvenirs

November, 1993
(increased depth of field)

Ruth has arranged and labelled most of the Bali photos in the blue album.

> *Dewi wearing the Nirvana's welcome lei.*
> *Dewi in the plunge pool.*
> *Dewi in her new slippers and sarong.*
> *Gusti and Murni farewelling us.*

'Our time in Bali didn't last very long,' Dewi says, scanning the photos. 'I wish we bought more souvenirs to help us remember.'

'Have to think about the luggage allowance when you're flying.'

∞

When the breeze had blown open the curtain of her room window, she'd thought she'd seen the cantilevered roofline of a Balinese temple above the new brick fence on the eastern boundary. But it was just the new neighbours' poolside pavilion, built in her absence and seen through her waking dream of Bali a few mornings after she and Dewi had returned.

In the kitchen, Dewi had already packed into her schoolbag peanut-paste sandwiches and the bundle of brightly painted pencils ornamented at their ends with hand-carved birds or fish, purchased the day of their departure from two wide-eyed Balinese girls about her age. She kissed Ruth's cheek and left ahead of time for once, eager to boast about her holiday to her classmates.

∞

After unpacking and washing, Ruth had swallowed a painkiller just before she'd heard the brisk clipping of heels across the verandah, followed by a firm knock. She opened the door to Mrs Robbins, scrutinising Dewi's pyramid of empty cat-food cans at the end of the verandah.

'Good morning, Ruth.' Ruth kicked their shabby op shop suitcases behind her bedroom door and closed it. Mrs Robbins glanced at her dressing gown and peered inside the house, her small, hazel eyes as unequivocal as full-stops.

'Hope I didn't get you out of bed. Just wanted a little chat about Dewi again. The only free time I have today.' Her smile revealed frosted-pink lipstick on her incisors.

'Come in. Cup of tea? Sorry I don't have anything I can give you to eat,' Ruth said, ushering her to the sofa. 'Haven't done the grocery shopping yet.' Ruth was glad her voice was reasonably audible, supposed Bali had done it good. The teacher waved her apology away, looking slightly relieved.

'No, thanks.'

A muted crunch under Ruth's foot as she sat on the other end of the sofa. She looked down to see a dead dried frog under her bargain Balinese slipper. She surreptitiously moved the frog under the sofa with her foot so Mrs Robbins wouldn't see.

'I'm a little concerned Dewi's been missing too much school,' Mrs Robbins said. 'She seems a bit anti-social every time she returns after an absence.'

'Oh? She was keen to go this morning.'

'She was happy enough at first. Gave everyone a sweet little carved pencil from Bali. Burst into tears a few minutes later and refused to speak or come out of the book corner.'

'Oh.' Ruth kept the dismay from her voice. 'Well. I know she *is* a bit *withdrawn* socially. She's worried, you know.'

'What about?'

'About what will happen to her, I guess. My prognosis is bad. Recurrence of breast cancer. I had to tell her.' Mrs Robbins glanced at David's dressing gown slipping down her shoulder on her breastless side; averted her eyes to the dust on the floor, the pile of clothes, the unwieldy pile of National Geographic magazines she'd brought home from the op shop for Dewi over that year.

'I see. You're probably eligible for help from various agencies. Social Securities, you know. Silver Chain.' The teacher cleared her throat. 'Child Welfare.' Ruth's throat tightened. 'Foster parents could be organised for Dewi. I know a good Christian couple just out of town who do wonders...' she stretched her hands outward as if she were rolling out a banner.

'No,' Ruth murmured.

'No?'

'It's important not to take children away from their home unless absolutely necessary, don't you think?'

'Unless their parents are unable to care properly for them. Par*ent*.' The teacher looked at the mess on the floor again. 'For whatever reason, of course,' she added hastily. 'I mean, some of them have good reasons. *You* have good reasons, I would say.'

'I'm still perfectly capable of looking after my daughter.'

Mrs Robbins glanced again at the top of the pyramid of empty cat-food cans through the window. She tapped her watch and sprang to her feet.

'Time to go already!' she said cheerfully. 'Try not to let her take more absences than necessary. It makes it hard for children to keep up socially and academically, and more difficult for them in the long run.'

There'd been two fleas on the teacher's ankle as she departed.

∞

Only a few blank pages remain in the blue album, its spine just visible between the full pages. Ruth flicks through the holiday photos to the shot of Murni and Gusti, their hands pressed together in front of their bowed heads.

I don't know which country I belong to, she'd confided in them on the day of departure. The couple had glanced at one another. After a slight hesitation, Gusti had replied: *Cultivate the land within. Nandurin karang awak, we say in Balinese.*

We pray for you always, Ruth and Dewi, Murni had called as they'd climbed into the taxi to the airport. *To be blessed wherever you are.*

Their gift to her isn't something she can photograph, or that can be held in her hands like a souvenir. It's immeasurable and weightless, a gift she unwraps now she finds herself feeling out of place and alone. A gift she can carry with her to the end.

Dewi running towards her future?

December, 1993
(images accidentally erased on film)

All the night noises: roos thudding softly around the orchard, the wind in the trees, the low rhythmic roar of waves breaking in the bay. The scratching in the ceiling's noisiest of all – possums or rats? Rats had gnawed through the electrical wires of Pete's house a few months back. Ruth lies awake listening, worrying about losing power, Dewi, money.

Her bed-lamp comes on straightaway when she tries it. The blank negative-strip and proof sheet lie underneath it. She'd accidentally opened the camera's back after photographing Dewi along the riverbank a few days before. Wrecked most of the film.

No point in focussing on the negatives, Mel the pharmacy assistant had quipped through her brightly lipsticked smile, but at least she hadn't charged her for developing the film. Ruth holds the negative strip up to the lamplight, but everything except the first frame is a completely transparent pale orange, any trace of Dewi obliterated. And apart from the first print of her own fingers as she'd focussed the lens, the proof sheet's blacker than the night on the other side of her window pane.

She rises and lets herself out through the back door. The stars like grains of sugar twinkling in the dark bowl of the sky. The Southern Cross and Milky Way; a waning moon setting over the sea as she walks on the sharp, frosted grass around the house, trying to tire herself enough to sleep. Soon the constellations begin dimming and a muted pre-dawn sheen like pewter spreads from the eastern horizon. She hears the verandah boards creak under someone's feet. Heart hammering, she tiptoes across the grass and peers around the corner of the house.

Dewi, reclining in her wicker chair. Still dressed in her pyjamas, the subdued lustre of the sky in her hair and skin.

'Good morning. Can't you sleep?'

'Nope. Happens a lot lately.'

'You too, hey. Any idea why?'

A brief pause, as if her daughter knows, but thinks better of telling her.

'Nope.'

'Not to worry too much. Sleeplessness just happens sometimes. Plenty of exercise during the day is supposed to help.'

'Yeah. You working this morning at the shop?'

'Yes. What about you?'

'Nothing.'

'Want to come in with me?'

'Nah.'

'Dewi? Would you mind doing the washing up for me sometime later today? I felt too sick to do it last night.'

Dewi sighs in exasperation, unlocks her long legs.

'I hate you sometimes, Mum.'

I hate you, Mum. Dewi had told her that a few times as a preschooler. It hadn't worried Ruth then, but now it stings her with the force of an adult's carefully aimed insult.

'Why?'

'Because you're not trying your hardest.'

'At what? The housework?'

'Not to die.' Dewi winces, then looks relieved, defiant, even. As if the truth's finally out.

'Dewi! I'm doing everything I can to live as long as I can. Of course! What makes you think I'm not?'

'Well. You're not trying lots of different medicine and stuff.'

'That's because the trial drug made me too sick. There aren't any medicines that will keep cancer away for long when it gets to this stage, Dewi. All I can really do is eat and exercise to stay healthy as possible.'

'I'm sorry, Mum. I don't really hate you. I don't know why I said that.'

'It's okay. People think and say those kinds of things sometimes.' As if what they're both going through is typical. 'What do you want for Christmas?'

Probably their last one together. What gifts could possibly be enough?

'Nothing. I-i-i just…wish…' she shrugs helplessly. 'That you wouldn't die.'

'Me too, Brave Star.' She wishes silently for more wisdom to help her guide them through their waking nightmare. She wishes for more money. Maybe it'd help buy some temporary remedy overseas, or at least a good counsellor for Dewi. She knows there are important things she should say to her daughter, but she's too tired to think clearly. 'You'll get over the sleeplessness,' she says instead. As if she can make it happen just by saying it. 'We both will. Sleeplessness comes and goes. People say things they don't mean when they're tired. Just listen to Roberta and Jack and Finn. People do it all the time.' She should ask Dewi what else's worrying her, but Ruth can't face any more big questions right now. And maybe her words are enough for Dewi at that moment, for she goes to her bedroom and is asleep by the time Ruth goes inside minutes later. Maybe that's all her daughter wants: words that remind her again of her place amongst the living.

It isn't as easy as that, of course. *We all make mistakes raising our children,* Ruth'd heard her adoptive mother consoling a young visiting minister's wife once. *We have to leave it to God,* Grace had concluded, her eyes and palms upturned. Back then, Ruth'd found her adoptive mother's words lazy and inadequate.

But maybe Grace was right. If you're a mother for more than a few years, Ruth reflects, you will hurt your child, and you will feel hurt by her. You will fail in ways neither of you see, as well as in ways you see all too clearly and try your best to fix. But there's no fixing this.

Nearly every morning during her last months of adolescence on the mission, Ruth had walked to console herself with a view of the world beyond its fences. After they'd returned from Bali, she'd walked as much as she could to try to get a view of life beyond her illness. Maybe the exercise would help prolong her life, too. She forces herself along the green river path daily, trying to ignore the signs of development encroaching on the wilderness.

'D'you want to come with me?' she'd asked Dewi if she was home. Usually, Dewi refused and shut herself in her room, burdened with homework and things she would not speak about.

Pretty much age-appropriate behaviour in these circumstances, Doctor Vincent had said. *Adolescence approaching.*

But early one evening as Ruth set out for her walk, Dewi had run from her bedroom ahead of her, across the orchard to the river, her hair and face flushed by the descending sun. A chance to spend time together! Ruth had grabbed the camera and taken a few quick shots as she followed.

But Dewi waved frantically at someone standing on the path ahead.

'Just catching up with Finn!' she turned and called over her shoulder, sprinting faster than the old camera's fastest shutter speed.

Ruth had kept walking. It was all she could do to help her sleep, blunt her anxiety about her daughter's future, put distance between herself and the realisation that her time with Dewi was running out even faster than she'd thought.

∞

Ruth can't bring herself to throw away the proof sheet of the obliterated shots of Dewi. She can still see her, radiant along the river path that evening, the light and wind streaming through her hair as she ran towards Finn. *Amazing. When I die, this memory of her will be lost forever.*

Trying to capture things that fly, she scrawls under the proof sheet's numbered erasures late at night. She tucks it inside the back cover of the blue album and looks out through the living-room window. The dark river, defined only by the reflections of far-off stars and the boat-shaped moon on the ocean's horizon.

Despite the relentlessness of her life's passing, despite the disintegration of the cottage and her body, despite everything, there were moments like this when a kind of grace descended on their precarious home. In these moments, it seems to Ruth that her life with Dewi has somehow sunk below the usual surface activity of the town, roads and vineyards into a quiet, truer place. Here, Dewi and she are beyond the reach of illness and death.

River of time. Sea of life. Please carry us.

PART THREE

The Green Album

First loves

January, 1994
(time on the scale of breathing)

From the doorway, for a few minutes, she watches Dewi sleep in the moonlight, the edge of her pillow over her head, as if she's hiding from something. Ruth'd swallowed some of the strong painkillers earlier in the evening to make her breathing easier. She puts their handmade Christmas decorations away carefully in the biscuit tin; some of them are eight or more years old. She drags the dead Christmas tree branch outside.

On the way back to the living room, she finds an unexpected photo on the darkroom threshold, way more detailed than she'd thought possible. It must've been taken by someone when she wasn't looking. It shows David and her standing on a green hill teeming with life: a little girl and a younger boy running under a flock of birds; Yoko Ono chasing iridescent insects amongst wildflowers and grass. On the horizon a city beckons, tall glass towers shimmering.

Strange I've never noticed this photo before. Where is it?

As the painkillers wear off, she realises that this image is not a photograph; not even a memory of an experience that she and David shared. It's a summing up of the life she might've lived with him but didn't. It's a dream she'd lost when he left. It's nothing but a drug-induced illusion. She cries herself to a flat exhaustion and dozes.

Wakes gasping for air.

Deep breath in. Hold steady. Breathe out. She hears David's voice, clear as daylight. Sees his face for just a moment.

She goes to the kitchen still struggling to breathe, calms herself with warm milk. Swallows more painkillers. When she finally falls asleep, she hears his voice in her dreams, but he's nowhere to be seen.

A few hours before dawn, she'd woken on the bathroom floor to more voices.

– *Uh-oh.*
– *Deep breath in.*
– *We will be borne up by the wings of prayer.* Fred?
– *Bicarb soda's best for sweat stains.* Grace.
– *Don't be shamed, Ruth.* Nelly.
– *We pray for you, forever.* Murni?
– *Hold steady. Breathe out.* David.

'Mu-u-um! Mummy! Don't die! Not yet! I want to tell you too many things!' Dewi, her sweaty hand finding Ruth's. 'And I want more photos of you. And I-i-i-i... don't leave me yet, Mum! Please!'

'Get Roberta to ring Doctor Vincent,' Ruth gasped. The bathroom tiles pressed into her cheek.

'But what if you die while I'm gone?'

'I won't.'

'Promise?' Dewi whimpered.

'Promise.'

But she'd left already, slamming the back door and running across the paddock.

When she could hear Dewi no more, darkness flooded Ruth. She resurfaced after what felt like years, gulping air. By the time Dewi returned with Roberta, she'd steadied her breath enough to whisper.

'Someone should put the phone on for you,' said Roberta.

'Can't afford it.'

'Can't afford not to.'

Doctor Vincent arrived and listened to Ruth's chest through her stethoscope, her lips pressing together harder, the longer she listened.

'Sounds like you're drowning.' She shook her head and looked at Roberta. 'Needs her lungs drained. At the very least. I'm taking her to the hospital.'

'Who'll look after Dewi?' Ruth murmured.

'She can stay with us,' said Roberta.

Dewi tapped Ruth on the shoulder.

'I don't want to,' she whispered. 'I want to go with you.'

'Your mother needs a rest, Dewi,' said Doctor Vincent. 'Help her out to my car?'

The moonlight felt cold on Ruth's skin as she shuffled across the grass, the unseasonal frost crackling underfoot.

'Please *hurry*! Don't let my Mummy die!' Dewi opened the car door and pushed Ruth towards it.

After Doctor Vincent shut the car door behind her, Ruth tapped on the window.

'Dewi. Be good for Roberta. I'll be back soon,' she'd rasped through the gap.

Dewi's face pressed up against the glass, searching her mother's eyes for the truth.

'Promise?'

∞

Underneath the oxygen mask and the painkilling drip, she'd dreamed that she'd become two women. One was named Ruth, the other had an unknown Balinese name. Ruth was wrapped in bandages and brown paper, a parcel waiting for dispatch. She dragged herself up to the hospital roof to be posted into the sky.

Below her, the unnamed Balinese woman slept as if she'd been sleeping all her life. She woke as an unexpected visitor entered her room.

'Hullo,' he said. His quiet diffidence, his attenuated fingers and slender, low-hipped body. The broken lines on his forehead, his sun-streaked hair and creamed-honey skin, almost atonal with his hesitant blue eyes.

Do we remember anyone else's face for as long as we remember our first love's? Searching David's, she found everything, yet not enough.

'Where is it, the truth of what went on between us?'

'It's part of the river now,' he smiled.

She tried to tell him all the things she wished she'd told him when she'd lived with him, but her voice kept coming and going.

'Don't worry,' he said. 'We're all so complicated. All we can do is use whatever light's available to see each other. And when the light's poor, you have to hold your breath and the camera steady to get a clear image.'

Deep breath. Hold steady. On this they'd always agreed.

'But when it's too dark, we've got to go beyond appearances,' she murmured.

'Don't worry about dying, too much,' he said. 'Death also is beautiful, believe me.' Then his eyes dimmed, and the warmth of his skin faded. She'd opened her eyes as wide as she could, trying to keep him in focus, but there was only the night-shift nurse, readjusting the oxygen mask.

'I'm losing my voice, but I am ready to speak with him,' she'd said to the nurse, who didn't seem to hear her at all.

After the nurse leaves, Ruth closes her eyes against the darkness of the hospital ward, waiting for the earth's rotation to turn her towards the sun and Dewi again.

> *A lifetime is one moment*
> *between my two little breaths.*
>
> *– Chade Meng*
> – Oriental Wisdom 1976 Pocket Diary.

Dewi and Ruth's
dune grass mementos

February, 1994
(so much unfinished)

A few mornings after Ruth's return from hospital, she's woken before dawn by the warbling of magpies. Since hospital, her world has taken on an intense clarity; even this dim sky and familiar birdsong. The light and wind in the trees and on the river are so compelling she's not been able to read the pamphlets on legal aid, child fostering and cheap funerals the hospital social worker gave her. She walks around the orchard listening to the magpies as the sun rises and gilds all the lives waking in the valley. It's almost too much for her, the breaking of the day.

Inside, she inserts the photo taken by Roberta two days before into the first page of the green album, makes toast, boils two eggs. Nearly seven o'clock. She watches her daughter sleeping. When she touches her cheek, Dewi opens her eyes with a start, her oceanic gaze immediate and focussed.

'Is everything all right?'

'Everything's all right, Dewi.' They both know the half-truths necessary for getting on with the day.

Dewi barely takes her eyes off her as they eat breakfast. What's she looking for? More breathlessness, Ruth guesses, signs of her mother's life ending.

'Why aren't you eating your egg, Mum?'

'It's for you. I've already eaten,' she lies. Swallowing anything but liquid's too difficult.

'I'm full.'

'Put your school uniform on then, Brave Star.'

'I'm too afraid to go to school. In case you…' Dewi presses her palms against her eyes.

'Die? I'm not dying yet, Dewi.'

'Don't be afraid to tell me if you know when you might die. Because it's *scarier* for me *not* to know.'

'I honestly don't know exactly, Dewi. I'm so sorry. I guess no-one knows exactly when they'll die. I'm sorry if that's frightening for you.'

'It's like being in the dark alone when I was little.'

'It helps to breathe a few deep breaths and steady ourselves against the darkness.' Though Ruth'd found him again only in her dreams, he had taught her that. 'A clearer picture develops, sooner or later. Even in darkness.' Dewi nods, brushes her hand across her eyes. 'How'd things go when you stayed over at Roberta's this time?' Still searching for a home for her daughter.

'Roberta and Jack were kind. They let me come back here.'

'Why?' Ruth tries to keep the alarm from her voice. 'Did you stay here on your own?'

'Don't *worry*, Mum. They had me over for every meal. But I was bored. Finn played with his mates most of the time,' she shrugged. 'He's just a *boy,* after all. And my bed's more comfy than their couch.'

Listening to the kitchen clock ticking while Dewi gets dressed, Ruth recalls the mission's old van, dented where the *E* of the Joiner's crudely painted *Eternity* met the end of their abbreviated timeline. How different would time, life and death seem if she and Dewi lived in a Balinese village? Gusti had said that a person could be reincarnated over and over again. Believing that, would you fret so much about your life coming to an end? And would Balinese villagers look after Dewi better than Roberta and Jack?

Dressed in her creased uniform, Dewi points to the latest photo in the album.

'Nice shot.'

They'd been sitting near the round dune after her return from hospital, while Ruth plaited three strands of the shiny dune grass around Dewi's wrist to make a bracelet.

'What would you call those colours?' Dewi points to the grass and trees in the photo.

Ruth tells her the names David taught her.

'The younger grass is viridian green at the tips, dark phthalo-green underneath. The older strands are yellow ochre and grey.' Her pulse quickens with the colours of new life and old growth. 'The paperbarks are cadmium yellow on the tips of their foliage, mixed with phthalo-blue underneath. Their trunks flake white tinted with burnt umber.' All the colours of this world. Would it take even longer than old age to know them all?

Dewi fingers the bracelet of dune grass still fastened on her wrist.

'I'll make this last forever,' says Dewi. 'And you'll keep wearing yours, won't you? Even though I didn't make such a good one.' All the ends coming undone.

∞

A northerly breeze blew a smoke haze across the valley from a fire; probably some farmer burning-off, Ruth guessed as Roberta waved from across the paddock.

Time to ask her. Ask Roberta if she could check on her mornings, and afternoons just before school finished, so Dewi wouldn't be alone with her when she died. Ask Roberta if Dewi could stay at the Murphy's after she died, until…Until what?

'You okay? Other night was pretty heavy.' Roberta exhaled the smoke from her joint slowly.

'Yeah. Thanks for your help. Roberta? If you don't see me around during the day, would you mind just checking inside the cottage for me before school's out? Just in case…'

'Sure, honey,' Roberta replied. But her eyes were narrow and red-veined, and Ruth guessed she wouldn't remember.

Time to make other arrangements for Dewi. Time to put the last photos and words for her into the album. Time to plan my funeral. Yet she couldn't bring herself to begin these final things, because she was still hoping for the best, despite everything.

∞

Balinese dance is inseparable from religion. One dance tells of a young woman who's very ill. When she prays to Durga, the goddess of death and destruction, Durga tells her that the price of her health is the sacrifice of her child. When the young woman recovers, one of the goddess's followers puts her in a trance and enters her body, causing her to beat her child and tie her to a tree in the jungle.

The young woman wakes from her trance to find herself immortal. But she finds eternity is unbearable without her child. The young woman overcomes her grief and sense of hopelessness, and after an immense struggle, she outwits the goddess's wrath. Finally, she is able to release her child from death, too.

Ruth puts down the Bali travel guidebook from the op shop, considers the snapshot Roberta took of her with Dewi on the dune. *These photos the only immortality I can hope for. What if I go mad just before I die, like the Joiners said my mother did? What if Dewi finds me dead when she's alone? What if I look awful, some terrible expression on my face? What if the last image she has of me is so frightening it's more real for her than this photo?*

She writes under the snapshot: **After the grass bracelet and I have gone, Dewi, remember all these times we showed each other that love endures, even when so much else seemed lost. Remember all those moments we made each other.**

Dewi hurries in from the school bus.

'You're still here!'

'Let's dance!' Ruth says.

Dewi looks at her with disbelief.

'*Really?*'

'I danced with you before.'

'I re*member*. I mean, aren't you too sick now?'

'I feel good today.'

'Yay, Mum!'

'*Mr Tambourine Man?*'

'Okay. But be careful of your *breath*ing.'

The record-player needle jumps a scratch or two before settling into the song.

'C'mon!…*waving free…*'

'Yay, Mum!'

'Yay, Dewi!'

'Both hands!'

They spin and gather the late-noon sunlight pouring through the open door, even Ruth making it all the way through the song.

'Mum? Maybe you're getting better.'

'I feel good right now!' Steadies her breathing.

'But you won't get better forever?'

'I'm sorry, Dewi.'

'Let's keep dancing,' says Dewi, fiercely blinking away her tears.

'Yes!'

And they spin faster, but neither of them can forget what they want to forget about – all the tomorrows.

Blurred portrait of Dewi's parents

February, 1982
(insufficient light)

When Ruth hears the gruff woman's voice call her name early in the morning – as she inserts into the green album the photo of her and David that she'd saved from the flood all those years before – she knows who it is before she opens the door.

'Katy. Come in.'

But Katy shakes her head, looks over Ruth's shoulder into the house.

'Better out here.'

'I'm just making a cup of tea. Bring one out for you?'

'Lotsa milk.'

'And four spoons of sugar, right?'

She pours Katy's tea into the biggest mug.

'How're you, Ruth?' Katy asks as they sit down on the verandah chairs.

'Okay.'

'True?'

'Well. Time's running out for me, I guess.'

'Nothing they can do?

'Nothing.'

'Maybe our old people's spirits will help you.'

How Ruth wants to believe this, but can't even begin. It hurts too much, that kind of hope. She looks at the river instead. They talk about all the new building around town, the clearing of more bush upriver, the disappearance of species, whether to give the grinding stone and cutting tool to the town's new museum when it opens. She recounts the Aboriginal myths about the young lovers' spirits that Jack had told her after David disappeared.

'We believe in spirits, but nothing like those rubbish stories,' scoffs Katy. 'Too many white blokes around here pretending to have Aboriginal knowledge.' At the newly released blocks of land on the way to the new neighbours' place, a car spins its wheels in the gravel and grinds to a halt. 'Who that red-faced man in the white suit gettin' out of that silver car?'

'Des Gilbert. The real estate agent and town councillor. His wife Eloise is my boss.'

'Ah, that bloke I seen flogging the fancy houses along the river. Never gets his fancy new four-wheel-drive dirty.'

'Big houses, little houses. Des does them all.'

'Big house, little house, no house,' shrugs Katy. 'The thing is with Lost River, no-one really feels at home here.'

'Do *you* feel at home here?'

'The river, the bays and country all around here my home. But white men made too many of us orphans in our own country.' Katy glances into the cottage again. 'Too many places haunted now.' She takes the last mouthful from her mug.

'Another cuppa?'

'Nah.'

'So what brings you here this time, Katy?'

'Just passing through my old peoples' country like always.'

'What's it like, always just passing through their country?'

'Too sad. What else can I do? Too expensive for me to own a home around here. Where's your true home, Ruth?'

'Nowhere, really.' Not even Bali. 'This is as close as I get to having a home.' A flicker of anger crosses Katy's face. 'Doesn't belong to me the same as it belongs to you though,' Ruth said hastily.

'That's all right. You passing through even quicker than me. These days we all just passing through.' Katy startles when she hears Dewi's footsteps inside the cottage. 'Hafta go now. But I'll be back soon.' She jumps off the verandah, waves and lopes away northwards along the riverbank.

Watching her disappear behind the peppermint trees, Ruth wonders why Katy's afraid. She wonders if Jack had been trying to console her with his stories about Aboriginal spirits, or just trying to impress her. She wonders about the damar kurung bird Gusti had mentioned. She wonders about spirits that fly and after-lives, all those other people's beliefs and consolations just beyond her grasp.

Dewi's already in the kitchen, looking at the photo Ruth'd inserted the night before.

'Sorry, Dewi. Talking to Katy.'

'*O-o-h!* Missed her *again*! Why doesn't she stay for long?'

'Not sure. She reckons there are ghosts around here.'

'That's funny. I was just thinking about ghosts.' Dewi's eyes widen. 'D'you think there *are* ghosts around here?'

'If there are, they're not noisy or frightening enough for me to notice. What were you thinking about ghosts before I came in?'

'I was just thinking the faces in this photo look like ghosts.'

'Why d'you say that?'

'They're sorta smudgy. But this is you, isn't it? I can tell by the hair. Who're you with?'

'Your father.'

'*Ohhh!*' Dewi scrutinises him so closely her nose almost touches the print. 'Why didn't you show me before?'

'His face is so unclear.'

'Have you got *another* one of him? A *colour* one?'

'Sorry. Only an accidental black-and-white double exposure where you can't see his face at all. You'll have to imagine him.'

'Who do I look like most?'

'You have blue eyes like his.'

'Mum. Do you believe in ghosts?'

'Not really. Maybe people just get afraid of their own past and future sometimes?'

'So you won't come back to haunt me.'

'I don't think so. It's probably just as well. I'd probably pester you. Boss you around. *Dewi, tidy up your room. Do your homework.* Would that scare you?'

'Nope. I'd just say, *don't be silly, Mum!* Anyway. I read somewhere that ghosts can't talk.'

'Well. Shall I tell you some things that I *really* want you to listen to? To remember every day after I'm gone?'

'Like?'

'Like…look after yourself, Dewi, at least as well as I looked after you before I got sick. Stay away from people who don't treat you well. Don't let anyone...make you do things you don't want to do.'

'Except school, right?'

'Right. You have to keep going to school. Work hard. All those sorts of things that'll help you make yourself a good life.' She hears the Joiners in her voice, clears her throat. 'Help you get an interesting job when you grow up. Maybe go to university or technical college.'

'Yeah, yeah, yeah. But *rrr-eally*, Mum. This photo *is* kinda scary. The blurring makes your eyes and Dad's look like big holes cut out of paper or something. Something thinner than skin.'

'D'you want me to take it out of the album?'

'No. It's the only one of you together. He's even blurrier than you. Why?'

'He set the camera on delayed shutter release so he could get a photo of us both, but there wasn't enough light and he was moving too fast.'

'Was he running?'

'Yes. To make it into the picture on time.'

'Not running away?'

'No.'

'*Really* sure about that?'

'What makes you think he was running away?'

'Finn says he ran away. Roberta told him.' Dewi pulls a strand of hair across her eyes. 'If David knew I was in your tummy, would he have stayed? Would he be happy to be my Dad?'

'I have no doubt about that,' says Ruth. It's the only reply she can give to the flicker of hope in her daughter's face as she puts her half-full lunchbox in her school bag.

Neither of them had revealed much about themselves to the other in their brief time together. During her years on the mission, she'd developed the habit of keeping her thoughts to herself. And David had often hidden behind his knowledge of light and photography when he spoke to her.

'There are things in the air around here that diffuse and scatter the sun's rays. Dust, smoke.' He'd fixed the camera to a tripod, focussed the lens on the dune overlooking the river. 'See how the sunlight's retreating quite fast? Another minute and you'd have to take a new light-meter reading before shooting.' He released the shutter.

The grass-silvered dune. A family of ducks flying over the inky, fish-rippled river, stark against the white frieze of paperbark trees.

'So beautiful,' she'd said.

'Almost looks like Aboriginal country again. The way it would've before the settlers made the rest of this countryside English; clearing as much wilderness as possible, turning it into fenced pasture and sandplain. The main street looked like a wild-west movie scene in a 1920s photo I saw in the library. Bakery, hotel, three shacks and a post office stuck in the middle of bare sand.'

He'd turned the camera on the tripod towards Ruth, run, and reached her as the shutter clicked. Just in time to be in the same frame, but not soon enough to be seen clearly.

∞

When they'd sat on the wicker verandah chairs the next evening, he'd told her even harder things about Lost River.

'Those hills look so soft and green in the day,' she'd commented.

'Yeah. But under all that foliage they're hard limestone full of caves and sinkholes.' He drew a packet of tobacco papers from his pocket. 'Be careful. A few people have fallen to their deaths over the years. Some locals say native animals and horses have a second sense and avoid them, but every few years someone discovers an animal skeleton at the bottom of a sinkhole.' He rolled a thin skein of tobacco tightly in a paper. 'They've found the fossils of extinct species, too. Jawbones of carnivores, thigh bones of kangaroos taller than a man.'

Though it was summer, the breeze from the sea gave her goose-bumps.

'How cold does it get here in winter?'

'Lost River has long, frosty winters. Summer's too short down here. All sorts of fads take hold when winter comes. The wealthy people from the city wear their designer ski jackets when they come down.'

'Does it ever snow here?'

'Never. The travel agent does a good trade in package tours to Bali and other warm places. The unemployed sell more dope to the wealthy.' His hand shook slightly as he held his cigarette to his lips.

'Do any Aboriginal people still live around here?'

'Not now. Not as far as I know. One or two descendants of the old local tribes come through in spring to pick wildflowers to sell in the city. Only a few traces of their ancestors remain. You hear their language in the name of a stream, see a few old scars in tree trunks they used for making tools. The main street and the scenic tourist road just around the corner were laid about a century ago over the tracks the tribes walked between campsites.' The match briefly illuminated his face as he lit the cigarette. *A man who finds it easier to talk about hard facts than personal things,* Ruth had thought.

'I found some stuff in the local-history files in the library. A photo of the men chained together by the early settlers to make roads and clear the wilderness they'd lived in a few years earlier. A few words of dialect collected by one of the first English settler families. About a decade later, wells and fenced farms covered sites where the local tribes were massacred and another river used to run. No-one else would've been more completely cast out.' His eyes had darkened as he'd stared into the night.

In the darkroom a day or two later, they'd watched the details of his photographic prints forming in the tray of developing solution. *Like embryo cells growing in fast motion,* she'd thought as the pale, rounded dune emerged in the first print. His small wind-up egg-timer buzzed on the shelf. He lifted the print dripping from the plastic tray, frowned slightly.

'Developing solution gets exhausted quite fast. That's often the problem when your prints suddenly go flat.' He floated the print in another tray.

'What're you putting it in now?'

'The fixer, to keep it permanent.' He turned the egg-timer on again. 'Bromide and silver build-ups limit the life of fixers. If a print hasn't been properly fixed, or if the fixer contains too much silver, the emulsion will dissolve and fall off the print before the washing is finished.' They stared through the shallow fluid at the print rippling under the red light. 'This one's a bit pale, I'd say. Not enough texture showing in the sand and grasses.'

'Anything you can do about that?'

'See if giving it more printing time on the enlarger improves it.' He turned to the enlarger shaped like a miniature construction crane behind him, twisted its timer dial. 'Give it a couple of seconds more light. But the best way to get a perfect print is to begin with a perfect negative. If the print's lacking in contrast like this, I usually need to adjust my camera settings. Expose more carefully for subject luminance.'

'How do you expose for subject luminance?'

'Something like this dune will reflect up to ninety-percent light, which can obliterate detail and make too much contrast between lights and darks, so you need to give it a bit less aperture to *under*-expose it. Slight negative under-exposure will reflect more texture in the dune, but too much under-exposure will turn a white dune grey. You have to find a compromise that best shows the most important things in the photo.' He turned back to the developing-solution tray. The fluid rippled over their blurred faces. 'This one didn't get enough light. Some of the earliest photographic portraits needed such slow exposures that the people in them left their place in front of the camera too early without knowing it. Sometimes nothing appeared in the finished print except the backdrop.' He lifted their portrait by the corners and watched the fluid run off its edges into the tray. Their faces, refusing definition. The grey bank of cumulus clouds looming behind them in the photo looked more certain.

'Is this a photo of us beginning to appear or beginning to disappear?' she asked.

'Don't know,' he'd shrugged. 'Impossible shot.'

∞

His face, when he didn't know she was watching him. *I never did work out how much light to shine on his sadness. Bright light can drown us as surely as water.*

Ruth steadies her hand, writes in the album above the fleeting portrait of them together: **Your father and I met late in summer. We were under-exposed and moving too fast; the darkness had already begun.**

Ruth, ready to swim

February, 1982
(minimum exposure time helps avoid camera shake)

Eating toast on her unravelling wicker chair, Dewi turns the page to the photo of Ruth in her op shop swimsuit a few weeks after her arrival in Lost River.

'You've got your arms over your chest as if you were trying to hide your boobs.'

'It was cold,' Ruth lied.

'Why's this photo look a bit shaky? Not as blurry as the one of you together, though.'

'Your Dad took it. Maybe he was cold, too.'

She can just hear the river gurgling over the waterfall in the dense forest upriver, slowly looping through the paperbark trees as it approaches the cliffs and the sea. The drawl of two men floats up from the river to the cottage.

'See that plastic raft? On special, fifteen dollars at Target last week.'

'Not making much headway in this wind, but.'

'Yeah, well, there's always *someone* showing off their luxury yacht.'

'Me goggles keep leaking.'

'Ya don't need goggles for windsurfing, mate.'

'Boughtem specially.'

'The thing about windsurfing is, mate, it's like sex: embarrassing the first few times you do it, but after a while, it all comes together.'

Dewi giggles, hand over her mouth. She leans forward to hear more, but the men have drifted too far downriver.

'Why'd that man say sex's embarrassing the first few times, Mum?'

'Maybe because you're not sure what you're doing? But maybe it isn't always embarrassing at first. Maybe it just depends how you feel about yourself and the other person.'

At first David's silences hadn't worried Ruth too much. Fred Joiner had been mostly silent when he wasn't preaching or telling her how to be good back on the mission; and she'd guessed David was tired after work and preferred music to talking.

One Sunday after she'd lived two or three weeks in his home, David had abruptly turned off the singer crooning *Hey, Mr Tambourine Man* on the record-player.

'I'd like to dance like that one day,' she'd murmured shyly in the silence.

'Like what?'

'Like in that song. On the beach. Waving my hands…'

'I can't dance,' he'd said peremptorily.

'Me neither, I guess. I've never tried.'

'Bob Dylan's dangerous sometimes.'

'Who's Bob Dylan?'

David looked sidelong at her.

'You don't know who Bob Dylan is?'

'Someone famous?'

He laughed softly.

'He's the singer on the record. You're kind of inexperienced, aren't you? But you sometimes *talk* like someone much older than you look.' He turned to face her.

'Why's Bob Dylan dangerous?'

'His songs make us feel dissatisfied with our limited little lives, but there's nowhere else to go for some of us,' he muttered.

'But this is such a lovely place.'

'I thought that a few years ago. Shifted from the city soon as this cottage came up for rent. S'pose small town mentality blights the view wherever you are.'

She could find no reply to that.

'What'd you do in the city?' she asked, too enthusiastically.

'Took photos for advertising.'

'Wow.'

His half smile, bemused and concerned.

'You *are* a bit naive, aren't you? Nothing much good about that job. Imagine taking photos of the view out there to help real estate agents sell it for development? Or taking photos of underfed young models in designer-label garments to help sell clothes to wealthy, middle-aged women?' He'd stared at the view through the window, yet his eyes had seemed unfocussed.

∞

That evening, humidity from a low-pressure cell drifting down from the north. A softening in the air.

'I can't dance, but you can swim with me in the bay if you like.'

'The waves are sort of scary.'

'The warm current's still in. Or we could swim in the river instead.'

'If it's not too windy.'

But her reluctance was due to more than the weather.

No rain had fallen in the time she'd spent with him, and the rainwater tank was low. But the small hard tomatoes and green globes of cabbage glowed like dusty jewels in the day's last light, and the pale tassels of corn-silk danced in the sea breeze. Just before dusk, she'd helped him carry buckets of the muddy river-water up the steep riverbank to the wilting vegetable garden, the muscles at the back of her legs and shoulders tightening and aching.

A rosemary cutting had flourished, but one evening when they'd dug their hands into the newly moistened earth to retrieve the onions and potatoes David had planted months before, they felt small as marbles, still full of the day's heat.

'Leave them,' he'd said disconsolately. 'Things would be different if the stream was still flowing.'

'Why'd it stop?'

'It all depends who you ask,' he'd muttered, scowling in the direction of the block next door. A few people in sarongs or Indian dresses drifted between the two mud-brick and timber houses. 'Don't expect a straight answer from Jack and Roberta Murphy. Stoned off their faces most of the time. Our closest neighbours, but they're on another planet.'

The boiled potatoes and tinned tuna Ruth'd bought in town with the last of her stolen mission-chapel coins had only half-filled the two enamel plates at dinner that night. David ate her attempts politely. She'd mentioned the dead reed she'd noticed in the hardened mud on their side of the fence the day before.

'Yeah. The Murphys told me there was no water this side of the fence when they bought their place,' he replied wryly, 'even though I pointed out a few reeds and dry mud when I first came here. But even if I *could* prove they dammed up a stream that flowed here, what would that do to our neighbourly relationship?'

Don't give in so easily, she'd almost told him. *Talk to them.*

Instead, she and David had kept their distance from one another whilst washing the dishes, as if afraid they might contaminate each other. Both too aware of their foreignness, lacking any clear sense of entitlement, anxious not to offend those who'd settled before them.

∞

'Ready for a swim?' he'd asked as soon as he returned home from work the next day.

The yellow, daisy-print, 1950s swimsuit she'd brought home from the op shop concealed more of her than the newer nylon ones. Behind the closed door of her bedroom, she'd pulled the leg elastic low over her thighs, tugged the bodice up high as possible and tied the neck straps tightly. Despite the ruching, the bodice looked too big for her. Arms crossed over her chest, she met him on the verandah.

'Antique bathers,' he said. 'Wild. The river's warmer than the sea today.'

They scrambled down the bank. She tightened the swimsuit's neck straps again as he waded in.

'The river's pretty clean here because the sea comes in at high tide,' he called over his shoulder. He freestyled into the middle. 'Aren't you coming in deeper?'

'I'm not very good at swimming.' She'd only learned how to float and dog-paddle in a waterhole near the mission.

'Know how to tread water?' She shook her head. 'A good survival skill, treading water. Come in a bit more.' Her feet sank through the top layer of fine, pale-green silt into the coarser sand as she waded in waist-deep and knelt so the water covered her chest. 'Come in till you're standing with it up to your shoulders at least!' he laughed. 'No crocodiles in this river.'

'What about sharks?'

'Just me and the property developers. Okay. Now move your arms and legs like this. That's it.'

But her muscles clenched and her limbs sank and she swallowed water.

'It's okay,' he laughed, 'I've got you.' She'd never been held like that by anyone. His hands were steady under her arms, but she'd scrambled to stand on her own two feet on the riverbed.

∞

The next evening after dinner, a bird had called low from the eucalyptus tree between the orchard and the closest dune. *Lone-ly. Lone-ly*, she thought it sang.

'Hear that mopoke? Means the weather'll be getting colder soon. They fly through here on their way north for winter. Feel like a walk to the river mouth?'

The twilight viscous as molasses; cicadas still clicking in the reeds. A fish jumped, the osprey dropped to the ink-blue river. Grasping her last catch of the day with her talons, she flew back to her nest on the cliff.

'How old are you, Ruth?'

'Eighteen-and-three-quarters,' she lied.

'Really?' He patted her hair appeasingly. 'Sorry. It's just that you look younger than you speak.'

'Oh, my Asian genes, I guess. How old are *you*?'

'Twenty-eight. And one-quarter.' Grinning, he ruffled her hair, grabbed her hand and led her into the last of the light. As good as dancing, she'd thought as they rounded the dune to see the low sunrays magnified in the waves.

'Should've brought your camera.' To make that peerless moment last. 'This sea looks like it goes on forever.'

'It's actually two oceans. The Indian and Southern oceans meet on the other side of that cape.'

'But if you take away the names, it's all just one ocean really, isn't it?' She could feel it in her blood, the river flowing into currents from the rest of the world; the mingling of waters and other transparencies. Everything that catches light and turns it into something more substantial. Something you might touch. Maybe even love.

∞

David opening the back of his single-lens reflex camera to load a roll of film. When he'd pressed the release button, she'd seen the shutter behind the lens's glass eye open and flood the camera's dark cavity with an instant of light.

∞

'Gotta take photos of the locals at the agricultural show for the district newspaper. Want a lift into town?'

'Thanks.'

'Hop in.'

A seam of rust along the bottom edge of the ute's door, a scattering of broken shells on the dashboard, entrails of soft cotton waste erupting through a split in the red vinyl-seamed seat. The interior smelled of sea, paint, hay. The engine coughed once before starting. Between them on the bench seat, a map of Lost River, worn to illegibility at the fold lines.

'Do you like taking photos of people?'

'People are complicated. I only photograph them when I'm desperate for money these days. Not many opportunities left for that, though, now everyone in town's got Instamatic or Polaroid cameras.' He'd barely accelerated when he reached the bitumen, as if unsure what lay around the bend. 'And the pharmacy in the town down the highway's doing cut-price film processing on their new machine. The days when the hands developing the images are the photographer's own are coming to their end.'

Surges of cicada song through the car's open windows.

'What do you aim for when you take photos of people?'

'Their noses. Or their warts.' Their laughter mingled in the warm breeze. 'Seriously? I s'pose I try to capture something distinctive about each person in my photos.'

'D'you mean sort of like…capturing their spirits?'

Shadows of tall-trunked trees flickered across their faces as the car passed a stand of dense forest.

'You could say that.' He glanced curiously at her. 'Your mother was Balinese, you said? I went to Bali once a few years ago to take photos for a magazine. Y'know some older Balinese believe photographs of people can be used to steal their souls?'

'How d'you capture something distinctive about a person?'

'S'pose I try to establish some kind of connection with them beforehand, so they're not putting up too much of a false front when I take the shots. Wait long enough and people reveal themselves. It's not only a visual thing, but sort of intuitive too, sensing it just before it happens. Otherwise, by the time you see it and press the button, it's too late.' He glanced in the rear-view mirror. 'Sometimes there's a spark of something in their faces as they look at the lens. As if they've realised something about their place in the world.'

'If you think about it,' she said slowly, 'I guess nothing is as unique as a person's face, really.'

He grimaced at the gears crunching as he turned onto the main street. 'After a few years of taking photos of people, you see that everyone becomes history, one way or another.'

When he'd pulled up at the edge of the Lost River football oval, the vertical creases between his eyebrows had deepened as he looked towards the crowd. People chatted over scones and tea at the Country Women's Association stall; a man in a white coat judged cows being led by farmers around the oval's periphery. On a makeshift catwalk constructed from bales of hay, next to the goal posts, Eloise Gilbert and two of her friends modelled evening gowns.

'Oh no. The town gossips and upholders of the status quo,' he'd muttered, walking away from Ruth as he spoke. 'Might be best if we go our own way for a couple of hours, Ruth.' Almost as if he was trying to distance himself from her.

'I'll make my own way back.'

'Okay,' he'd called over his shoulder, without looking at her again.

∾

Had he been trying to hide something? She'd wandered down the main street to the grocer's, walked aimlessly up and down the aisles, staring blankly at the shelves before buying bread, more tinned tuna, tomatoes and milk. Weighed down by something besides the shopping, she'd found a shortcut home across sun-yellowed paddocks shrill with cicada song and glare.

∾

Even inside the cottage, the trilling of cicadas had been inescapable as the sun climbed towards noon. She'd chewed on a piece of dry bread before putting on the swimsuit and walking downriver. Beyond the river mouth, the osprey swooped into the cobalt-blue bay and rose slowly with a silver salmon squirming in its talons. Almost as big as the bird, the fish swung its tail so hard that for nearly a minute the osprey could barely ascend.

After it landed in a rock cleft beyond her sight, Ruth paddled into the pale-green silt of the riverbed. Bream fingerlings sucked gently on her toes. She stuck her belly out and pushed off with her foot into deeper water, spreading her arms wide. As she lay there, the water rising just over her ears and encircling her face, she closed her eyes and saw David's face, patient and kind as he taught her how to tread water. After a minute, the edges of her body and mind seemed to merge with the river, but his face persisted. Then a sudden darkness loomed behind her eyelids. *It's just clouds passing over the sun,* she thought, *or the osprey again,* but when she'd opened her eyes and stood up, the sky was a bright, birdless blue all the way to the horizon.

∞

On the way to the river mouth late that afternoon, when he'd returned from the show, David had gripped her arm suddenly, pointed to a pair of white birds circling overhead.

'Red-tailed tropic birds. Better keep Yoko inside. They're rare around Lost River now. Their nesting sites have been bulldozed for car parks and holiday houses. They're usually alone, except in their breeding season. They spiral high above each other like that when they're courting, using the updrafts from the cliffs to get more lift. Then they glide together a long way out to sea before returning to nest. See how the female's red tail-streamers have been broken during courting?' He focussed his lens on them, took three quick snaps. 'Shutter speed's probably not fast enough. They go back to the tropics during our winter. When the young are old enough, they drop out of the nest into water, or manage to become airborne. Their parents abandon them. They have to learn to fly quickly. A young chick'll usually wander alone over the oceans for a year before returning to breed in the area it was hatched.'

'How does it find its way back?'

'Instinct, I guess.'

Shirr-iigh, one of the birds circling above them called, *shirr-iigh*.

'Hear that? Their courtship song.'

'Sounds like a woman crying,' she'd said.

She'd been silenced by the sudden fear in his gaze. Watching the two birds spiral upwards together, she had hoped for courage, certainty, safe journeys for them all.

In the photo he'd taken of her in the yellow swimsuit, Ruth notices for the first time that birds are just visible on the horizon, coming from places she and David had never been.

A person is not a bird or a fish, but a person is freer than he or she thinks, Ruth writes under the photo.

Curtain lifting on Dewi's father; the beginning of song

February, 1982
(double exposure)

Dewi has the album open at the first photo Ruth'd ever taken. A shot of his breeze-blown bedroom-curtain superimposed over a face. Only the man's cloud-strewn hair, narrow shoulders, and chest are clear above and below the lace curtain.

'What's this?'

'Double exposure. An accident. The only photo I tried to take of your father.'

'Can't see his face. Looks like a veil.' Dewi glances at her. 'Mum? Why didn't you and Dad marry?'

'We didn't know each other well enough.'

'But you were in love with each other.'

Breathe in.

'Well.'

'Weren't you?'

Breathe out.

'Guess I was.'

'What about him?'

'I don't know for sure. I never asked and we never told each other. Not in words, anyway.'

∞

The waning moon on a late-summer evening smelling of freshly mown hay and eucalypt; the air skin-temperature in the thicket of weeping trees where they'd entered the sandy foot-trail. He'd picked one of the trees' long leaves, crushed it, and held it near her face.

'Nice smell.'

'Commonly known as peppermint trees. Botanical name's agonis flexuosa.'

They'd walked the track through the thicket and around the base of the grass-silvered dune. Across the river, the small island of reeds and papery-trunked melaleucas, centuries old.

'I've tried to paint the colour of moonlight along this trail. Is it a cool or a warm colour? I've never worked it out.' He'd turned to her, stopped walking. 'The moonlight on your skin right now's really...*something*.' When he'd touched her cheek lightly with his fingertips, she'd turned away, for fear he might read things about her that she didn't want him to know.

Lone-ly. The mopoke calling again from high in the marri tree further along the track.

'How about a swim in the bay tomorrow before the breeze comes in?'

'What about the waves?'

'We'll stay shallow so you can just go over them. If they're too big, dive under them. I'll show you. If you try to run away from the big close ones, they get you.' The sandtrack rose suddenly to reveal the setting half moon floating on the waves like a boat. 'Let's just sit for a while.'

He smoothed the ground under the marri tree for her. His arm, warm and light around her shoulders. Their pulses counting the moments. Everything in its place in their little world. Stars, crickets, nightbirds' songs, the river lapping at the reeds. The mingling of their breath as he pressed his lips against hers. The waves arriving on the shoreline at last.

– *No,* hissed Fred and Grace.

She tensed, turned her face away again so he couldn't see her apprehension. The waves receding, exposing her nerves in their wake.

'It's okay,' he said. 'We don't have to go any further.'

For a moment she'd wished she could tell him the whole story of her life before Lost River. But she'd bitten her tongue and buried her story so he wouldn't see that she was cheap, rubbish, unlovable.

Sometime in the early dark hours of the next morning as she dozed in bed, her window and door open to catch the breeze, Ruth had seen a tall shadow shift across the living room towards her doorway. She lay still as it reached the threshold of her room, suppressed a scream. A man, she was certain. Through her window, the setting moon cast a nacreous sheen on his bare arms. He paused at her door.

She could only just make out his eyes, darkened and enlarged by shadow. He seemed to be looking towards her, but his face was impassive as he swayed slightly on his feet. For nearly a minute, she heard nothing but his steady breathing.

'David?' she called finally. He didn't respond, and his face remained expressionless. She counted to thirty before he turned, pulled her door closed behind him and walked away. Though it seemed he hadn't heard her, she sensed that a kind of refusal had occurred.

∞

At breakfast the next morning, he'd greeted her in his usual quiet, slightly preoccupied way; resumed chewing his toast. He handed two pieces on a plate to her.

'Why were you standing at my door late last night, David?' She couldn't make her voice any smaller.

He looked disconcerted. 'Was I?'

'You can't remember?'

'I don't remember standing at your door, that's for sure.' His eyes candid and slightly surprised.

Ruth pushed her toast around her plate. 'Maybe you were sleepwalking.'

'Must've been.'

'Have you sleepwalked before?'

'Not as far as I know.' He frowned slightly. 'I have sleepless nights sometimes.'

'Since when?'

'Since I was a teenager, really. Getting worse in my old age,' he joked feebly.

'I have that, too.'

'Old age?' he smiled.

'Sleeplessness.'

'It's a strange thing, sleeplessness. Your waking life feels slightly nightmarish and your dreams stay with you all day.'

'What d'you think makes you sleepless?'

'What makes *you* sleepless?' he countered evasively.

'Worrying about the future, I guess.'

He'd brushed the crumbs from his hands onto his plate, patted the back of her hand. 'Try not to. Often it's just our past making us worry unnecessarily about where we're going.'

On hot days like that one, vapours rising from the eucalyptus trees on the ridge made the distance even bluer.

∞

The circle of confusion. A term some photographers used, he'd told her that afternoon.

'Only one plane of any photo we take appears absolutely clear. Everything nearer or further away from the camera will be a bit less clear. That's called the circle of confusion, but if it's below a certain size, the eye won't detect it. When a less clearly focussed point in an image becomes large enough, we perceive the circle of confusion as a blur. Every photo has a circle of confusion, sometimes so confined it's a tiny, almost invisible point; sometimes so big it blurs the whole picture. If we have a high tolerance for lack of clarity, we mightn't notice even a relatively large circle of confusion.'

As he spoke, she thought of her lost name, her lost mother and lost place of birth. She thought of the Joiners' harshness during her life on the mission. Maybe all that had demanded from her a high tolerance for lack of clarity. Maybe that'd become her habitual way of dealing with life. Maybe she'd always live with confusion.

She'd shut her eyes tightly for three seconds, opened them as wide as she could. Trying as hard as she could for clear-sightedness.

'Teach me how to use the camera.' It'd sounded more like a demand than a question.

He'd let her wind on a new roll of film; shown her how to focus and use the camera's automatic light meter.

'That's it. See how the needle's pointing to quite a slow shutter speed? When it's dim like this and you're not using a tripod, you have to concentrate on holding your breath and the camera steady as you press the release button, until the shutter closes again.' He'd stood at the end of the verandah side-on to her, gazing at the river, apparently unaware she was staring at him through the camera. The light meter's needle wavering on the side of the view-finder.

She'd read his face only in covert glances before. She focussed on it as closely as she could through the lens. She could see his youthful desire to get on with life. But she thought she could also see a man much older than twenty-eight years in his world-weary eyes, trying to come to terms with some memory of failure or loss.

'Breathe in and hold steady,' he said, facing her directly. 'Press the shutter button.' The paler cloud of his hair and face against the darkening cumulus. 'That's it. Breathe out.'

'I get it,' she said. 'I get it.'

∞

They'd left the camera in the cottage and walked nearly the same path as the previous evening. Where the path forked near the dune, they lay on the cool sand under the gnarled marri tree. The mopoke called again in its branches; this time another one replied from across the river.

He put his shirt under her head, lay on his side next to her. Face to face, hip to hip.

'Since you've been here…I've felt calmer than I've felt for ages.' He paused. 'When I'm with you, anyway. But when I'm not with you, I sometimes think…I shouldn't be with you at all.'

'Why?'

'Can't say exactly. It comes and goes.'

His words should've been a warning, but she gave up trying to make sense of them as he began stroking her hair. He named a few constellations in the sky and retraced them tentatively on her arms, waist, hips, thighs until she felt her body burn bright.

– *No,* admonished Fred and Grace. He'd noticed her tense suddenly.

'What's wrong? Tell me what you're thinking?'

'Nothing,' she lied. *Let go,* she told herself, *let go.*

'Tell me what you want, Ruth?'

No-one had asked her that before.

'You.'

Who was most shocked by her declaration? It'd sounded to her as if it were spoken by someone else. His face looked suddenly unresolved, the stars of the Southern Cross seemed to shift in the patch of sky above them. Bearings lost.

And then; and then. His kisses, uncertain but tender. His hands, awkward but gentle, guiding her towards some wordless song. His attenuated limbs, low hips. Body of Christ. Searing pain. And then again. They uttered a cry together that seemed to come from a long time past, yet reach far into the future.

The gnarled paperbark trees timed the river as it flowed past the ancient cliffs to the sea. He closed his eyes, gave a single sigh that sounded almost like a sob and took a deep shuddering breath before opening them again. As if he'd been trying to calm himself.

'All the shades of darkness,' he said.

'Eternity,' she murmured. But she could barely bring herself to meet his eyes.

'You okay?' Broken shells shifting on the sand underneath them. 'What's wrong?' he persisted.

'Nothing.'

'Have I hurt you?'

'No.'

'Are you in pain?'

'No.'

'Do you want to see a doctor?'

'No.'

'Ruth? I tried to be careful. I'm so sorry if I've hurt or upset you. Talk to me?'

The mopoke above them no longer received any reply from the one across the river. Beating its wings rapidly, the lone bird ascended into the sky before free-falling into the dark valley and out of sight.

After taking her only photograph of him, she must've accidentally pressed the shutter release again without winding the film on properly. She'd only realised her mistake months after he'd disappeared and she'd had the film developed for any clues it might offer about him in the days before he'd disappeared.

Ruth writes underneath the double-exposure of the curtain billowing from his open bedroom window across David's face:

Dear Dewi,

Your father was a tender man. He and I loved each other as far as it's possible for two damaged young people in such a short time. We shared pain, but joy, too. They say a bird's nerve centre is where its song begins.

The end of the path Dewi's parents walked

February, 1982
(limited depth of field)

Leaving the album open on the verandah at David's photo of the twilit dune, Dewi and Ruth paddle in the half-moon bay late in the afternoon. Arcs of silver fish; gardens of kelp, samphire and wrack are illuminated in pale-green waves like film transparencies by the sun behind them, just before falling back into the darker water.

'Why did he go?' Dewi asks, the waves delivering and taking from under their feet.

He'd arrived home late the evening after they'd made love, sat on the verandah and looked across the valley silently before saying he was sorry, so sorry. That he'd be ashamed to admit to anyone else what he'd done to her, that she was too young. He'd turned to her, said he hoped that in time she'd be able to forget about him, move on. Stunned, she didn't know how to reply.

– *You were too easy with him. Too cheap,* chorused Grace and Fred.

– Like your mother.

– How can you expect a man to respect you? How can you expect a man to love you?

A tiny light had hovered between the bush and orchard, zigzagged haphazardly towards the verandah.

'A firefly,' he'd mumbled as it drew closer. 'Rare around this time of the year.' The firefly alit on the rusty drainpipe against the verandah post. They watched it crawl slowly up and down for several minutes, its body growing gradually dimmer.

'Its light's going out,' she said.

'Must be sick I s'pose.' He cleared his throat. 'I've decided I'm going away. A month or so. Tomorrow. You can stay here. It'd be best for you to think about living without me in the long term. I'm not a very nice person.'

'*I* like you,' she murmured.

'You wouldn't say that if you knew me better. I'm sorry.' He placed his hand briefly on her forearm. 'Would you mind feeding Yoko?'

'Where are you going?' she murmured.

'A fair way from here, I s'pose you could say.' She couldn't see his face clearly in the dark. 'Don't worry. I've already been there before.' The firefly rose suddenly, hovered dimly around them for a few moments before embarking on a trajectory they couldn't see to its end.

He walked past her to his room. She stood outside his closed door. *Please can we talk,* she wanted to say. *There's something you're not telling me. There are things I should tell you.* But the silence behind his door intimidated her. The boards on the verandah under her feet felt even more unsteady than usual as she walked out.

The pale dune glowed in the moonlight against the dark foliage and grasses, but she could no longer see the path clearly. When she'd reached the dune, she turned back to look at the cottage. All its lights were out, as if it'd been blinded. Suddenly that place of her new beginning seemed like the end of the world. As if nothing in her life would ever be promising again. As if there would only be gradations of darkness.

She looked at the other house-lights twinkling upriver as she walked. When she eventually returned to the cottage she stood outside his bedroom door for a long time again, but still no sounds came from the other side. She left her own bedroom door open and lay on her bed, listening for him. Yoko stalked in and out a couple of times, mewing softly. Ruth didn't sleep until the first birds of the new day began singing.

When she woke mid-morning, he'd gone. His knapsack and hat no longer hung from the coat hooks on the back door. He'd taken the bulkier clothes from his wardrobe and folded them into a box. But his camera and watch remained on the living-room mantelpiece, their round glassy faces unseeing.

Walking into the kitchen, she saw he'd put the Dylan record on the table with a folded note for her. *To Ruth from David,* he'd written on the Dylan cover. The folded note said again that he was sorry, that he regretted deeply what he'd done. That he'd mistaken her dependency on him for love.

But I do love you. More than anyone I've known, she'd replied to the river, because he'd left her no address to write to him.

∞

The Balinese believe there are many skies. In one of these skies a Goddess of the underworld lived, and in another sky lived a God who created beauty from light and earth. They had to move through immeasurable distance to find one another: through the sky perfumed with flowers, and through the sky full of snakes that appear to humans on earth as falling stars. The God and Goddess finally met in the sky immediately above the earth, which the Balinese call the floating sky, where love lives. But even when the God and Goddess held each other in the floating sky, they were unable to bridge the distance created by their unshared pasts. When the God departed to the flame-filled heaven where his ancestors lived, the Goddess became lost in the dark-blue sky with its sun and moon that Westerners call space. There she wept for him, until her tears washed her back down to the underworld she'd come from.

∞

Ruth has no answer to Dewi's questions about his reasons for leaving. She'd missed the details in the darkness. She hopes Dewi will make these photographs of her parents' time together lead to more hopeful stories.

Ruth inserts into the green album David's final photo of the grass-tussocked dune at evening, the winding track they'd last walked together only just visible at its base before it turns towards the cliff and disappears. His smile in the twilight, so fleeting she'd miss it forever.

The cave of the unknown

exact date not clear
(impossible to see the details of darkness)

All these years later, Ruth finds herself talking to him as she watches Dewi turning cartwheels in the orchard. *Look how beautiful our child and the day are. Even if loving them was all you could do, I wouldn't have minded. I would've looked after you.*

In the past year, Dewi's legs and arms had taken on the gangly awkwardness of adolescence. Would she become too tall to turn cartwheels easily? Ruth puts the last of his photographs in the green album. She writes under his photo of the dark cave entrance near the cliff: **I grieved for your father and everything I knew about him. And I grieved for everything I would never know about him.**

How much should remain concealed from their daughter?

∞

David had been gone several months when Ruth'd looked through the back door to see Roberta walking across the paddock, her auburn hair aflame in the afternoon sun, her purple, crushed-velvet dress in disarray. Next to her the town policeman, unsmilingly upright in his permanent-press uniform.

'Constable Bill Collins,' he muttered, glancing at the slight rise of her belly through her t-shirt.

'Hiya, Honey,' Roberta said apologetically, her eyes bloodshot and brimming with tears. Bill Collins turned over a page in his notepad and concentrated on writing something.

'Full name?'

'Ruth Mary…Smith.'

'And you lived with David Mathews here only a month or so, Miz Murphy tells me?' Why did he want to know? Ruth glanced at her neighbour.

Roberta grabbed her hand and sobbed: 'You wouldn't think that such a talented, sensitive man would do that to himself. Or maybe it helps explain why he did.'

'Did what?'

'He must've crawled into that cave near the cliff and just waited for the cold to get him.'

'Get him?'

'The cause hasn't been established yet, Miz Murphy,' said the policeman sternly. 'It's impossible in some cases to ever establish the cause.'

Roberta squeezed her hand harder.

'David's dead, Ruth honey. They found him inside the cave near the cliff. He was facing towards the cottage. He would've been thinking about you.'

'How do you know it's David?' Clutching at the last thin straw of light.

'His brother's identified the body,' the policeman said.

The cold darkness rushing into her ears and eyes. At first she hadn't recognised the whimper rising to a low, animal howl as her own. Roberta held her until her weeping subsided, offered her a used tissue from her pocket.

'Can you tell me anything unusual you noticed about his behaviour before he disappeared?' the policeman asked.

Ruth shook her head. Too cold, too numb.

Bill Collins spoke to his highly polished shoes but didn't succeed in keeping the embarrassment from his voice. 'What precisely was your relationship to David Mathews?'

'I-i loved him.'

'De facto.' Holding his pen to his notebook, Bill Collins glanced at her belly again and looked away as if he'd smelled something bad.

'We didn't have enough time...'

'Can she see his body if she wants?' Roberta asked.

'His brother's already arranged for the body to be sent to the city for the funeral.'

'We didn't have enough time together...' Her tears dissolved her speech, the crisp, blue outline of Bill Collins's uniform and the red beacon of Roberta's hair. But glancing over her shoulder at his darkroom, she'd seen in an instant of blinding clarity David and everything about him she already missed.

After Bill Collins and Roberta had left, Ruth had walked down to the bay under a sky as cold and fissured as marble. Although it was an unusually windless autumn afternoon, the ocean's surface looked bumpy all the way to the horizon, as if jostled by some subterranean force.

Enormous waves broke out near the point. Wading into the calmer bay almost up to her shoulders, the clear water magnified her brown toes against the pale sand. A sea snail dragged its unwieldy home on its back, away from her. She toed the edge of the deep reef-edged trough. No safe foothold there. It would take her only seconds to let the current take her away. No-one would see.

A sudden swaying, almost like the onset of vertigo. She looked up just in time to see an enormous wave pushing steadily towards her, its undertow strengthening and pulling her. So dark it was almost black at its base, way bigger than her.

You can go over the top of waves, or dive under big ones, she heard David say again. *If you try and run away from the big ones, they get you.* But the looming wave looked far too big to either jump over or dive into. Paralysed, she closed her eyes and waited for the wave to carry her out of her depth and into drowning.

But the wave didn't even close over her head for a second, barely reached her chin. It only moved her along a few inches before letting her go and spending itself in the shallows. Just another abandonment.

She waded back to the shore strewn with shattered shells, and walked back along the dune path; turned around to look just once more at the sun setting over the bay he'd swum in nearly every day she'd known him. At the very moment the glowing edge of the sun sunk below the darkened sea, a plume of foam leapt and twisted upwards like a dancer from a breaking wave, catching the last of the light before dispersing into spray, vapour, invisibility.

Ahead of her, the waning moon had just risen over the hills and paddocks. Night too soon; already she'd known it would last too long. She'd stumbled, wet and shivering, to his precarious cottage near the bend of the river, and it had seemed she was entering orphanhood all over again.

∞

Ruth'd lain awake through most of the night following the news of his death. She kept opening her eyes to the dying of his light, thought she could hear the closing bars of *Simple Twist of Fate*. Any minute now he would speak to her, surely. But a dour angel from the illustrated Bible of her mission childhood appeared and raised its wings, blocking out any traces of him. Finally, she'd slipped under a wing to sleep an hour or two.

In the wan morning, Ruth wondered who she could talk to about him. She thought about trying to ring his brother. To say something, at least. To say what? I loved David, too?

Unfed and unwashed, she'd crossed paddocks and fence-lines, startling grazing Friesian cows and grey kangaroos. She'd entered Lost River's main street as the first shopkeepers began opening their doors. Inside the peeling, red-framed payphone box with its weather-scoured panes of glass, she'd found the name Luke Mathews in the city phone directory, put some coins in the slot and dialled the number. But when a man answered, she put the receiver down quickly. What would her grief be compared to his family's? She'd known David less than two months; his brother would've known him all his life.

∞

She could tell by the glances of townsfolk that the news of his death had already got around. She tugged the front of her shirt to hide the slight rise of her belly, but this left her back exposed. They said nothing to her when they saw her; some of them crossed the street to avoid her. Had her peculiar loss marked her as a threat to their soundness and routines?

In the supermarket, three middle-aged women had been full of opinions. The bread aisle between Ruth and them was no barrier to their gossip.

'He must've just sat there until he died.'

'How long?'

'Wouldn't have taken long for a skinny bloke like him. Record cold nights for early autumn.'

'A week, maybe.'

'A fortnight, max.'

'He might've survived if he hadn't been so thin.'

'He seemed pretty down sometimes.'

'Bit happier when that Asian girl moved in.'

'Cold and depression slow the circulation and spirits.'

'Drugs can do that, too, you know.'

'For *sure*. He lived in Ferguson's old farmhouse.'

'Next door to that block where those hippies built their shacks.'

'Cannabis. At the very least.'

'Or coulda been money.'

'Or love.'

'He didn't have much of those.'

'Unless you count that Asian girl.'

A sudden, appalled silence as two of the wives had glimpsed Ruth between the loaves of Wonder White and sliced multigrain. She'd retreated down the aisle and hidden her face at the milk refrigerator, staring at the small cow standing green and alone in a pasture of spikes on the label.

∞

Grief had made the everyday seem strange and far away – the people she spoke to, the clothes she sorted in the op shop, the food she ate, even her heartbeat. A couple of evenings after David's body had been found, Jack Murphy told Ruth a story about the dead.

'The local Aboriginal people believe that sometimes the spirits of dead people take the form of red-tailed tropic birds,' he'd said, smoking a joint in his hammock. 'Reckon the spirit's face looks like the face of the dead person but smaller; that the white feathers around its feet muffle its footsteps. Make a kinda rustling sound. These spirits live in the caves near where that other river used to flow.' Jack'd finished his joint and exhaled in her face until she felt lightheaded and slightly nauseous. 'I've seen one of those feathered spirits around there myself since Davo died. Maybe it'll appear to you like that. Don't be afraid if it does. Just his spirit on its way back to its true home.' As Jack sighed and looked across the paddock to the other side of the river, Ruth realised that some of his stories probably weren't authentic Aboriginal stories as he'd claimed, but about his own yearning to belong.

∞

Trying to sleep in her bed with the full moon shining on the white-quilted rise of her belly that night, after hearing Jack's story, Ruth thought she heard the rustle of feathered footsteps outside her window. When she heard David's voice call her name, she was too frightened to look out the window. She pulled the quilt over her head, pulse thumping, hands over her ears.

The voice and footsteps had gone when she finally removed her hands from her ears. Only the wind in the trees; the loose corner of roofing tin lifting and falling. She recalled her adoptive father Fred Joiner's biblical stories of people cast out into the wilderness. In Fred's sermons, wilderness meant loss of home, faith and sanity. Only foreigners and mad people wandered in the wilderness, beyond hope unless they came home to God.

Suddenly, the back door of the cottage had opened and slammed three times. Wind gusted into her room. Pulse beating heavily in the silence, she tiptoed down the dark passage, staying close to the wall.

The back door was wide open. Above her, a white gull in the black sky struggled to fly against the wind. Closing the door and pushing a chair against it, she'd been certain she was crazy and outcast. A disintegrating shack rented by a dead man the only home she had.

It'd taken her hours to drift off to sleep again. Sleep, too, had been filled with David's face, footsteps and voice, and she'd woken around dawn with him tolling in her, hollow as a bell.

∞

In the following days, Ruth had sensed his spirit in every silence and shadow, yet it'd evaded her. She'd taken wrong turnings looking for it in the cottage, bush and town; thought she'd seen it hanging amongst the clothes in his bedroom and in the op shop, or thin with starvation in the grocer's aisles. She'd abandoned her groceries in the shopping trolley before reaching the till; gone home empty-handed.

And what was home? His vegetable garden looked improvident and full of empty spaces, despite her attempts to water it since he'd left. The old fruit trees: who'd pruned them so cruelly they wept sap instead of fruiting, and why hadn't she noticed that before?

Inside, nothing but coldness, empty cupboards and inconsolable hunger in every corner. She went to his bedroom again. When she opened his wardrobe and the cardboard box, only the smell of washing detergent rose from his clothes. But on his bedside table, she noticed two of his sun-bleached hairs entwined in the teeth of his blue plastic comb. She'd inhaled his fading, sweet oiliness before returning the comb to the exact place he'd left it.

Back then, only the life she'd shared with David had seemed substantial, beating in her like another heart. It'd seemed the moments she'd spent with him would last longer than all the years of her life.

∞

'Why did you put the photo of the cave in this album?'

'It's where your Dad died.'

'Oh. You never found out what he died of, did you?' Dewi asks.

'No-one knew for sure.'

'How come?'

'Sometimes it's very hard to tell.'

'What was he doing in the cave?'

'Sheltering, probably.'

'What from?'

'Bad weather, maybe.' It's only half a lie.

'Shame all his photos are black and white,' Dewi says, closing the album.

'Sometimes, Dewi, you have to imagine the colours.'

After cremation, Bali

November, 1993
(accidental exposure)

After taking a painkiller in the early hours of the morning, Ruth's sleep is interrupted by garishly lit people in long white robes and black rags fighting with each other. They look like the saints and sinners from the illustrated Bible in the mission classroom, until one of them turns suddenly and rushes towards her, sarong flapping, toothless mouth huge and speechless, a black hole into which Ruth might fall.

Her mother? Or one of the beggar women in Bali?

Panicking, Ruth switches the bedside lamp on. The hallucination disappears.

She turns to the few Bali holiday photos remaining in the pharmacy envelope on her bedside table. Who'd taken that shot of tiny lights in darkness so dense you couldn't tell if it was water, sky or earth? Was it a snapshot of a far-off village, or fireflies in the flooded padi fields? Then she notices the glowing skeletal frame of the distant cremation tower, sees the tiny lights are its embers falling through the Balinese night.

Another knock on the door. More authorities? Ruth had looked at the alarm clock on her bedside table, heart sinking as she realised she'd slept through Dewi's departure for school. Footsteps. A shadow against the curtain. She pulled the sheet over her head; lying still until the steps clicked briskly across the verandah and down the gravel track. A car whirred away onto the road.

Under the front door, she found a small white card.

Can Help called today. Can Help is an outreach service of the Child Welfare Authority, set up to support children at risk. Please ring Phoebe Collins at your earliest convenience to find out how we can help you.

Children at risk. Had Mrs Robbins been spreading the word?

∞

Dewi had slammed the back door in her rush back from the bus that afternoon.

'Guess what? There's a *reea*lly nice new girl at school. Amy. She's invited me to her place to play.'

'That's great!'

Dewi hesitated. 'She's our new neighbours' girl.'

'Oh!' Ruth tried to sound enthusiastic. 'She can come over here to play, too.'

A flicker of consternation on Dewi's face. She opened her mouth to say something, closed it again before going to the verandah and gazing over to the new neighbours' place.

'Mm-maybe another day,' she'd replied half-heartedly.

∞

Already some of the Oriental Wisdom quotes in the album are coming unstuck, but most of the photos hold firm. She's losing her grasp of time though; can't get the remaining photo dates or sequence right. So many unfinished yesterdays.

The magpies' throaty warbling continues through the full moon night. As the analgesics wash through Ruth, her hallucination of the embers falling from the Balinese cremation tower is obliterated by another one of floodwaters swamping her burning body.

Forgetting. It's what she wants. It's what she dreads.

PART FOUR

The White Album

Dewi on her way to her new friend's

December, 1993
(shutter release too late?)

Ruth glimpses herself in the kitchen window, pale and gaunt as a ghost. Refusing to be fooled by this apparition, she sits with Dewi as she eats an apple and flicks through the albums. All those moments of her daughter's life already flown. The mantle-piece clock chimes the half-hour.

'Twelve-thirty!' Dewi exclaims. 'Don't wanna be late for Amy's!'

On the doorstep, Ruth sniffs Dewi's freshly washed hair smelling of their rosemary rinse and Home Brand Shampoo, kisses her on the forehead as she sets off to Amy's place. Her daughter turns and waves, her eagerness for the journey showing in her smile, her arms open wide to the horizon beyond their small home.

'Keep spreading your wings!' It's all Ruth can think to say to her, moving towards a future she won't be part of. The mother steps back, lifts the camera and presses the button, practises letting go of her child again.

Roberta and her bonfire

December, 1993
(ghost images and flare spots)

'Why didn't I see this fire?' Dewi asks when she opens the white album to the photo of Roberta next to the unwieldy tower of clothes, highchair and tricycle burning against the night sky; her face glowing with flickering flames and something like triumph.

'Roberta lit it quite late at night. You were asleep.'

'What are those?' Dewi points to the scattering of bright circles across the print.

'They call them ghost images or flare spots. Made by lens surface reflections entering the camera and film.'

∞

Ruth had been woken that night by an explosion much louder than Jack's home-brew bottles usually made. An orange glow danced around the bedroom walls. She listened carefully but heard only loud crackling. Through the window she saw flames in the paddock. She walked barefoot across the spiky summer grass to find Roberta nonchalantly leaning against a rake, hose in her hand. Ash and sparks eddied above her rickety tower of unwanted belongings.

Roberta shouted over the roaring blaze.

'Jack and me got those jobs as guides with the tourist bureau. We'll have more money! A new life!'

'Wow!' Ruth rasped. 'So this is your way of celebrating?'

'We're sick of living in a time warp. Time to get rid of all this old crap. We'll buy new things and renovate the house.' Silhouetted amongst the flames, a broken guitar rested against the back of Finn's old highchair. Two strings snapped, releasing a fountain of sparks, one low and one high note, just audible above the crackle of the flames. *The Best of Leonard Cohen, The Free Wheeling Bob Dylan* and *Ravi Shankar Sitar* records melted like black icing over a pile of jeans, tie-dyed t-shirts, Indian dresses and blouses, the little brass bells on their bodices tinkling one last time in the updraught before melting. A Peruvian woollen poncho blackened and released an odour like singed hair; a tuxedo from the op shop stiffened on its wire hanger for a second before slumping over a bubbling nylon negligee. Chapters from the Murphy's past, reduced to windborne odours and particles.

At the base of the fire amongst some old shoes, plastic tentacles flailed in the updraught before shrivelling and withdrawing.

'What are those?'

'Just negatives from years ago.'

'Oh no! Keep the photos!'

'We'd sooner forget those days.'

'All that history going up in smoke!'

'Trust you to say that! Ruth, the biggest hoarder of them all. It's not enough just to keep what you're given. You have to *choose* from what you're given,' Roberta said, sweat on her face, an evangelical gleam in her eye as strong as Fred Joiner's had ever been.

Ruth had no reply. *Do those old things mean more to me than they do to Roberta because I've lost touch with where I came from?*

Looking into the flames blackening Finn's preschool tricycle and the artificial daisy wilting on Roberta's straw sun hat above a smouldering velvet coat, it had seemed to Ruth that forgetting the past was another kind of death.

∞

A Saturday; the road's crawling with tourists' cars. Ruth can only just carry the rack of her Lost River postcards up the driveway to the old weatherboard bus-stop shelter facing the road. She leaves the postcards with a locked money box chained to the shelter.

The sea breeze blows ash from the remains of Roberta's bonfire. Watching the particles blow east on the breeze, Ruth recalls the Balinese cremation and the death customs Gusti had described. *I'll tell the funeral directors that I want my funeral to be a celebration, for Dewi's sake.* Helium-filled balloons seemed popular with the children when she'd walked past one of the old dairy farmer's funerals at the Lost River cemetery recently. *But who will shelter her during and after my burning? And who will help her find my blessings in the ash and silence?*

Dewi defending home

January, 1994
(exhaling before releasing the shutter prevents camera shake)

When Ruth sees the photo she'd taken of Dewi standing proudly next to her new hand-painted warning sign the following week, she doesn't know whether to laugh or cry.

A few days before Dewi made that sign, Merv Ferguson had stood on the verandah holding the same khaki towelling hat he'd always worn. His faded overalls stretched across his belly.

'Sorry. Just letting you know I'm selling the cottage to finance our retirement and medical bills, luv. So sorry. I know it's bad timing with you being so ill and all.' He turned to look at the river. 'Way things are going, this view's worth more than all me cows and milk. Guess some silvertail from the city'll buy this tiny block and put a mansion on it. Really sorry about this. Me and Ivy's going up north on a caravan trip after we see the specialists. Catcha bitta sun. Des Gilbert's handling the selling for us.

I've told him not to shift you out till you get something better.'

Ruth gripped the door jamb for support.

'Where will we live?'

Ferguson held his hat in both hands and twisted it in the middle. 'Stay until it sells if yer like. Who knows, new owners might keep you on as a tenant. Best to keep your antenna up for somewhere else meantime, and I've asked a few people to look out for an easier place for you. So sorry, luv. Me and Ivy's getting old. Need the money to live in the city close to medical specialists. The old ticker's giving me a bitta trouble, the missus has diabetes.' He put his hand on his paunch. 'All Ivy's cakes and scones. Can't help it.' Patting the back of her hand lightly, he'd put his old hat on but couldn't get it to sit right as he walked away.

Ruth had closed the front door and leaned against it, as if it were the only friend she could depend on.

∞

When Ruth had gone to the opportunity shop the next day, the enormous red SALE sign in its window surprised her. A small queue of locals, including Roberta, waited on the front step for her to open the shop. They surged through the door past her.

Eloise was already inside in the back room, fingering her permed blonde helmet of hair, straightening her suit in front of a mirror.

'We're having a sale because we're closing both the shops down,' she said. 'Not enough profit.'

'My job?' Ruth murmured, grateful that the painkillers had numbed her.

'Don't worry. You can probably get sickness benefits.'

'Bitches,' muttered Roberta as two younger women grabbed an armful of jeans and t-shirts. 'I wanted those.'

'They're all vultures,' Eloise whispered to Ruth. 'Have you noticed how people with money are so much *nicer*?' She grabbed her plump purse from under the counter, held it tightly under her arm. 'I'm off to catch bigger fish. Department store stocktake sales start in the city tomorrow.'

'There's more stuff out the back in boxes,' Ruth murmured to Roberta after Eloise left. From the counter she heard cartons tearing, zippers hissing on jeans, press studs popping as Roberta tried things on.

'Thanks, Ruth. Sexy nighties. Nice woman's skirt-suit. And the safari suit could be good for Jack. You know he wrote me a song and bought me a gorgeous red rosebush yesterday?' she confided almost shyly as she emerged from the change room. 'Got the van parked out the back. Take a raincheck on these?' She hurried through the back door with her arms full of clothes.

Ruth scooped into a pile all the discarded garments. Seagull came in and leaned on the counter, idly fingered the strands of false pearls and pendants on chains while Ruth sorted the pile.

'How're ya *feeling* after hospital?' The feathers on the ends of Seagull's plaited fringe spiralled in the breeze coming through the door. She stared at the lumps under Ruth's collarbone. Ruth felt the difference between Seagull and her, sharp as a knife.

'Happy to be back and breathing easier.'

'Your voice sounds like you're running out of puff. And look at those new lumps under your neck! What are you going to *do?*'

'Wing it, I guess. Nothing else I *can* do.'

While Seagull tried on shoes and dresses in the change room, Ruth thought she glimpsed something she'd lost years before. Almost the colour of the golden light David had shown her through the camera on their first meeting, the garment looked like a piece of happiness amongst the pile of drab cast-offs. But when she tugged, it tore, and she held just the yellow silk sleeve from the dress Eloise had advised her against on her first day in the op shop. Where had it been all these years? She held the sleeve to her face, recognised Eloise's stale perfume and sweat immediately. She folded the sleeve with the dress, put them under the counter, took a deep breath and tried to sort through her jumbled thoughts as she sorted more clothes, but they broke into separate voices again.

— *Death.*

— *No-one will ever buy that one.*

— *Unfashionable.*

— *Made in Asia.*

— *Cheap.*

— *Bad quality.*

— *Serve something greater than yourself.*

Is that my past or my future speaking? Ruth wondered. Seagull emerged from the change room and looked curiously at the lumps again; stuck her tongue into the inside of her cheek.

'I got a lump in the side of my mouth. An ulcer, cos I don't get enough money to eat enough nutrition.'

'Well. Look after yourself, Seagull. Don't sell yourself short.' Seagull's gull tattoo had a shallow scratch across its tail.

'Whaddya mean?'

'Don't expect anyone to save you,' she replied gently. 'Especially someone like Des Gilbert. If we don't rescue ourselves, we stay unrescued.'

'Don't know what the fuck you're talking about, Ruth. Your meds must be scrambling your brain.' Could Seagull be right? Maybe the red stiletto that had fallen from Des's car a few months ago wasn't even Seagull's. 'I'll take these.' Seagull had avoided eye contact as she stuffed a dented heart locket and false pearls into her pockets, and turned towards the op shop door and all the living she had to do.

The clunk of something heavy by the front door and the shuffle of receding footsteps had woken Ruth the next morning. Groggy with sleep, she took too long to dress and open the door. On the doorstep, a cast-iron pot full of baby carrots, potatoes and lamb stew – a shimmering rich treasure, nothing like the mission's impoverished stews. Receding up the road, Merv and Ivy Ferguson's old truck, towing their caravan somewhere warmer.

At the end of the op shop's last day, Ruth had stood with Dewi behind the op shop counter and looked around after the customers had taken the things they wanted. All those abandoned fashions and whims; all those outdated household effects, books and records. The remnants of a bottle of *Je Reviens* perfume, sheets of music titled *Hallelujah*, a porcelain figurine of a young man and woman dancing, their hands chipped.

'Can I keep these?' Dewi had found the two china wall-ducks missing a wing and their drake.

Some things we want even when they're broken.

∞

Early the next morning, someone had knocked harder and faster than ever before on the cottage's front door.

'Time to face the music, Ruth.' Des Gilbert, his ginger hair and sunburned face florid against his cream suit and white shirt. 'This property's not gonna sell with you in it. And you can't afford to live here now you don't have a job.'

'Merv Ferguson told me I can stay until it sells. At least.'

'You're not the tenant, legally speaking. Your name's not on the lease. This house is a health and safety threat and an insurance liability with you living in it. I'm not prepared to risk it. Management's in my hands now Fergusons are away.' He poked a cracked verandah board with his white shoe until it splintered. 'I'm a real estate agent and a town councillor and I know all about property and real estate law, Ruth. You gotta respect property.' What had Katy told her? *Just passing through my old people's place.* 'People work hard and pay good money for property,' Des droned on as he broke a small piece of the wood with a kick. 'You wouldn't want to impede Merv Ferguson's right to realise the full value of his real estate investment, would you?' He turned over the piece of wood with the toe of his shoe, revealing fine silvery tunnels on its underside. 'Look at that. Riddled with white ants and dry rot.' He nodded towards the garbage bags on the other end of the verandah. 'A vermin trap. Bulldozing's the best thing for this dump, anyway. Bulldozing and nice new fences increase block value. You gotta move out.'

'You know I have a daughter to care for. Eloise must've told you I'm ill.'

'All the more reason to shift, luv. Try looking on the bright side. Now you can live somewhere low maintenance.'

'But there are no other cheap rental places around here anymore. You of all people should know that. I can't look after my daughter and myself without this house.'

Des scratched his sunburned scalp and clapped his Panama hat back on his head. 'Times change. Yer gotta keep up with them or get out. Look, I'll give you a month. That's more than I need to, legally.' He scrutinised Ruth's face. 'Yer never did tell Eloise exactly where you came from. Maybe you could go back to your family?'

Eavesdropping behind her, Dewi had stepped back into the shadows.

∞

Taken a few hours after Des Gilbert's visit, the photo of Dewi and her hand-painted paper sign on the front door:

Dear Mr Gilbert
We are trying our best to live clean and tidy.
Do not mess us up.

Dewi stands holding David's old paintbrush solemnly at arm's length in front of her, like a sword.

Old friends' new lives

February, 1994
(kinder light)

The photo of Roberta and Jack in their business clothes from the opportunity shop: Jack in the safari suit, Roberta in a navy-blue pencil skirt and jacket with padded shoulders, teetering in her op shop high heels on the gravel. They each have a red rosebud from the bush he'd bought her in their lapel. Roberta has hennaed the grey in her hair. The crimson lipstick makes her grin look a bit crooked.

Focussing the lens on Roberta and Jack early that morning, Ruth had thought she'd seen what David meant when he talked about *that spark of something* in people's faces.

'Smile!' she coaxed her neighbours.

Jack grinned. Roberta looked at Ruth beseechingly in the moment before she pushed the button, as if to say: *Be kind. Show me in the best possible light.* The shutter opened and closed on their self-consciousness. The capture of their flickering flame of awareness, by darkness.

Would dying be like that?

Jack and Roberta's self-consciousness had disappeared as soon as she'd replaced the lens cap. They'd slid into the tourist bureau's new, white sedan, waved, and set their eyes on the road ahead, grinning as if they'd found their place in the bigger picture.

'Bye! It's been great hanging out with you!' Ruth watched them glide on automatic transmission all the way up the road and towards their future as guides to Lost River's good life.

∞

Walking as fast as she could from Doctor Vincent's to try to reach Dewi before she boarded the school bus home, Ruth had been surprised to hear her daughter's voice, quiet but determined, coming through the doorway of the new supermarket.

'Ex-*cuse* me. Do you have any food you don't want, please?' Ruth ducked into the laneway to listen. 'My Mum's sick. Too sick to cook and she doesn't have much money. And I want to feed her to make her strong.'

Voices murmured, plastic bags rustled. Her face burning, Ruth swallowed hard. Embarrassment and pride, she'd never felt them all mixed up together before.

'*Thank* you! Very, very *much*,' Dewi chimed. She came out carrying a loaf of bread, knob of polony, and some other less-visible items in a plastic bag, her expression serious and too old for her years.

'Hi, Dewi,' Ruth murmured as casually as she could.

'Mum!' Dewi quickly held the bag of food behind her back. 'What are *you* doing here?'

'Coming back from Doctor Vincent's.'

'Why?' Anxiety sharpened Dewi's face.

'Oh, just a check up.'

'What did she say?'

'Nothing new.'

'You're not hiding anything from me, Mum?'

An apple dropped out of the bag behind Dewi's back, rolled between their feet.

'No. What are *you* hiding?'

'Nothing.' Dewi bit her lip. 'It's supposed to be a surprise for you.'

'A surprise! How lovely. Walk home with me?'

'Don't look while I put this into my schoolbag?'

'Promise.' Ruth looked away while Dewi stuffed the supermarket bag into her knapsack.

'And we'll walk this way,' Dewi whispered, 'so the supermarket people don't see you.'

'Okay,' Ruth agreed. *Is she worried they'll think she was lying, or that I asked her to beg for food? Or is she just embarrassed by my appearance?* 'You're in charge.' But her daughter had looked too uncertain to lead the way against the oncoming traffic.

∞

'Roberta looks *really different* dressed for her new job! But she still has quite a sad face,' Dewi comments on the photo as she serves her dinner of polony and tomato sandwiches.

'You're right. Dewi, promise not to tell anyone this?'

'Promise.'

'Roberta had her first baby taken away from her by hospital and welfare authorities when she was sixteen.' Because she wants to show Dewi that others have survived loss, too. Maybe that'll help take the sharp edge from Dewi's grief in future, help her extract some understanding from her tears once the worst is over.

'Why?'

'She was so young. She didn't get on with her parents very well. She had no money. The hospital social worker persuaded her it was the best thing to do. She told me she'd felt unable to go on after they took the baby. But she *did* keep going, and made herself a life.'

'I guess lots of people are heroes in their own way,' muses Dewi.

'You certainly are. What a meal.' The thick slices of polony and tomato, the crooked slabs of bread.

'Thank you,' Dewi says with satisfaction. 'I've wanted to try polony again since I had some at Amy's.'

'Y'know, I can always give you money for food, Dewi. And I'll give Roberta some money to buy us food if I'm feeling too sick.'

'Okay.' Dewi considers the photo of Roberta and Jack again. 'Sometimes the ones who don't *look* like heroes are the bravest.'

'Yes. A face without light is so easily overlooked.'

Ruth writes under the snapshot of Roberta and Jack: **Darkness can be as important as light for defining people.**

Making it through the storm

March, 1994
(unclear transparencies)

Dreams of Dewi and her missing the school bus, the town bus, the Greyhound bus, the flight to Bali; never quite making it to happiness, wherever it was.

Late that night, a storm rattles the cottage's weatherboards and tin roof, coats the windows in a thick film of dust and salt by morning. Ruth wakes to windborne drizzle drifting across the valley. The verandah roofing-tin bangs more loudly than before. Dewi's sign has blown off the front door and disappeared. The dusty living-room window bears the imprint of fleeing creatures blown off course: insects, a bird, a bat. Another kind of negative.

∞

'Follow the river,' Ruth had murmured to herself, trying to catch more sleep after Dewi left for school. But someone knocked so hard on the door that it rattled.

'Who's there?' she called.

'Police.' It wasn't Bill Collins the policeman's voice.

She pulled on David's dressing gown over her nightshirt, opened her bedroom door to find Des Gilbert had let himself into the living room through the front door, key in hand.

'Hey! You have no right to invade my home like this!' she shouted, prodding him in his cushiony chest with her thin finger.

'I already gave you much more time than I should've, Ruth. Tell you what else I've done for you.' His voice, overflowing with charity. 'Gotta friend in welfare to tee up a women's shelter for you in the city. Nice and handy to a school. You and your daughter can live there till you get a State Housing Commission place. Can't say I haven't cared for you, sweetheart. Paid your wage all these years. Come to help you shift now.' He wiped the fine beads of sweat from his top lip. 'Truck's waiting.' He opened the front door wide, pushed the sofa onto the verandah.

'You have no right,' Ruth repeated, pulling the sofa back towards the door. Just before she reached the threshold, a verandah board splintered under her foot and she fell, a rush of panic stinging her sinuses as her face smashed down so hard on the doorstep that she felt nothing else.

∞

She saw no faces, just the hovering shadows of two men as she regained consciousness, tasted her own blood. Closed her eyes again because she couldn't open them properly.

'She's a liability to herself and Merv Ferguson. I warned her, but she didn't want a bar of it. I gave her much more time than I needed to.' Des Gilbert's voice shook with the strain of proving his fairness. 'Yer can't reason with a mad woman.'

'You're a wanker, Des,' the other man said.

She thought she heard more voices, as if every authority in the town were giving an opinion on her but had merged into one indistinct drone. Felt the wetness of her nightshirt against her thighs; a wave of shame as she realised she'd wet herself. She pulled David's dressing gown around her tightly so they wouldn't see the wet patch, wondered if they could smell it. Put her head down again to stop the shadows pressing against her.

– *Sleep, Ruth. No shame,* the voices of Nelly the mission cook and the unknown woman sung softly, and for a while she obeyed them and it seemed another night passed.

When she opened her eyes again, her nightdress bodice had fallen open. Had the men seen her scar and all the lumps? She tugged the bodice closed.

'The lease is still current,' the other man said. 'You're way out of line, Des.'

'Me and Eloise've bent over backwards to help her. Paid her for doing next-to-nothing for years.'

'Just running two shops and doing all the mending and cleaning. With her next-to-nothing wages and the profit she made you in your antique shop over the years, you must've been laughing all the way to the bank.'

'Bullshit. That's not all we did for her, either. Gave her clothes. Lined her up with somewhere to go next. You can't say we treated her badly.' Des's voice shook again. 'But she needs more help than we can give her now. She's not just sick physically. She's sick in the head.'

'I'm…not…sick in the head,' Ruth gasped, but her mouth was awash and her words slurred. When she spat, a small, white thing landed on the verandah in a skein of her blood and saliva. Her tongue went to the bleeding hole where her incisor had been. 'I'm…not…sick in the head,' she tried again, scrabbling for her tooth, seeing double.

The other man stooped and picked something up.

'Got it.'

'Give it back,' she sobbed.

'Ruth.' The other man's gentle voice. 'It's me, Luke. I'll look after your tooth for you. I'll put it in a jar of milk and get you to hospital. Don't strain yourself talking. You just rest.' He began shouting. 'If you don't call her a fucking ambulance right now on your fancy mobile phone Des, I'll sue the hell out of you for negligence and breach of lease. And I should tell you, Merv's not selling this part of the block anymore.'

'Whatcha mean?'

'He rang last night to say he's keeping the cottage and the orchard in the family. So you can bugger off from here and devote your energy to selling the paddock up the road.'

'Not what the contract said.'

'Better talk to Merv Ferguson. He'll be paying your commission.'

I'm not sick in the head, Ruth had repeated to herself as the voices of the two men grew more strident, *I'm sick in my body but I'll never be sick in my head,* a promise to herself and Dewi before she slept again.

∞

Minutes after she'd let herself into the cottage after returning from hospital that afternoon, another knock on the door.

Luke, his hair and voice even smoother than usual.

'How're you feeling?'

'Okay,' she croaked.

'They didn't save your tooth.'

'Got bigger things to worry about,' she shrugged.

'Meant to ask. How was Bali?'

'Bali seems such a long time ago now.'

'Find any family?'

'Didn't even find my birth certificate.'

Across the paddock, Jack began strumming on his guitar.

'How's Jack's band going?'

'The Night Mares? They only lasted a few months. Broke up when Pete went travelling overseas. But Jack still likes to keep his hand in.'

'Lucky you. How's Dewi?'

'As well as can be expected. She worries.'

'She must be growing up.'

'She'll be twelve this year.' With no mother to celebrate her birthday, guide her through the confusion of adolescence. Ruth looks away, swallows her sob. 'How old's your son?'

'Four-and-a-half. Danny. Speak of the devil.'

Margo burst through the door with a little boy behind her, groceries and a pot of soup in her arms, hair damp with rain. Danny, stocky, dimpled at the knees and cheeks like Margo, olive-complexioned like the Mathews brothers. Margo's pregnant belly filled her dress like wind in a sail.

'Hi, Ruth,' she said quietly. 'Thought I'd make some scones to go with the soup, if that's all right with you.'

Over Margo's shoulder, Ruth saw Dewi dragging her bag and her feet in the gravel until she noticed Luke's car. She hurtled down the driveway but halted abruptly on the back step when she saw Margo and Danny.

'Hey!' Danny yelled excitedly from the kitchen doorway. 'A very *big* girl!'

'You must be Dewi,' said Margo, beaming.

'Yes,' murmured Dewi, looking at her own feet.

'I'm Margo. Luke's told me so much about you. I'm really glad to meet you at last.'

Dewi glowered at Luke and stepped away from him when he patted her shoulder.

'*Mum!* Your eye's all swollen and bruised. What are they doing here?' she whispered.

'You remember the photo of Margo. This is Luke's family.'

'And yours,' said Luke. 'I'm your uncle, so Margo's your aunty and Danny's your cousin.'

'If you think you can put up with us. We eat a lot and we've got really bad manners,' said Margo.

'Y'know Merv and Ivy Ferguson?' Ruth asked Dewi. 'They're Margo's grandparents. Margo and Luke are staying in the Fergusons' house up the road while they're away. Margo's making us scones.'

'Mum! What's happened to your tooth?'

'Don't be upset, Brave Star. Just a small accident.'

'What are you like at sifting flour, Dewi?' asked Margo, rummaging through the cupboard.

'What accident?'

'I fell over. Don't worry, Dewi. I only lost one tooth.'

'Bet you're not telling me the truth.'

'Promise I am.'

'Push this flour against the sieve with the spoon, Dewi,' said Margo, handing them to Dewi. 'That's it. Get all the lumps out.' Dewi stirred the flour so vigorously around the sieve that a cloud rose, dusting her face and the table.

Danny sat on the laminex chair chortling at her. 'A *funny* big girl.'

'I can't get every single lump out,' Dewi said.

'Doesn't matter. S'all good. Throw it into the mix,' said Margo, cutting a knife through butter. 'D'you wanna help rub the butter into the flour?'

'Roberta says butter's animal fat and bad for you,' Dewi muttered.

'Bitta wickedness does everyone good.'

'I don't know how to rub it in.'

'Between your fingers like this.' Margo's plump fingers worked lightly at it. She winked at Dewi. 'That's it! My Gran always says, "Don't worry if your cooking's not perfect, the chooks'll love it even if the people don't."'

Ruth gave up attempting to hide the hole in her smile from Dewi. And Dewi grew more content as she followed the recipe and listened to Margo's family stories; some tried and true things.

∞

Already the imprints of the flying creatures on the dusty living-room windows have become fainter. Ruth wonders if the flying creatures ever made it home in the storm. But Luke's snapshot of Dewi with her hands in the mix is perfectly exposed, the two mothers beaming over her shoulder, one of them with something missing from her smile.

The sound of the water says what I think.

– Chuang Tzu
– Oriental Wisdom 1976 Pocket Diary.

Dewi in the golden hour; eleven-and-a-half years old

March, 1994
(illumination without detail)

Dewi appears at the far end of the paddock, chasing Seagull's stray hens. Her face is a pale-sepia jewel, haloed by hair incandescent with setting sun. Ruth grabs the camera, but it's impossible to focus clearly on such radiance. Never mind. Illumination doesn't depend on seeing all the details. The click of the shutter slower than a heartbeat.

∞

Luke had been alone when he visited again that morning. His face looked as creased as his shirt, as if he'd been sleeping hard.

'Where are Margo and Danny?'

'Merv and Ivy's house.' Only then did she notice Luke had a large document under his arm, precisely folded. He pushed it to the back of the table as he insisted Ruth listen to what David had told him, long distance, from the Lost River post office pay phone the day before he'd disappeared.

'I think you need to know. I think it might help you.' Speaking fast, as if he was afraid she'd stop him again, Luke told her his brother had sounded exhausted and distraught. When he'd asked him what was wrong, David had confided that he'd gone against his better judgement and had sex with a young woman, too vulnerable. That she was living with him. That he already knew their relationship wouldn't work because of his past. He'd said he couldn't ask her to leave because he felt responsible for her, and because she had no money, friends, or family to stay with. At that point, he'd run out of coins for the phone.

As Luke spoke, the walls of the little cottage seemed to fall away, exposing her. How could she bear this?

'So, it was my fault he died.' Her voice was higher than it'd ever been, almost inaudible. 'It wasn't an accident.'

'No. You mustn't think that. That's not the point at all. The investigations into his death were inconclusive, you know.' Something flickers in Luke's eyes. A judgement? A lie? Mercy? Luke lowered his head and voice so she could barely hear what he said next. 'If it was anyone's fault, it was mine. I should've helped him, but I didn't realise how desperate he was.'

'Do you know *why* he was so desperate?'

'I told you the problem began in his past. I didn't realise he'd been so messed up by that.'

'Inga?'

'Longer ago and far more traumatic than that.' That flicker in Luke's eyes again. 'Look, I can't tell you any more about that. Enough to say it clouded his judgement with you, okay?' Luke's hands were outstretched, as if he was pleading. 'I promised him I'd never tell anyone else.'

'Something to do with your mother's death. You already told me that much before. Might as well tell me the rest.'

'Look Ruth. I'm sorry. It wouldn't help you to know what it was, anyway.'

'Yes, it would. It'd help me to know before *I* die.'

He rubbed his forehead with the heel of his hand.

'You're tougher than you look, aren't you Ruth? Okay. Our mother *suicided*, okay? David found her.'

'How...?'

'Hung herself. She'd suffered from depression all our lives.'

David's fear of the bird call that'd sounded like a woman crying came back to her.

'I'm so sorry,' she whispered.

'He couldn't shake the image of how she looked when he found her. Not a pretty sight, from what he told me.'

'Do you think that's why...beauty was so important to him?'

Could there ever be enough light to cut through that kind of darkness?

'Never thought of it like that, to be honest. He was my brother. So close I guess I couldn't see him clearly. He did tell me the memory of her face when he found her resurfaced whenever he had...some kind of intimacy with a woman.'

David's single sob after they'd made love came back to her next, clearer in the remembering than it had been at the time. The way he'd steadied his breath and closed his eyes, as if struggling to calm himself. So there'd been something more than their skins between them, even then.

'Ruth?' Luke touched her on the back of her hand. 'Listen to me, Ruth. I'm still getting to the most important things he said about you and him. I tried to tell you years ago, remember?' He spoke more quietly but even faster, as if he was afraid she might shut the door on him again. 'He told me he loved you, that he would've always loved you. But he realised he wouldn't be able to love you in the way any normal guy would. Said he was afraid of any woman being dependent on him.'

Luke reached for his document, fumbled with the edges but couldn't unfold it. 'He was too unsure of himself in too many ways. He had other problems, too.' Luke looked her in the eye. 'You were not one of them. The problems were inside him.'

She couldn't stop thinking about the night she and David had made love. Their silence afterwards and in the hours that followed. All those words held back, all those moments they might have confided in each other. Had he been as frightened as she was of the unexposed past flooding their moment of light and dimming it forever?

'I see,' Ruth said, though she'd only glimpsed a sliver of the indecipherable picture. 'Things I'd sooner keep in the dark about my past, too.'

For a moment Luke looked as if he might ask her about that, but he concentrated on unfolding his document.

'When it's too hard to make sense of the past, the best thing's to look to the future. Here are the plans for the new house.'

Uh-oh. Luke, too, has plans for me. A new house. Over my dead body.

Ruth tried to focus on the plans but they looked like a maze to her, full of impenetrable complications.

'Designed to combine privacy and openness,' Luke said, 'much better suited to the Lost River climate than this old shack.'

He wants me out so he can bulldoze our home and begin build-ing his own, but he's too cowardly to say so. New house in time for the new baby. Ruth felt the trembling begin at the base of her spine and spread through her like after-shock waves.

'North-facing with lots of glass to let in the light. It'll be high off the ground with an undercover area for parking. Pale rammed earth, recycled pine floors and stainless steel. I want to begin building it soon,' he said.

'After everything David did to this one?' She leaned against the wall for support. Looking at the door David had sanded and oiled, she recalled his long slender hands and his careful touch.

'But it's riddled with white ants. And it wasn't built to withstand flooding,' said Luke.

'It floods only once in a blue moon, the old locals reckon.'

'You never can tell. You need somewhere easier to live, anyway.'

'Hang on a minute, Luke. The best thing would be to wait. Let Dewi have more time in this house.'

'Wouldn't it be healthier to help her move on?'

'Don't you think kids in her situation deserve as many memories of their parents as possible?'

'You really can't let go, can you?'

– *Sick in the head*, she heard Des Gilbert explain. Ruth breathed deeply to steady her shaking. *Sick in my body, but not in my head.*

'You're a wanker, Luke.' Another voice had entered hers. 'Coming on like our bloody saviour when you're going to obliterate the few traces of Dewi's father she'll ever know. The house that's sheltered her since she was born.'

'But I'll help you shift. Financially, too.'

'You silly man. Can't you see? Shifting'll cost me something far more valuable than money. I'm nearly out of time and energy, Luke. It's bloody hard trying to keep my spirits and energy up, even without everyone interfering. I can't look after Dewi without this house. I'm stretched as far as I can go without breaking.'

'Calm down, Ruth. There's no need to demolish this if you don't want to. The Lost River Council's just approved these plans for the new house higher up on the block, above the flood-line. Plenty of room for both houses.'

As he smoothed the document on the kitchen table, his meticulously drawn lines wavered until Ruth could barely see them. She closed her eyes. Her daughter's small hands, clasped together as she'd tried to pray that day in Bali. Is that what Nelly had meant when she said as the mission closed down, *our true home is something we carry with us?* But Dewi's gesture of prayer had looked way too fragile and tentative to shelter her. Not even the strongest painkillers and Luke's kindness allowed Ruth to forget that when she died, Dewi would lose the only person who really cared for her.

'You okay?' Luke touched her on the wrist. She quickly withdrew her arm from him, opened her eyes.

'I'm fine.'

He smoothed the plans and showed her his new house would be high-ceilinged, angled to catch the best views and sunlight in winter, shaded in summer. Its exterior sympathetic to the angle and colour of the limestone ridge; its roofline lifted slightly at the eaves, almost like wings. He pointed to the windows.

'These thin, adjustable aluminium shutters will keep out the glare of midday but allow the early-morning and late-afternoon light to illuminate the living areas. And there's this wall running the length of the living room to hang David's paintings and photos.' He pointed to a small square near a sketch of the intersection of the driveway and road. 'Maybe a little gallery, when we can afford it.'

'His paintings and photos belong to Dewi. You're not going to sell them.'

'Just prints of his photos. And yours, if that's okay. The postcards. Maybe some other local arts and crafts.'

The plans wavered before her eyes again.

'You don't understand, do you Luke? No-one understands. What can I do? What can I do?' The shutter jamming. 'God, what can I bloody do?'

'About what?'

'What can I do about Dewi?'

Luke pointed to a room adjacent to the living room on the plans. Modestly sized, but with a large window facing the river valley.

'This is Dewi's bedroom, of course,' he said. 'She can live with us after you die, if that's okay with you.'

– *Breathe out.*

'You okay? Let's take this slowly, shall we?' Luke said.

'Slow's fine with me. Thank you,' she whispered, barely able to catch another breath, shaking with something between disbelief and relief.

'Margo suggested it, actually. Not that I hadn't thought of it. I'd just assumed you might have…other plans for Dewi?' The branches of the trees scratched at the window as the sea breeze picked up.

'Nothing. I have no-one else she can go to.'

'I promise I'll look after her. I can organise legal papers for you to sign. If that's what you'd like, Ruth.'

'Thank you. Thank you. Thank you.' She couldn't make her hoarse voice sound grateful enough.

After she blinked hard a few times to clear her eyes, she could just see something else. Maybe planning his future house had been Luke's way of trying to deal with his grief over his brother. Not an attempt to erase the last traces of David, after all.

And she saw that Luke's future house would be filled not only with light and children, but with the finely attenuated presence of his wilderness-roaming, lost forever, infinity-seeking brother.

∞

Homes, photographs, stories, paintings. All memorials we make to help us find our way back to love after loss. Death takes from us, but maybe it shows us what endures, too.

She flicks through the albums, one after the other. All those lives. All her beloved ones, rising and sinking with each turn of the page like the moon and sun with each day.

Loving these people is the closest I've been to eternity. If we do not love, our lives are over before we know it.

Yet we can never know everything about each other. Maybe that's a blessing. More is felt than can be revealed.

A Balinese mother
and the names she gave

Your Balinese grandmother when your mother was born, 1965
(the past finds the present)

In their roadside mailbox a few days later there's a manila envelope, a small bulge in its bottom corner, Balinese dancers on its postage stamps. Ruth shakes it gently. A faint rattling sound, somewhere between emptiness and promise.

Opening the envelope at the kitchen table, at first she doesn't register the names on the thin yellowed certificate inside. But when the tarnished copper-filigree flower brooch and the small black-and-white photograph of a thin, young Balinese woman fall into her lap, her pulse falls too.

The woman in the photo appears to be sitting in a hospital bed, the same brooch fastening her kebaya above her breast. She doesn't look at all crazy, as the Joiners had implied. She looks barely adult, but her gaze at the newborn in her arms is ancient with sorrow. Yet from the depths of sadness, her mother smiles at her.

Mother: *Ni Ketut Sriutami, age 17 years.*
Nationality: *Balinese*

Father: *Name and age unknown.*

Nationality: *Australian*

The name Ruth's mother had given her blurs as she reads it, its faded, ornate blue script like a horizon on the birth certificate.

How long had her mother's gifts waited for her?

She puts her mother's photo and the certificate in the white album.

My name is Kadek Ketut Murni Sriutami, she writes under her birth certificate, ***and it is Ruth Mary Joiner, and I forgive everyone who's misunderstood who I am.***

Her mind is a home as spacious as the world, and the unknown woman's voice has stopped echoing in it.

She'd dreamed that afternoon of loud voices approaching her as she lay wrapped in a white cloth in the Bali night.

'Kadek Ruth! Kadek Ruth!' Their clamour grew louder until she thought they'd trample her underfoot; a scream rose in her throat but she knew it'd come out as a whisper and be lost in the din.

Only when the voices surrounded her did she realise they were disembodied. Her suppressed scream became a song that ascended with the other voices into the sky. She sang for the joy of being one of many voices. She sang for Dewi, David, Luke, Margo and Danny. She sang for her mother, Roberta, Jack and Finn; for Nelly, Lizzy, Fred and Grace Joiner, and all the other people from the mission and Lost River. She sang for Murni, Gusti and everyone in the orphanage. She sang for her life, in case her voice disappeared forever.

My name is Kadek Ruth, she'd concluded as she woke. Both rivers making their way to the sea. The search for togetherness nearly over. *I've been lost, but now I'm found. I have come the long way home.*

∞

Even the faintest traces of where we come from can give us the courage to continue our journey, she writes under the certificate and photo sent from Bali.

'My Bali grandma,' says Dewi when she sees the photo, and her face says everything else.

Life after life

Morning, March 15th, 1994

'Someone's hung a wreath of dune grasses at your window,' says Roberta, opening the bedroom curtain wider to show her.

'Dewi.'

'*Gorgeous.* Sort of a bigger version of the bracelets you made together. And someone left these dune berries at your front door.'

'Katy,' Kadek Ruth murmurs. 'If you see her...'

'*Say hello?*' sings Roberta.

'And tell her I said goodbye.'

'Do you want your Balinese names on the plaque above the dates? Or just Ruth Mary Joiner?' asks Roberta.

'Kadek Ruth'll do.'

'1965–1994, right?'

Does it matter exactly how her ashes are marked? *We're all just passing through these days.* Had Katy said that? Maybe, Kadek Ruth thinks, the name, nationality and years we're given are not as important as how we try to live our life. That all-too-short dash between the dates of our birth and death.

∞

After Roberta leaves and Dewi goes to Amy's, Kadek Ruth dozes on the living-room couch. She dreams of trying to control the enlarger and its timed light in the darkroom, so she can reprint all the photos to capture the full detail and depth of their lives for Dewi, but it's hopeless. She wakes thinking she never really learned properly from David how to do that – would never know now.

But she knows about the enlargement of moments. She looks out the living-room window for a minute and sees twelve years of her life: the bend in the river where she first met David; the cliff above the rim-stone pool where he'd talked about the waiting and work of centuries; the path they'd walked to lie together under the old marri tree; the orchard and verandah where their wide-eyed daughter played and grew and made wishes.

So many events from the past and hopes for the future in each new moment.

Dewi and her friend Amy come up the track in the outlandish dress-ups Ruth'd brought home years ago from the opportunity shop. The bodices and skirts of the gowns a bit too big for them, billowing like sails in the sea breeze. Amy had never had dress-ups at home. When she'd first seen the dresses, despite the dust motes rising from them, she'd cooed and stroked the velvet and satin, the extravagant sequins, gathers and frills.

Watching the two girls laughing and singing in the orchard, Ruth recalls Lizzy and herself dressing up in the mission's donated clothes. She wonders if Lizzy married the old man she was promised to and if she'd had any children; if she'd managed to keep them on the outstations, away from the authorities and churches. She sees Lizzy's face and body full and young; hears her low voice and laughter as they'd shared their dreams of womanhood. She can't imagine Lizzy, Dewi or Amy ever getting old.

And herself? She's so weary she feels as if she's growing old by the minute. She pauses between words as she begins writing the letter.

Dewi, my brave star;
now it's come to my last chances
to tell you the most important things,
I don't know what to say.

I hope the photo albums will speak to you long after I'm gone. Some of the bracketed words under the prints are echoes of your father's voice.

She ties a purple ribbon around the digital camera and manual Luke brought her the day before. She's too tired to learn how to use it now.

The paintings and cameras are yours, too, and anything else in the house you choose. I wish I could leave you more useful possessions; the few I have are mostly second-hand and mightn't serve you well. I wish I could leave you more wisdom, but the little I have would've also been second-hand for you and mightn't have served you well, either.

It's dawned on me lately that useful wisdom isn't given, but instead gleaned by us, bit by bit, as we make our own path through our own wilderness.

And happiness, I wish I could give you more of that, too. Thank goodness you're so good at making your own.

I've lived long enough to learn that we do better in life if we find ways of dealing with grief. Loving people, creatures, wilderness; or making a home, a garden, pictures – any of these can help us find our way again. If we don't keep loving and making, all we're left with is a sense of loss and time passing. And that's too sad for words.

Brave, strong Dewi, I hope you will move on from my death by making whatever you want of your life. That's the kind of life after death I really believe in.

Love

She signs **Mum** for the last time. Adds **Kadek Ruth** in brackets before tucking the letter inside the white album's back cover, next to the spaces for her last photos of Dewi, still waiting inside David's old camera for development.

Through the window, she can just see her weathered scratches on the verandah post, marking the days since David's disappearance. Recalls how he'd closed his eyes and steadied his breath after they'd made love. How he'd taught her to search for the fleeting image and hold the camera still before releasing the shutter. How Dewi closes her eyes and pauses before blowing out her birthday cake candles.

So much care and hope in all our waiting.

She writes on the bottom of the last album page: *So much depends on what we choose to see. Finding happiness in what remains, you've always known how, Dewi. And in these new photos of you, it's clear you're already on your way to life after life.*

Because her photographs aren't only a record of her daughter's past. They carry her hopes for her daughter's future, too.

The last uncaptured images

Evening, March 15th, 1994

Dewi standing at her mother's twilit bedroom door. Her small hands pressed together in a roof-shaped attempt at prayer; her fragile try at sheltering from grief, so dependent on the wind changing soon.

Another photograph not taken.

So many important moments pass unrecorded. No memory or album is ever complete.

∞

Her last breezes come from the Indian Ocean, through the tall trees of this country she loves although it's not really hers.

Her last moon a pale gold leaf rising in the east.

∞

After she hears Luke, Margo and Dewi walk onto the verandah to watch the evening, Kadek Ruth searches David's painting of the river valley and Dewi's hand-drawn copy, both on the wall opposite her bedroom door.

Oil paint, liquid medium, wax crayon. Deep ultramarine those horizons, as warm as blue and distance can be. Not just a place between earth and sky. A place between living and dying. A way of letting go.

Her window's open.

Deep breath. Focus on infinity.

Her pulse slows, her heartbeat gathers her in. A faint click, like a camera shutter opening to the small family waiting outside the cottage to farewell her:

Hold steady.

She lingers over Dewi's sun-kissed cheek, her untameable hair.

Let go.

She's surprised that letting go feels such a blessing. Ahead of her, fences and boundaries give way to the colours of happiness spreading from her last moments into infinity. Entering those colours, she merges with leaves, air, river, sea; endless transparencies, all in a moment of light.

RELEASE

After checking that the old flower-shaped filigree brooch is properly fastened to the bodice of her purple dress, the girl walks with knock-kneed grace across the orchard towards the river. The grass bracelet encircles her wrist as she leads her uncle by his hand.

The girl's aunt sits on the verandah of the new house trying not to cry into a tea-towel as she feeds the new baby. At her feet, her son does a jigsaw of a bird sitting on eggs in a nest. In the vegetable garden next to the new pump, the elderly tortoiseshell cat curls her tail like a comma in the air. She's too slow and fat to chase the insects and occasional birds flying through the open windows of the old weatherboard cottage, where honey from a small native bees'-hive drips from the main bedroom's ceiling onto the bare iron bedstead.

The bush below the orchard runs down to the river, the only strip of wilderness left next to the new time-share holiday apartments upriver. The cat watches the girl and the uncle walk towards the river.

'If you just look ahead and focus on the river, you can *really* believe we're still in the wild,' says the girl.

'It's good to focus on the river,' the uncle nods. 'Your mother and father would like that.'

When they reach the small metal plaque he'd hammered into the top of the riverbank that morning, the uncle gives the girl one of the two grey plastic boxes he carries under his arm, helps her slide the lid of hers open before his.

'You ready?' She nods. He steadies his voice with a deep breath. 'As ready as we'll ever be, hey? One...Two...' He pauses deliberately.

'Let go,' the girl says. Her mother's and father's ashes eddy on the breeze and mingle with each other before falling towards the river, the sea, the end of another too short Lost River summer.

You wouldn't know from the small metal plaque that her father had tried to capture the light on the river valley before it changed forever; or that her mother had found herself by finding the value in unwanted people and things.

'Just in time. Tide's in. The river'll carry them out to the sea,' says the uncle.

'Just in time,' the girl agrees, looking at the photo at the base of the plaque bearing her parents' names and dates.

In that copy of the photograph taken by her father soon after he met her mother, both their faces and arms appear blurred. So even if you look closely, it's unclear whether the young woman and man were about to embrace, or to take flight alone.

END

ACKNOWLEDGEMENTS

My gratitude to the following people for generous reading, advice and encouragement during the research, writing and editing of this novel:

Susan Strehle; Susan Ash; Judith Lukin-Amundsen; Linda Martin, Suzannah Shwer and Katie Connolly; my agent Jenny Darling.

Thanks to Terri-ann White for her continued support of my writing and her perceptive reading of the manuscript; to Anna Maley-Fadgyas for this novel's wonderful cover; and to everyone else at UWA Publishing for their hard work.

Hollis Dwyer told me about the cat he encountered in a remote part of north-western Australia, whom he drove to his motel room where she unexpectedly gave birth.

Judith, Anne, Catherine and Mark Lazaroo; Ken, Sophia and Tom Rasmussen; and many other wonderful family and friends inspired this book in countless ways.

I am grateful to the following organisations for their assistance:

The Literature Board of the Australia Council for a grant that enabled me to write much of this novel; Murdoch University for allowing me time to research and write.

The following texts informed this novel:

Miguel Covarrubias's *The Island of Bali* (Oxford University Press, Kuala Lumpur, 1974 edition; originally published in 1937) contains information about Balinese myths, dance, funeral customs and ways of thinking about life and death that informed several passages in my novel. The two stories Ruth reads in her travel book are not authentic versions of Balinese stories, but they do mention characters from Balinese stories and myths noted in Covarrubias's book; specifically a god who lives in 'the floating sky' and a goddess of the underworld (p. 7 of the 1974 edition of Covarrubias); and Durga the goddess of death (pp. 340–341, Covarrubias). The story about the acutely ill woman who has to sacrifice her child to Durga in order to live is based on a myth sometimes performed as a dance in Bali, according to the website http://www.indo.com/interests/dance.html (p. 4, accessed 2/06/2011).

The quotes from various Eastern philosophers at the end of some chapters were extracted from *Wisdom of the East 2008 Calendar*, Andrews McMeel Publishing, Kansas City.

The old tin shop sign Ruth finds inside the opportunity shop is based on the wording of a shop sign photocopied in the Local History Files (volume 2) in the Augusta-Margaret River Public Library.

The hand-painted words on the mission van were recreated from words on the side of a van I once saw in Fremantle.

Different versions of some of the passages about Ruth and Dewi's visit to Bali were published in my short story titled 'Someone Else's Bali' in *Meanjin*, volume 69, number 3, 2010, Melbourne University Press; and in my short story titled 'Cocooning' in *Amerasia Journal,* volume 36, number 2, 2010, University of California, Los Angeles.

NOTES

Lost River, its township and hinterland are fictional constructs, although some details of their history and geography are drawn from several actual places in south-western Australia. All characters in this novel are fictional.

The character Jack Murphy claims to tell authentic Aboriginal stories, but these are syntheses of his own stories and wishful thinking with his misinterpretations of Aboriginal stories, as other characters imply in this novel.

www.ingramcontent.com/pod-product-compliance
Lightning Source LLC
Chambersburg PA
CBHW060427030726
47495CB00003B/774